MARIANNE
BOOK 2
The Eagle and the Nightingale

MARIANNE
BOOK 2
The Eagle and the Nightingale

JULIETTE BENZONI

Translated by Anne Carter

UNABRIDGED

PAN BOOKS LTD : LONDON

First published as one volume called *Marianne* in Great Britain 1969
by William Heinemann Ltd.
This edition published 1971 by Pan Books Ltd,
33 Tothill Steet, London, S.W.1.

ISBN 0 330 02738 7

Printed in Great Britain by
Cox & Wyman Ltd, London, Reading and Fakenham

CONTENTS

CHAPTER ONE

The Night at Butard

The town berlin belonging to the Prince of Benevento sped as
swiftly as the rough-shod greys could draw it along the promenade de Longchamp, deserted at this late hour. It was eight
o'clock in the evening. In summer, the promenade would have
been crowded with horses and carriages for some hours yet but
the dark, the cold and the snow had long since driven Parisians
indoors, the bourgeois to their supper and cards, the fashionable world to the large parties which took place almost every
night at this time of the year. Yesterday, it had been the Prince
de Cambacérè's, tonight it was the Duc de Cadore's, who had
replaced Talleyrand as Foreign Minister. This, thought Marianne, was no doubt the reason why Talleyrand was sitting
beside her in the berlin rather than dressing for the Duke's
ball.

Ensconced in the mulberry-coloured cushions which
matched the paintwork on the great wheels of the carriage, she
stared out indifferently at the snow-covered landscape. Longchamp was quite familiar to her now from many drives with
the Princess and little Charlotte and she did not greatly care to
know where she was being taken. Talleyrand had told her that
morning:

'Tonight, I mean to take you to the house of a very good
friend of mine, and a great lover of music. I want you to be
beautiful. Not that that will be difficult but I should like to see
you in pink.'

It was the first time the Prince had expressed any preference
with regard to her clothes and Marianne was surprised, especially since, until that moment, she had believed his taste to
incline rather towards cold colours, like blue and green, and
she had no pink dress.

'You shall have one tonight,' the Prince assured her and sure enough, later in the day a gown had arrived from Leroy which, though extremely simple, Marianne thought perfect. The dress was made of very pale pink satin, frosted with silver but with no other decoration. With it went a great hooded cloak of the same stuff, quilted and bordered with ermine, and a matching muff. The effect, on her, was stupendous, as was proved to her by the smile of satisfaction bestowed on her by the Prince as she came down to meet him.

'I believe,' he told her, 'that tonight will be another triumph for you – perhaps your greatest triumph of all—'

Marianne's voice had certainly earned her a very flattering degree of success at private parties but it was a success which bore no relation to what she hoped to meet with in the theatre. She had the good sense to realize that what she had achieved so far was simply a fashionable success, and by its very nature fleeting. For some time, too, she had been feeling less confident of herself, and had worked with less enthusiasm at her singing. In addition, there was the persistent black cab always on her heels wherever she went. It was beginning to haunt her, like some inescapable presage of disaster. She had thought once or twice of going out on foot to see if anyone would approach her but she had not dared, held back by a fear which she could not have explained. What was more serious was that, although she had mentioned it in her report, Fouché had made no comment and now Marianne did not know what to think. The Prince had not mentioned it, either. It was all very bewildering. It was in her mind to go and see Fouché in the morning.

It was eight days now since the scene with Jason Beaufort and in spite of her expressed determination to forget him, Marianne had not yet succeeded in doing so. Whenever she thought of the American, it was with such a host of contradictory feelings that she felt quite lost. Anger predominated, and resentment, all the more bitter because she had been tempted to accept his offer. She was still too young to remain unaffected by the magic of certain words. Jason had awakened in her a desire for this new life he had described for her, a free life in a new world full of sunshine and warmth. Perhaps he really meant it when he said he wanted to give back a little of what he had taken from her? And, with that thought, Marianne was sometimes on the point of going to him. One morning, when she was out doing some errands for the Princess, she even asked the coachman to drive down the rue Cerutti. She had seen the Hôtel de l'Empire at number twenty-seven, a building of some elegance with a number of vehicles outside it, and for an instant she had been tempted to stop the carriage and get out, to ask this strange man whom she hated but who fascinated her—

But then she had changed her mind. Why should she believe Beaufort's word? He had robbed her of everything, had dared to barter her love and modesty. Who could say if, once they were at sea, he would respect his promise and not claim the shameful rights which he believed were his? And how much more when they were together at the other side of the world! After all, what reason could he have for saving her and from what? What was this danger with which he threatened her, if not some imaginary bogey intended purely and simply to make her fall more readily into his snare? Only that morning, Marianne had received a short, unsigned note.

'*I am here for another week. To find me after that, you should inquire of my friend Paterson, the American Consul at Nantes. Think again, I urge you, and come with me. Time is short—*'

Marianne had merely shrugged and tossed the note into the fire. Today, she did not want to believe Jason Beaufort.

The berlin crossed the Seine and Marianne put her face to the window, rubbing a clear patch on the misted glass with the tip of one gloved finger.

'Are we going out of Paris?' she asked. 'Is it much farther?'

In the dimness of the coach, she could see little of her companion, though she could smell the faint scent of verbena. Since leaving the rue de Varennes, he had seemed to be asleep.

'No, not much farther – the village we are going to is called La Celle Saint Cloud. The friend we are to visit has a most delightful château there. It is a charming house, one of the prettiest I know. The King used it formerly as a hunting lodge—'

It was rare for Talleyrand to be so lyrical. Marianne's curiosity was aroused. It was very strange, this former hunting lodge, tucked away in a village that, however close now, was certainly well out in the country. Until now, Talleyrand had taken her mostly to fashionable Parisian hostesses such as Madame de la Laval, Dorothée de Périgord, and the ladies of Bellegarde. But this was quite an expedition.

'Will there be much company?' she asked with assumed indifference. 'Who will be there?'

The Prince coughed as though pondering his reply but when he spoke, his drawling voice was as smooth as glass.

'No indeed, there will not be much company. Before we get there, my dear child, there are one or two things I must tell you. This is no great party. The friend to whom I am taking you is called simply Monsieur Denis—'

Marianne raised one eyebrow in surprise.

'Monsieur Denis? Denis de—'

'Nothing. He is – a bourgeois, very rich and extremely able and also a very old friend from a time when things were – difficult. He is also an unhappy man suffering from a recent cruel bereavement. To some extent, the visit on which I am taking you is one of charity.'

'Dressed like a princess, and in a ball gown at that, to the house of a man in mourning? Surely, I ought to be more soberly dressed?'

'Mourning is in the heart, my dear child, not in the apparel. In the darkness which surrounds him, M. Denis needs to see the dawn. It was my wish that you should be that dawn.'

Something rather too unctuous in the Prince's tone increased Marianne's already awakened curiosity. He sounded over-enthusiastic and not wholly sincere. Who was this bourgeois person who owned a former hunting lodge and who one visited dressed as though for a ball? She was immediately agog to know more.

'I wonder that your Highness should take so much trouble

for a man so far removed from him. Is he really an old friend?'

'Very old,' Talleyrand said quite seriously. 'You would be surprised how many bourgeois I number among my acquaintance, and even among my friends. There are a good many even in the imperial court, although dressed up, I grant you, in high-sounding titles.'

'Then why has this M. Denis none?'

'Because such things have no interest for him. He has no need to be count or marquis. He is – himself, and that is enough. Tell me, Mademoiselle Mallerousse, I hope you are not shocked at the thought of singing for a bourgeois?'

She sensed the mocking smile in the shadow of the carriage.

'Of course not,' she murmured. 'I only hope he is not one of those former members of the Convention, a regicide—'

'He would not be my friend,' Talleyrand interrupted her with some severity. 'You may rest easy on that score.'

Under the cover of the fur rug wrapped about their knees, the Prince's hand sought Marianne's and held it gently. Lowering his voice to a more confiding tone, he added:

'You will discover that people in this country sometimes do funny things, but never without a reason. What I ask of you this evening is a personal service, a favour, if you like. This man's name is not a noble one, but his heart is and his grief deserving of your sympathies – to the extent of forgetting to mention it to our friend Fouché, eh? He need not know of this visit—'

Marianne's brief uneasiness subsided but curiosity remained, sharper than ever. Although it made little difference to her who she sang for, having promised the Prince to do so when it was his wish, she was now impatient to arrive and see what kind of a man this M. Denis could be for the Vice-Grand-Elector of the Empire to hold him in such regard.

'I am sorry,' she said gently. 'I will be pleased to sing for your poor friend.'

'Thank you.'

The berlin was now climbing quite a steep hill. The horses had slowed down considerably but Lambert, the coachman,

was holding them with a sure hand so that they did not slip.
The glass in the windows was misting up and in the well-padded
interior of the carriage silence fell again as each relapsed into
their own thoughts. Marianne remembered suddenly that as
they left the house she had not noticed whether the intolerable
black cab was still there but then forgot about it once more
and her mind turned instead to the mysterious M. Denis. She
was glad she was not obliged to mention him in the tiresome
daily reports which it was still her painful task to write although, thanks to Talleyrand, they had become a mere formality. But why had Fouché said nothing in reply about the black
cab? Unless it belonged to him. After all, why not?

White against the black background of the forest, the pavilion
of Butard seemed dreaming on the shores of the frozen lake
which spread below its terrace. Soft golden light came from its
tall windows to lie in bright splashes on the crusted snow. Its
low pediment decorated with a relief of a hunting scene
loomed out of the night and the woods like an enchanted
place. It may have been her sharpened curiosity which
made her expect wonders, but Marianne was captivated by it at
once.

She scarcely saw the footman in dark livery who lowered the
steps for her when the carriage had passed through the gates
into the circular forecourt, and she made her way to the open
doorway like one in a dream. She stepped into a small entrance
hall, decked with flowers and pleasantly warm from a good fire
burning in the wide hearth. A staircase vanished into shadows
above. But Marianne had no time to look about her very
closely. Before her, the footman was opening the door into a
blue and white salon with a domed ceiling surrounded by a
frieze of cupids playing among the leaves.

The pretty, delicate lacquered furnishings belonged to the
previous century. They were upholstered in blue and white
striped silk and gave the impression that their chief purpose
was as a foil to the huge bunches of iris and pink tulips that
were cunningly arranged on all sides. A large baroque mirror
over the fireplace gave back a reflection of the room in the light

of tall, pink scented candles. Bow windows looked out across the balcony to the frozen lake and the causeway running across it. Marianne's eyes had gone straight to the lovely old harpsichord that stood by one of the windows. The wooden floor, covered by a big Beauvais carpet, creaked softly under the pressure of Talleyrand's stick and limping steps. The room was quite empty. But then a door opened and a man appeared.

Thinking that this must be the mysterious M. Denis, Marianne looked at him with interest. He was of medium height, fair and far from good-looking, with sharp features and brown eyes that squinted slightly. But his face looked open and intelligent with a naturally kindly expression that appealed to Marianne although she was a trifle taken aback by the bright green clothes for a man supposedly in mourning.

He held out his hand, smiling, and came quickly to meet the new arrivals.

'A positively military punctuality, I declare! How do you do, my dear Prince, and so this is the young lady.'

'Yes indeed, my dear Duroc, this is Mademoiselle Mallerousse whose matchless voice you have often heard me praise. Is – M. Denis not yet here?'

'No, not yet,' answered the man addressed as Duroc, 'but he will not be long. In the meantime, I have ordered a light supper for you. I thought you would be cold after your long journey.'

He led Marianne with the utmost politeness to a mauve velvet sofa near the fire and helped her off with her cloak. Slightly overawed by the extreme elegance of her surroundings and also by the unmistakably military bearing of this stranger with the bourgeois name, Marianne submitted in silence. Her confusion at his frankly admiring glances made her drop her eyes so that she missed the glance which he exchanged with Talleyrand. The prince declined to part with his furred overcoat.

'No thank you. Mademoiselle Mallerousse will be glad to warm herself but I must be off.'

Marianne, who was warming her hands at the fire, started.

'What! Is your Highness leaving me?'

He crossed over to her and taking one of her hands in both his, dropped a swift kiss upon it.

'I am not leaving, my child, I am entrusting you. I must go back. My old friend the Baroness de Stael has been given permission to travel to America with her son. She passes through Paris tonight. I wish to say goodbye to her and see her off on her journey to Morlaix where her ship is already waiting. But have no fear. My friend Duroc will look after you like a father and when you have finished charming our poor friend he will see you taken home in his own carriage.'

'I hope you do not doubt that,' Duroc said with a warm smile, 'and that I do not frighten you, mademoiselle?'

'No – no, not at all,' Marianne replied, returning his smile with an effort. She thought he seemed very nice but she was bewildered. Why had Talleyrand not told her he would not be staying with her? He had never behaved in such a way before. However, with his usual subtlety, he must have realized what was going through the girl's head because he leaned on his stick and bent down towards her.

'I feared to alarm you and startle your timidity before you had seen this reassuring fellow! To tell you the whole truth, I wish your voice to be a surprise for my friend Denis. When you hear the sound of his carriage outside, then start to sing – but don't tell him that I am responsible for this pretty surprise.'

'But – why not?' Marianne said bewilderedly. 'If you think it an agreeable surprise, then he must be grateful to you—'

'Exactly. I do not want his gratitude – or not at the moment. He shall know the truth but not just yet. For the present, I want no other feelings, however slight, to interfere with the pure joy that he will have in finding you.'

Marianne understood less and less but she was highly intrigued. What a strange, complicated, mysterious man the Prince seemed to be. And why should he think it necessary to speak to her in this rather over-emphatic way, that was so unlike his usual manner? She was grateful to Duroc when, in his own way, he expressed her feelings.

'You have some funny ideas, sometimes, Prince. But you would not be yourself if it were not so. Have a safe journey.'

Watching her temporary host go with Talleyrand into the hall, Marianne wondered what could be this Duroc's position in M. Denis' household. Was he a relation? Or merely a friend? Was he perhaps the brother of the lady for whom the mysterious bourgeois was in mourning? No, the green suit made it equally unlikely that he was the dead woman's brother. A cousin perhaps, or a childhood friend entrusted with the running of the house – no, certain mannerisms, a way of holding his head, even the way he walked, the tread of a man more used to boots than pumps, made it certain he was a soldier. Duroc's return interrupted Marianne's musings. He was accompanied by a superior servant of some kind, dressed in black and pushing before him a small table on which a collation was set out. Under his powdered wig, the man's round pink face reflected all the grave solemnity becoming in the servant of a great house. He bowed to Marianne with a touch of condescension which astounded her. This Denis must undoubtedly be some frightful upstart, puffed up with conceit in his luxurious way of life, if even his servants felt entitled to give themselves airs. Like master, like men! M. Denis must be quite intolerable! However, Duroc was saying:

'Put that table in front of mademoiselle, Constant, and then leave us.'

'Am I to serve your—'

'No, no, that will do.' Duroc cut him short hurriedly. 'We will serve ourselves, I tell you—'

The butler retired with dignity but Marianne had not missed the unfinished address and wondered what title he had been on the point of giving Duroc. It seemed to her that, since the mysterious Denis had not yet arrived, she might take advantage of his absence to try and find out a little more about him. She gratefully accepted a cup of soup but refused any other refreshment.

'Should I not be singing when M. Denis comes in? He cannot find me at table.'

'That is so. But it will be enough to begin when we hear the carriage.'

Marianne glanced at the harpsichord.

'Must I accompany myself?'

'No — no of course not. What am I thinking of? Wait one moment.'

He was showing signs of increasing nervousness. Marianne sipped her soup and smiled inwardly. All things considered, the adventure was proving enjoyable and she was more and more curious to set eyes on this odd bourgeois whose arrival spread such panic in his household. Duroc returned a few moments later accompanied by a thin, austere-looking young man with long hair and a dark complexion. Not glancing at Marianne, the young man picked up the roll of music she had brought with her and sat down at the harpsichord. Duroc returned to his guest, looking considerably relieved.

'There, now we are ready. You may give M. Hassani any instructions you wish, but do not look for a reply. He is a mute,' he added in a low voice with a glance at the pianist.

A mute, now? Marianne began to wonder suddenly whether this M. Denis did not bear a false name, hiding something else. The owner of an ill-gotten fortune, perhaps, living luxuriously but discreetly deep in the woods, away from the prying eyes of Fouché's men, or else some noble stranger conspiring against the régime. Fouché had certainly implied that there were some doubts in high places as to Talleyrand's loyalty. There were suggestions that if he had not yet betrayed the Emperor, it would not be long before he did. This simple but unlikely name of M. Denis was almost certainly a cloak for some dangerous character, an agent of the Tsar perhaps, or even of England?

'What do you mean to sing first?' Duroc asked.

'An air by Paer — one I am very fond of.'

'M. Denis will be delighted. He too likes Paer who is, as you probably know, conductor of the court orchestra.'

'Has M. Denis been long in France?' Marianne asked the question point blank but with apparent casualness.

Duroc stared. 'Er — for some time, yes. Why do you ask?'

The sound of a carriage in the gravelled court outside released Marianne from the necessity of a reply which she might have found awkward to make. Instantly, Duroc was on his feet while Marianne hurried over to take up her position by the instrument, her back to the door. The impassive Hassani was already playing the opening bars as Duroc hastened out to the vestibule. All at once, Marianne found herself in the grip of an attack of terrible stage fright. Her hands were icy cold and she had to clasp them tightly to keep them from trembling while an unpleasant shiver ran down her spine. She cast a look of such desperate appeal at the expressionless pianist that he glanced back at her sternly. From outside, came the sound of voices, footsteps – she had to take the plunge or else ruin Tal- leyrand's great surprise.

Hassani's stern gaze became imperative. Marianne opened her mouth and was wholly astonished to hear her own voice come out, sounding as warm and relaxed as though the terrible fright had not gripped her throat at all.

> 'Oh joy comes ever slowly,
> But fleeteth fast away,
> While youth is sad and lonely,
> And lives but for a day—'

As she sang, Marianne was aware of a quick step in the tiled hall, a step which stopped short in the doorway of the room. After that, she heard nothing more but she had a piercing sense of someone there, watching her – the strange thing was that, far from making her uncomfortable, his presence seemed to her to release her from some unconscious anxiety, that it was friendly and reassuring. Her fright had flown away as though by magic and Marianne's voice soared forth with a warmth and fullness such as she had never known. Once again, music had come to her rescue. Its power over her was never failing, always fresh and constantly renewed. She let it carry her away, fearless and unresisting, knowing that the love between her and her music was real. There could be no betrayal here. The final words of the song fell like a sigh from the young lips:

> '. . . false flattering hopes are lost
> And love alone remains . . .'

It ended and silence fell. Hassani, eyes lowered, let his hands
slip down on to his knees and Marianne felt the spirit go out of
her. Feeling suddenly horribly nervous, she dared not turn her
head to the fire where she knew someone was standing. A voice
spoke brusquely:

'Excellent. Sing again, mademoiselle. Do you know *Plaisir
d'Amour?*'

She looked at him at last. She saw a man of slightly less than
average height, and rather fat without being in any way gross
or heavy. He was leaning on the mantelpiece, dressed in a black
coat, black stock and white kerseymere pantaloons covered,
she saw to her astonishment, with black marks that were undoubtedly ink stains. She could even see where he had wiped
his pen on them. They ended in knee boots armed with small
silver spurs. M. Denis' hands and feet were small and neat but
it was his face which held Marianne's attention. She had never
seen one like it. In colour, a very pale ivory, it had the classic
beauty of a Roman mask. His black hair, worn short and
straight, fell over his forehead, emphasizing the dark blue,
rather deep-set eyes. Those eyes were not easy to meet but
their expression was unforgettable. In his hand, M. Denis held
a gold and tortoiseshell snuffbox whose principal use seemed
to be to distribute snuff liberally over his person and everything around him.

'Well?' he said.

Marianne reddened, conscious that she had been staring at
him in a way that was scarcely polite and turned her eyes away
hastily.

'I do know it, indeed.'

She began to sing the well-known tune with a degree of
feeling that was beyond her control. Something was happening
in the inmost depths of her being, something she did not
understand but which made her identify with the music with a
passionate intensity of which she would never have believed
herself capable. But now, as she sang, she was not afraid to
look at M. Denis. She had never felt drawn to any man as she
did to him and, unable to hide the feelings which her mobile
face betrayed with absolute honesty, she kept her green eyes

firmly fixed on the stranger's blue ones so that the words of
love in the song seemed to be meant for him alone.

> '*As long as these slow waters glide*
> *Downstream by the meadow's side,*
> *I will love you . . .*'

But as the plaintive words of the lament fell from her lips,
she saw M. Denis slowly abandon his indolent posture, put
away the snuffbox with an impatient air and gradually draw
nearer. His eyes, too, never left her face. He was looking at her
intently, looking at her as no man before had ever dared to
look at her. And it seemed to her that if that look were suddenly removed, in that instant she would cease to live. Her eyes
filled with tears. She could feel her heart beating under the
frosted satin of her dress, so strongly that it seemed it must
burst. She was happy, troubled and frightened all at once, but
she knew that she could go on singing all night long only for
the pleasure of having him look at her like that.

When the last note died away, Marianne and M. Denis stood
face to face. Still without taking his eyes off her, he snapped his
fingers sharply.

'Go, Duroc. And you too, Hassani.'

The friend and the pianist vanished instantly but Marianne
had no thought of protest. It was quite natural, in the order of
things. In a few minutes this stranger with the ridiculous name
had become for her more important than anything in the world
and Marianne tried in vain to find a name for the feeling, urgent
and primitive, which overwhelmed her. It was as though she
had never lived for anything but this moment. Now, she did not
even want to know who this man was, whether he was really
called Denis, or whether he was some noble, perhaps dangerous person. No, he was there, and all was well.

She stood with her back against the harpsichord, gripping it
with cold hands, her bosom rising and falling as she watched
him come closer, and closer still. He smiled at her and she felt
her heart melt before the charm of that smile.

'When I was a child,' he said confidingly. 'I often wondered what it was Ulysses heard, tied to the mast of his ship, while his companions' ears were stopped with wax. He begged them to untie him so that he might throw himself in the water and swim to the sirens' voices. I know now what he felt.'

The sirens. Jason Beaufort too had likened her to the sirens — what was it he had said? Marianne could not remember exactly. Besides, was there still a Jason Beaufort somewhere? Had he ever existed? Had she herself ever lived before this minute or had she just been born?

In spite of his French name, the strange Monsieur Denis must be a foreigner. He had a slight accent which made her think of Italy. For an instant the thought that he was a foreign conspirator revived but Marianne dismissed it as of no importance. He could be what he liked. She knew already that he had become the most important thing in her life. The great emptiness which had brought her to the brink of accepting the future held out to her by Jason Beaufort was there no more.

Very gently, M. Denis took Marianne's hands and held them in his own, which were warm and firm. He was shocked to find how cold they were.

'You're frozen! Come close to the fire—'

He made her sit on the sofa, then placed himself beside her and drew the table towards them.

'You will eat something?'

'No – please, truly.'

'Don't tell me you aren't hungry. At your age one is always hungry. I used to eat – here, a little of this quail pâté, a thimbleful of Chambertin – Chambertin is the king of wines. I never drink anything else. No? This is absurd! You must prefer champagne. Now, a little champagne?'

'I – that is – I have never drunk it,' Marianne said anxiously, watching him fill a crystal glass with sparkling golden wine.

'Then now if ever is the time to begin!' M. Denis told her gaily. 'You will like it. There is not a woman in the world who does not like champagne! It puts a sparkle in the eyes – although,' he added leaning a little closer, 'it is true that yours need no such artifice. I have seen many emeralds not so bright.'

He poured the wine for her as he spoke with the dexterity

and attentiveness of a lover. A little nervously, Marianne set her lips to the glass, then she smiled. The wine was cold, sparkling and fragrant – altogether marvellous! Her host was watching her out of the corner of his eye and smiling.

'Well?'

'It is wonderful! May I have a little more?'

'Indeed you may!'

He laughed and refilled her glass. Then he began to eat hungrily and Marianne found herself following his example. All at once the room had become a very warm, cosy place. No sound came from outside. All was muffled by the snow. The two of them might have been alone together in an enchanted palace, or in a warm, hollow shell lost in some immense petrified forest. Marianne had never felt so happy and contented. She drained her glass and smiled at M. Denis. How nice and gay he was! It crossed her mind that he was in fact rather too gay for a widower, but then perhaps he might not have loved his wife as much as people thought. Or maybe the music had done him good, or – oh, after all, it did not really matter. The champagne inclined Marianne to optimism. Fatigue and nervousness were all forgotten. Her head was full of wild ideas. She wanted to laugh, without knowing why, to sing – even to dance!

'A little more champagne?' M. Denis asked. He had been watching her with a half-smile.

'Yes please! I – I should never have believed it could be so good!'

He let her drink half of it then gently took the glass away and moved closer to her.

'That's enough for the present. Tell me your name.'

The sudden intimacy in his voice seemed perfectly natural to Marianne. In a short time, they had become such good friends.

'Marianne. My name is Marianne Ma—'

'No. I want only your first name. The rest I shall learn later if I wish. But a dream should have one name and it is long since I addressed anything so pretty – you are beautiful, Marianne. Your voice enthralled me, but I am enchanted by your beauty.'

'Really?' she said happily. 'Do you really like me? In that case, you must tell me your name. Monsieur Denis is frightful.'

'I know. Call me Charles! You like Charles?'

'I don't care! I shall like it because it is yours!'

He had taken her hand and began kissing it softly, moving upwards gradually to the wrist, and then the arm and then the shoulder, putting aside the short, pink sleeve to reach its curve. The caress sent a wave of surprising happiness through Marianne. She gave a long shivering sigh and closed her eyes. Not for anything in the world would she have pushed him away, perhaps because she had known half unconsciously, from their first glance, that such a moment would come. The champagne had put just enough warmth into her blood to deaden the repugnance she had felt for men ever since that first unhappy encounter with Jean Le Dru. Besides, Charles was not really a man, he was a dream — a dream from which she had no desire to awake. She did not even wish to speak, only to listen to the awakening of her own body to feelings which made her long for more than kisses.

When he slid his arm beneath her waist and laid her back gently on the cushions of the small sofa, she sighed deeply and opened her eyes to see Charles' face very close to hers but closed them again quickly as their lips touched. He kissed her gently, his lips only just brushing hers in the faintest of caresses, kindling the fire in her blood with exquisite slowness. Her heart was beating as though it would burst her breast and she lay panting in Charles' arms, avid for yet more kisses and caresses.

His mouth against hers, he whispered:

'You want me? Say — truly?'

Her eyelids flickered, yes, and she slid her arms round his neck to draw him closer.

'There is too much light—' she whispered.

'Come.'

His arm went round her, holding close and drawing her to her feet to lead her across the room to where a small door was almost concealed in the panelling. The room beyond was small and blue and smelled of jasmine but though the bed was turned down, its whiteness was scarcely discernible in the light of the fire crackling in the grate which was the only illumination in the small chamber clearly made for love.

Marianne flinched instinctively at the sight of the bed but Charles stopped her mouth with such a burning kiss that she almost fainted in his arms. Leading her gently to the fire, he sat on a low chair and took her on his knees like a child. He unfastened the beautiful pink dress, murmuring to her all the while in Italian, charming, tender words of love and covering with kisses first her neck and shoulders and then, as his caressing hands softly put aside the lace shift, her breasts. There was such gentleness in his touch and in his words that Marianne very soon forgot all modesty or shame in the sheer pleasure of hearing his voice tell her she was beautiful.

At last, he carried her, naked and trembling, to the bed and laid her tenderly between the scented sheets where, in a moment or two, he came to join her. When, two hours later, she fell asleep in Charles' arms, relaxed and happy, Marianne thought with a contented sigh how little comparison there was between what had just happened to her and her unpleasant experience in the barn at Kérivoas. It was more than simply that she loved Charles while Jean Le Dru had meant almost nothing to her apart from her need of him. This man, to whom she had given herself so spontaneously, had really become her lover in every sense of the word. It was tonight that she had really ceased to be a girl. Charles' love and not the sailor's clumsy haste had made her blossom into a woman. She knew now what it meant to belong to someone. Nothing and no one could ever divide her now from the man who had given her true knowledge of love and of herself.

'I love you, Charles,' she had murmured sleepily into his neck as her eyelids dropped shut. 'I belong to you for always. Wherever you go, whatever may happen to you, I will follow, I will love you—'

He raised himself on his elbow and made her look at him.

'One should not say such things, *carissima mia* – we never

know what may be hidden behind the closed door to the future. I could die tomorrow.'

'Then I should die also — and we should still be together. You cannot know how much you have given me tonight — there's no help for it now. I belong to you — and you alone, kiss me, Charles, kiss me hard—'

Then he had caught her to him once more, so violently that she half cried out, and had made love to her again.

'It is you who have given all and you who gives thanks — *mio dolce amore*,' he murmured afterwards. 'You are right. Nothing and no one can undo this night. Sleep now, it is late.'

She settled obediently into the crook of his arm and closed her eyes. It was all right, everything was simple now. She loved him. He loved her. Who could prevent them being together always? He was a widower and, for the first time since that night at Selton Hall, Marianne remembered that she too was widowed.

Whether that blissful sleep was long or short, Marianne never knew but it seemed only a moment later when she woke suddenly. Charles was already sitting up in bed and in the dim light she could see Duroc murmuring something in his ear.

'What is it?' she asked sleepily. 'Is it already so late?'

'No. Be quiet. It is only three o'clock but I must go. Have the horses put to, Duroc. I'm coming.'

He was already leaping out of bed. Marianne clung to him with the feeling that her heart was being torn out.

'Why are you leaving me? Why must you go so soon? What is happening?'

Gently, patiently, he took her in his arms and kissed her eyes.

'Nothing is the matter. But I have a busy life, my heart, and not an easy one. Urgent business summons me to Paris and you must let me go.'

But still she did not let him go. This sudden departure in the middle of the night terrified her. It seemed to her she understood the reason all too well.

'Charles, I beg you — tell me the truth! You are a conspirator, aren't you?'

He stared at her in astonishment and then began to laugh, gently unfastening the arms linked round his neck.

'Since you have guessed, it is hopeless to deny it – it's true, I do conspire. But there is nothing you can do about it, so now, be a good girl—'

Kneeling among the ravaged bedclothes with the silky mass of her hair tumbled about her, she watched him with a feeling of desperation as he dressed quickly. She had not been wrong. Charles led a dangerous, fugitive life, and she could only accept it. Their love might not be easy in this land ruled by a tyrant but she would wait for him and if he had to flee, then she would fly with him.

'Promise me,' she said in a soft, loving voice, 'that if you are in danger, you will tell me. I will come to you in hell, if need be.'

He was tying his neckcloth in front of the tall cheval glass which stood in one corner but he turned and gave her a penetrating glance. Kneeling like that on the crumpled silken sheets, her skin gleaming like soft gold in the rich night of her hair, she was as bewitchingly beautiful as any pagan statuette.

'I promise,' he said gravely. Then, with sudden harshness: 'Get back into bed.'

Instead of obeying him, she stretched sensuously, like a cat.

'Why? It's too hot—'

The drowsy fire had begun to burn up brightly once more. In an instant, Charles was on Marianne.

'Because I have to go – and because you tempt me still, she-devil! Quick! Into bed with you!'

Half angry, half in fun, he began bundling her up in the sheets, wrapping her firmly in the blue covers until only her face peeped out, deaf to her cries of protest. Then, laughing, he kissed her.

'There! Now, be good. You can go home whenever you like. A carriage will be waiting.'

'But, when shall I see you again—'

'Soon, I promise you.'

'You don't even know—'

'What? Who you are? Or where you live? It does not matter. Duroc found you. He will find you again. Goodbye, *mio dolce amore*. Don't catch cold, because of your voice — I love you.'

He got up and went quickly to the door and opened it. Marianne called after him.

'Charles!'

'Yes?'

'Take care of yourself, please—'

He only smiled at her, blew her a kiss and then he was gone. And not until then did it occur to Marianne that she did not know the first thing about him.

She waited, listening for the sound of carriage wheels, then after they had disappeared into the night, she sighed deeply. Now, she was truly alone.

She fought her way out of the cocoon of sheets into which he had bundled her and got up. She was no longer sleepy and felt no desire to remain longer in the house which, now that Charles had gone, seemed unfamiliar, almost hostile. The pink dress lay like a crumpled dawn cloud on the carpet. Marianne picked it up and hugged it to her with a surge of gratitude. She could never forget now, that it was in this dress he had loved her.

She saw her reflection in the tall mirror and could not repress a start of surprise. She saw herself from head to foot, but did not recognize what she saw. That woman with the dark-ringed eyes, the mouth still swollen from his kisses, the provocative limbs, was that herself? She ran her hand slowly, experimentally over the thighs which Charles had caressed, realizing in some obscure fashion that the still innocent girl she had been when she came there was gone for ever. She was a woman now, she thought with a sense of triumph, a woman in full possession of her powers and the thought made her glad because the change had come about through him and for him.

A light scratching at the door cut short her meditations and sent her scuttling for the reassuring shelter of the bed-clothes.

'Come in,' she said.

Duroc's head appeared round a crack in the door.

'Forgive me for disturbing you but I wish for your instructions. Until what hour would you care to sleep?'

'I am not sleepy any more,' Marianne assured him. 'In fact, I should be happy to return to Paris at once.'

'But – it is still the middle of the night. And very cold!'

'I do not mind that. And it is best I should return. I do not know what his Highness will think at my coming home so late. He will never believe I have been singing all this time—'

'Indeed no, but—' Duroc added with a quiet smile, 'I think that Monsieur de Talleyrand was prepared for you to return late, even very late. I will order something warming for you and have the horses put to.'

As she sat in the brougham that was ferrying her back to Paris, Marianne was still wondering why Talleyrand should have been so certain she would come home very late. Had he thought that Charles would ask her to sing for much longer than he had done? Or – or had the cunning mind of the Limping Devil foreseen what would happen? Had he foreseen how deeply his friend would be drawn to her and how completely Marianne on her side would be won by him? Had he known that they would fall in love? Had he, in introducing her to Charles Denis, meant to give him simply the pleasure of her voice, or Marianne herself? With such a man, anything was possible, but as the horses carried her onwards at a steady pace she sent a warm, grateful thought out to the wily diplomat. She owed him the most beautiful night of her life, her first real love, because now, with the passing of time and the events which had taken place between, Marianne was able to see her brief infatuation for Francis Cranmere in its true light, a romantic schoolgirl illusion, the normal attraction of a very young girl for any good-looking man. She would never forget that it was Talleyrand who, deliberately or not, had thrown her into Charles' arms.

But now, she was in a hurry to be back. She would question the Prince, even if it meant being disrespectful. He must tell her everything he knew about Charles Denis. In her

new-found love, Marianne identified herself completely with the
man she loved. She wanted to live his life, even or especially if
that life was dangerous. All this, Talleyrand must tell her or
else she would apply to Dorothée who was surely bound to
have heard at least something about the strange Monsieur
Denis.

It was freezing hard now and the carriage windows were
thickly frosted over but wrapped in her coat and plenty of
rugs tucked carefully round her by kind Monsieur Duroc,
and a footwarmer under her toes, Marianne felt wonderfully
happy and comfortable. Duroc had begged her pardon for
being unable to escort her himself and deluged the coachman
with instructions, not to go too fast, take care the horses did
not slip, make quite certain the young lady reached home
safely, and a host of other things. Consequently, the man was
driving with great caution, due probably to the steepness of
the slope they were descending.

Somewhere over the fields, a church clock struck five. It
was answered from close by by the sound of bells ringing for
masses. There must be a convent somewhere near. After a
few minutes, driving on level ground, the carriage slowed
down and stopped. Marianne leaned forward in surprise, and
rubbing a clear patch on the glass, she saw a broad band of
water a little way off. They had come to the River Seine.
Suddenly, the door opened and the coachman looked in.

'You will have to get out here, madame,' he said. 'We have
to take the ferry.'

'The ferry? What ferry? We took no ferry when I came?'

'Because you came by the bridge of St Cloud. But they've
been rebuilding it for two years now and when it freezes as
hard as this it is not safe. Better to take the ferry. This is
Suresnes.'

Looking beyond the coachman's swaddled figure, Marianne could see a big barge with a lighted lantern on it waiting a little way off. But it looked quite empty and the air
which came in through the open door was so bitterly cold
that she shivered and huddled deeper in her rugs.

'It is much too early,' she said irritably. 'No one will take us across at this hour. Let us go back and take the bridge.'

'Not worth it, madame. The ferryman will take us, I promise you. It's early yet but he's already got people waiting on
the other side. Folk come every morning to hear mass with
the Trappists of Mont-Valérien. So if you'll be so good as to
get out. It's best the carriage should be as light as possible to
go on board.'

'Very well, if I must,' Marianne sighed, putting aside her
rugs regretfully. She gathered up her skirts and taking the
hand the coachman offered with an injunction 'to take care
and not slip' she jumped lightly to the ground.

At the same instant, a black cloth was flung over her
head.

CHAPTER TWO

The Riders of the Shadows

Marianne screamed but a hand was clapped roughly over her mouth outside the cloth and she quickly realized that all resistance would be useless. Terrified and half-suffocated, she felt arms round her knees and shoulders as she was lifted off the ground. A slight rolling movement told her that her kidnappers had boarded the ferry. A masterful voice spoke.

'Make it a little quicker, if you please. I'm damnably cold. The horses will be freezing on the other bank.'

There was another sound, as of a bag of money being thrown, followed by muffled, obsequious thanks and she guessed that the coachman had been paid. Certainly the coach did not come aboard. There was a noise of metal-shod wheels on the pebbled shore, a noise which soon faded and disappeared. Then there was nothing but the slap of water against the side of the boat.

Marianne was flung down on the bare planks of the deck but a strong arm still held her firmly pressed against an unknown chest. Marianne fought desperately against imminent suffocation and driving panic. Who were these men, and what did they want with her? Were they merely carrying her over to the other side or – she felt sick at the thought of the black water she had glimpsed briefly. She wriggled, trying to loosen the choking folds of cloth but the arm only clutched her more tightly.

'Lie still, little fool,' ordered the same commanding voice. 'Or I'll throw you in the water—'

The fact that he should threaten her with it meant that he did not mean to do away with her at once. Ever so slightly reassured, Marianne tried to fight down the feeling of suffocation but she failed. The material, a cloak it might be, was too thick to let even a breath of air reach her lips. She was being slowly suffocated.

'I can't breathe,' she managed to gasp. 'For pity's sake—'

'Take off the cloak,' a fresh voice advised. 'In any case, we are here—'

The thud of the barge striking the banks came just as the cloak was loosened round her head. It was only just in time. Half-fainting, Marianne gulped instinctively at the icy air while a heavily gloved hand slapped her sharply to revive her.

'She's fainted,' said the man with the harsh voice, critically.

'A faint may be worse than it looks,' the other answered.

Both voices sounded cultivated. They certainly did not belong to ordinary highway robbers, Marianne thought, her mind still working automatically. She opened her eyes and saw two men in black masks bending over her. They wore round hats and voluminous riding cloaks. They were now on the other side of the river and just underneath the trees of the Boulogne, which at this point came close down to the bank, she could see two other horsemen waiting beside a carriage she recognized all too readily.

'The black cab,' she said faintly.

One of the masked men laughed. 'So she had noticed it! You were right, she is much more dangerous than she seemed. Come now, we must be off.'

'One moment. Just because she is dangerous, we must make sure of her. Letting her breathe is one thing—'

'But what have I done?' Marianne protested as the second man was binding her hands swiftly with a silk scarf. 'Where are you taking me? And why?'

This was ridiculous! Anger was now beginning to overcome her fear, reviving her instinct of self-preservation.

'That, mademoiselle, you will be told when we reach our destination,' the man answered. 'For the present, you will best keep silent. We should not like to have to kill a woman—'

She was suddenly aware of the long-barrelled duelling pistol gleaming in the man's gloved hand, the muzzle pressed close to her left breast. The threat was serious.

'I'll be quiet,' she breathed.

'Good. Now, if you will excuse me—'

Another scarf was bound across her eyes, so tightly that no ray of light showed through. After this, her kidnappers took an arm each and guided her to the carriage. She felt other hands reach out to her from inside, and pull her up the steps. The door slammed. Marianne found herself sitting on a seat that was not uncomfortable. She could hear someone breathing beside her and guessed that this was the person who had helped her into the carriage. Outside, she heard someone say:

'The muff! There, by the water. We cannot leave it there. The chief said: "Leave no traces".'

'Why not? They might think she was drowned.'

'Leaving her muff carefully on the opposite side! Fool!'

A few seconds later, the door opened again and she felt someone push her bound hands into the muff. The man sitting beside her spoke for the first time and she repressed a shudder. His voice was like steel, hard and merciless.

'Such care for a renegade!'

'Our job is to take her, not to judge her,' the first man said firmly. 'If she is guilty, she will die, but she need not suffer unnecessarily. We have to get her to the chief in one piece!'

The door banged to and the carriage moved off, speeding to a gallop as it plunged into the thickets of the wood. Marianne could hear the four horsemen galloping behind. She wondered who was this chief to whom they were taking her.

The journey in the carriage was comparatively brief but it was followed by a much longer one on foot. Two of Marianne's captors seized her arms and half carried her along. The way seemed endless. And it felt to Marianne as though she were being dragged down a fearful, slippery and evil-smelling slope. The air was cold and dank as though at the bottom of a tunnel and a smell of rottenness assailed her nostrils. No light was visible below the bandage over her eyes, although the rubbing against the cushions of the coach had loosened it a little. Neither of her companions had spoken since leaving the river bank and Marianne found herself moving in a wholly dark and silent world. Only the strength of the hands holding her upright and the sound of men breathing told her she had not been spirited away by ghosts. From time to time, in the course of this nightmare journey, she heard the sound of a cat yowling or the trickle of running water somewhere. Her feet in the pink satin slippers felt like ice and were bruised unmercifully as she stumbled blindly along the stony path. She would have fallen had not the phantom riders held her up. Her blood congealed with terror and there was a tight ache in her throat. This hideous adventure, coming so soon after leaving the enchanted pavilion where she had known such happiness, was like a nightmare from which she knew that there was no awakening. She was like a trapped bird flinging herself against the bars of her cage but only succeeding in hurting herself.

A door banged suddenly. They had entered what must be a lighted passage because Marianne could see a yellow gleam of light. Then came some kind of muddy court or garden, followed by some crumbling steps. Someone whistled three times, then knocked twice on a door. It became suddenly warm. Marianne felt a floor beneath her feet. A smell of cabbage soup and sour wine filled her nostrils. At last, the bandage was taken from her eyes.

She looked about her fearfully. Five men stood around her wearing black masks and dressed in black, but with a certain elegance. There were two more, evil-looking fellows in dirty smocks and oilcloth caps. The figures stood out grimly against the background of a wretched wine shop, lit by two smoking lamps. The walls shone with grease and sweat, there were rickety tables, chairs losing their stuffing and, in one corner, an ancient trunk covered with moth-eaten fabric. Only the glasses and the row of bottles that stood on a shelf looked clean and new. But most of all, the prisoner was struck by the appearance of an extraordinary old woman who rose up suddenly out of the shadows, leaning on a cane. She was so bent and broken that she looked at least a hundred and on her powdered hair she wore a massive lace cap, torn and filthy, in the fashion of twenty years before, as was the greyish muslin fichu crossed on her breast. Her stained gown must once have been a handsome violet silk and a great golden cross gleamed on her bosom. The old woman's face was so criss-crossed and veined with wrinkles that it resembled the bark of some ancient tree, but although her sharp nose all but met her chin, the eyes, very nearly as green as Marianne's own, were bright and young like new leaves on an old withered trunk.

This ancient creature dragged her rheumaticky limbs painfully up to Marianne and looked her up and down with a wicked grin.

'Fine game, Baron! Very fine game—' she cackled. 'Satin and ermine, mark you! To say nothing of what's underneath! Do you really want to send all this to the bottom of the Seine with a stone around its neck? Do you know what a waste it is?'

A trickle of cold sweat ran down Marianne's back at the fearful sound of the old woman's cackling laugh. But the man she had addressed as 'Baron', who seemed to be the leader of the band, merely shrugged.

'The court will decide. I carry out my orders, Fanchon-Fleur-de-lis. I've had trouble enough laying hands on her. She never went out but by day and with a good escort. Until tonight's little affair.'

'We need not regret that,' another broke in swiftly and Marianne recognized the voice of the man who had been with her in the carriage. 'We were able to confirm what we suspected — that she was meant for him. We took her on the road from Butard. And God knows we waited long enough! He must have found her to his liking.'

Once again, Marianne's hackles rose at the cackling laughter of the old woman with the curious name.

'I've had enough of this!' she burst out suddenly. 'More than enough! Tell me, once and for all, what you want with me! Kill me if you insist, but do it quickly! Or else let me go!'

Her protests ended in a cry of pain as the old woman struck her sharply across the knuckles with the knob of her cane.

'That will do!' she snapped shrilly. 'Speak when you are spoken to! Otherwise, keep silent — or I might forget myself and kill you! And I'd be sorry afterwards because if the court will listen to me, my beauty, they'll give you into my keeping and I'll take good care of you. I have a little house at Ranelagh where I entertain some gentlemen of substance. Your favours would fetch a high price! An imperial whore! I hope he's a good lover, at least?'

'Who? What do you mean?' Marianne said in a choked voice.

'Why him, of course, the Corsican ogre! You must not be so modest. In the profession I have in mind for you, it will be something to be proud of—'

Marianne decided the old woman must be mad. What was she talking about? What was this about an ogre? In her bewilderment, she was even able to ignore the creature's sordid threats. Nothing made any sense.

'You are mad,' she said with a pitying shrug.

'Mad, am I? You wait—'

She raised her cane again but the Baron intervened.

'That's enough! I have already told you, Fanchon, it is not for us to judge. Leave her alone. We will go down now.'

'Maybe,' the old woman muttered obstinately, 'but I'll speak to the Chevalier. She'll see then if I'm mad! I'll tan the hussy's hide for her before I put her to work—'

'Must you really let this woman insult me?' Marianne cried angrily.

There was a moment's silence, broken only by the sniggering of the two men in overalls. The Baron took his prisoner by the arms.

'No,' he said sternly, 'you are right. Come – you Requin, open the trap – and meanwhile, let Pisse-Vinaigre outside make sure we have not been followed.'

One of the rough-looking men went to the back of the room and, grasping a large iron ring, lifted up a trap-door leading apparently to the cellar. The other went outside. The Baron untied Marianne's wrists.

'The trap-door is only wide enough for one,' he said briefly. 'You would fall otherwise.'

She gave him a pale smile of thanks and rubbed her sore wrists gently to restore the circulation to her frozen hands.

'You are very kind,' she said bitterly.

The man's eyes studied her closely through the slits in his mask.

'And you,' he retorted, after a moment, 'are braver than I thought. I prefer that.'

As he thrust her not unkindly towards the trap-door, Marianne thought that he was quite wrong. She was not as brave as he believed, in fact she was half dead with fright but not for anything in the world would she have shown her fear. Her pride kept her upright, her chin held high before these unknown men beneath whose masks she divined aristocrats like herself, men of her own class, even if by some absurd series of misunderstandings she had become their prisoner, though accused of what or why she did not know. In a way, she even felt a kind of impatience to find herself confronted with this mysterious court to which they kept referring, in order to find out at last why they had captured her and why they threatened her like this.

They went down a wooden staircase into the cellar in almost total darkness, illumined only by the candle held by one of the masked riders. The cellar was like any other, filled with barrels, bottles and a strong smell of wine. But in one corner underneath a rack which was moved with surprising ease, there appeared another trap-door, opening this time on to stone steps.

For all her show of courage, Marianne felt herself trembling as she made her way down into the bowels of the earth. She shuddered at the memory of the threats she had heard. A horrible idea came to her that perhaps these silent men were really leading her to her grave. From the anguish of her heart she sent out one desperate thought to Charles. He had promised her that they would meet again soon, he might be thinking of her at that very moment, unaware that she was perhaps being torn from him for ever. She saw all the cruel irony of a fate which opened the gates of death to her at the very moment when she had discovered love and happiness. No, it was too stupid! Marianne swore silently to fight for her life to the very end if only she might yet see Charles again.

About two dozen steep steps had echoed under their feet

when they came at last into a huge, decaying crypt with semi-circular arches. A fierce draught blew through it, making the torches which the riders had brought with them from the first cellar stream out wildly. Their booted feet rang ominously in the tomb-like vault.

The crypt was cut in two by a large black curtain. A gleam of light showed from behind it. Before Marianne had time to wonder what was there, it was thrust aside and a man appeared. He was of medium height with short, crisp, slightly greying hair but of his face nothing was visible except a long, pale nose, owing to his mask and to his thick, black beard. The man's neck and shoulders indicated the strength of a bull, but the eyes which shone through the slits in his mask sparkled so gaily that Marianne found it hard to believe her own. His hands clasped behind his back, displaying the pair of long pistols thrust through his belt, the newcomer strolled up to the prisoner, stared at her closely for a moment and then burst out laughing, which was certainly the last thing Marianne had been expecting.

'S'blood! What a beauty!' he began but his smile changed to a frown as the Baron gave an exclamation of annoyance then stepped forward and murmured something in his ear.

'Very well, if you insist! But I don't like it, Saint-Hubert, I don't like it at all. However, let's get on with it—'

The curtain was pushed aside completely to reveal a long table covered with a scarlet cloth, behind which four men sat facing them with an empty place in the middle for their leader. The bearded man sat down. Six candles stood on the table and these he lighted, revealing the faces of his companions who were also masked and sat as still as stone. But Marianne found her eyes drawn instantly to one of them. All too well she knew that strong, sardonic mouth, that rosy scar that ran up under his mask and in that instant, she knew why she had been kidnapped. One of her judges was Baron Hervé de Kérivoas, otherwise Morvan, the wrecker, the man whom Fouché had so incautiously allowed to escape. She had no eyes for any of the others. One only concerned her: the man she knew as her implacable enemy.

He did not move as she came in. There was no tightening of his features, no exclamation, but the eyes that fastened on the girl's face were bright with hatred. Marianne's only response was a slight scornful movement of her shoulders. She was not really afraid of Morvan. There was something unbalanced about him which made him weak, vulnerable perhaps. It remained to be seen what metal her other judges were made of. The four riders surrounded Marianne and marched her up to the table. All five remained standing and the leader's deep voice rang out.

'We are here,' he said solemnly, 'to hear and pass judgement on this woman who stands accused by one of our brethren of treachery, treason and intelligence with the enemy. Riders of the Shadows, are you ready to listen and pass judgement fairly and with justice?'

'We are,' judges and guards answered in unison.

'But I am not ready!' Marianne cried boldly. 'I am not ready to be judged by strangers for what crime I know not. By what law, by what right do you sit in judgement on me? And what wrong have I done you?'

'You shall know that,' the leader told her, 'when you have heard the accusation.'

'Not before I know with whom I have to deal. One who accuses should have the courage to do so openly, and a judge to pass sentence in broad daylight. I see nothing here but a dark, shadowy cellar and blind moles buried in the earth. My face is not hidden! Dare to show yours if you are really what you claim to be, if not true judges, at least real men!'

Some instinct, deep within her, drove her to defy these men. She found some comfort in it and even a kind of enjoyment.

'Silence!' one of the judges ordered. 'You need not know who we are. You only wish to see our faces the better to denounce us!'

'I understood,' Marianne observed with a disdainful smile, 'that I was not to leave here alive? Are you afraid of me? Afraid of one woman, a prisoner, alone amongst so many. Is that the truth?'

'By all the Gods, I will not have it said that a chit of a girl accused me of being afraid!' the leader cried. He tore off his mask and threw it down before him, revealing a bluff, joyous countenance which had clearly seen more than fifty summers. 'And she is right! What have we to fear from her? I am the Chevalier de Bruslart. Are you ready to answer me now?'

It was a name Marianne had heard more than once. The man's reputation was high in England for courage and loyalty. Sworn enemy of Napoleon, he had for years successfully eluded the unremitting efforts of Fouché and his men to capture him. His presence here was some assurance to Marianne that, if he were really the leader of these men, then at least she would receive something approaching a fair trial. She pointed to Morvan.

'You may ask this gentleman also to remove his mask. I am too well acquainted with Monsieur de Kérivoas – or perhaps here too he prefers the name of Morvan?'

Slowly Morvan removed his mask, revealing his mutilated face. He rose to his feet and seemed to Marianne enormous in this shadowy place.

'Insolence will not save you, Marianne d'Asselnat. I accuse you of having deceived me, of pretending to be what you were not by means of stolen jewels, of causing the death of one of my men and, last of all, of loosing Fouché's bloodhounds on my trail. Thanks to you, my band is decimated, myself in flight and—'

'I had no part in what has befallen you,' Marianne interrupted him quietly, 'and my jewels are my own. But suppose we were to mention your own activities which are my best excuse for anything I may have done. I accuse you of lighting false fires on the shore to draw unhappy vessels to destruction on the rocks on stormy nights, of robbing corpses and doing to death the injured. I accuse you of being that worst of all human fiends, a wrecker! If I deceived you, it was to save my life. That is my legitimate defence. If these men are, as I think, faithful subjects of the King, they should hold you in abhorrence!'

Bruslart's great fist slammed down ringingly on the red table.

'Silence! What we may think concerns only ourselves. We are not here to settle a quarrel but to pass judgement on your actions, madame. Answer me. Your name is Marianne-Elizabeth d'Asselnat de Villeneuve as you told this man?' He indicated Morvan. 'But you are living in Paris under the name of Marianne Mallerousse, a name given you by Nicolas Mallerousse, one of Fouché's most active agents. And you have been employed of late as reader to Madame Grand.'

'To her most serene Highness the Princess of Benevento,' Marianne corrected him proudly. 'You should have thought of that before you kidnapped me. Do you think that when my absence is noted in the morning there will be no search made?'

'No danger of that! The Prince will receive word this morning, by a very short discreetly worded note, that you have found such favour with – the person you know of, that your presence is desired for some time longer in that charming woodland retreat where you spent the night.'

Marianne acknowledged a hit, fighting down the pain she felt at this cynical reminder of the blissful hours she had spent there. Then another thought came to her. Fouché, who always knew everything, who had agents everywhere, surely he would learn of his star's sudden disappearance! Perhaps he knew already that she had been taken to La Celle Saint Cloud, although there was no reason why he should be watching the house of someone of no particular importance. But there was also a possibility that Talleyrand, deceived by the letter, would arrange for Fouché to learn of what, in his eyes, would after all be no more than an amorous escapade.

The Chevalier's cold voice interrupted the somewhat melancholy trend of her thoughts.

'Will you tell me, yes or no, whether you are indeed Marianne d'Asselnat?'

'Since you know I am,' Marianne said rebelliously, 'why do you ask? Are we in a court of justice? Are you a real judge?'

'So, you admit your name and rank – you admit them and yet—'

Bruslart paused. His bearded face twisted with sudden fury as he roared:

'—and yet, you, the daughter of a noble house, the daughter of two martyrs who died for their King, you have not feared to associate with the vilest rabble of this monstrous régime, you have dared to meddle with Fouché's police, to become an informer – and worse!'

So, he knew it all. In spite of herself, Marianne felt a red flush of shame sweep over her face. She understood that for these silent men whose eyes were fixed on her like so many daggers, that was her greatest crime, that she had seemed to come to terms with the régime of the hated Bonaparte. It troubled her like an unfair stigma. Could she make them see that they were wrong, that appearances alone were against her?

'Monsieur,' she said in a low voice, 'that I came to this country, that I have seemed to accept its laws and conditions, was because I had no choice. I did so to save my life. I can explain in detail, if you are willing to listen. But which of you has never tried to save his life at the cost of a lie? Which of you has never taken refuge in a borrowed name and character in such times as these?'

'We have lied,' acknowledged one of the judges who was still masked, 'and we have worn borrowed characters, but we have never betrayed our own people or compounded with the enemy.'

'I have never betrayed my own people!' Marianne cried passionately. 'It is my own people who have betrayed me. I was alone and helpless and I asked for help and assistance from one close to King Louis, and he rejected me without mercy, abandoning me knowingly to the worst of fates! But I have never compounded with Bonaparte's régime! I was brought up in England, brought up to hate him and I recognize his power no more than you. Whatever he made me suffer, I never betrayed the man I knew as Morvan. As for the tyrant who reigns here, I swear on my mother's grave, that I have always execrated—'

Before she could finish, one of the riders, the one who had been addressed as the Baron de Saint-Hubert, had rounded on her, his arm raised and his eyes alight with such a murderous fury that Marianne recoiled instinctively with a cry of terror.

'Renegade! Perjurer! Blasphemer! You should be burned alive for what you have just dared to say, for daring to soil your

mother's memory with a lie! You deserve to die in torment!
Miserable creature! You dare to say you hate Napoleon?'

Saint-Hubert's hand fell heavily on Marianne's arm. He flung
her violently to her knees and held her there.

'You dare to say? Dare you say it again?'

Marianne was white with shock but even now she refused to
give way to her fear.

'Yes—' she whispered. 'I do dare!'

Without releasing his hold on her arm, Saint-Hubert dealt
her a ringing blow to the head which sent her sprawling on the
ground.

'You filthy little vagabond! So frightened for your skin you'll
swear to anything! But your lies shall not save you, do you
hear? So you hate Napoleon, do you? Did you hate him so
much, tonight, at Butard?'

'At – Butard?' Marianne echoed dazedly.

'Yes, at Butard! At the delightful nest he keeps for his
amours and where you spent the night! Or perhaps you were
not in his bed? It was not he who made love to you, eh?'

Marianne's head reeled. Everything seemed suddenly to have
gone mad, the world was falling to pieces about her ears. In her
horror, she began to scream:

'No! No! It's not true! You are lying! The man I saw is called
Charles Denis! An ordinary bourgeois.'

'Will you not cease your lies? And to think that I admired
your courage, that I was ready to speak for you, perhaps to
help you!'

Mad with rage, the Baron was about to strike again but
Bruslart sprang forward suddenly and tore the terrified girl
from his friend's grip and thrust her behind his own broad
back.

'Enough, Baron de Saint-Hubert!' he said grimly. 'I am no
murderer, or persecutor of women! The girl is too frightened to
know what she is saying.'

'Say rather she's making a mockery of us all, Chevalier!
Leave her to me, I'll make her talk. Creatures of her kind deserve no pity.'

'And I say enough! There is something here I do not understand—'

He turned to where Marianne lay half unconscious, face
downwards on the ground. He helped her up and made her sit
on a low stool. Marianne's head was ringing like a cathedral
bell. She struggled unsuccessfully to collect her thoughts but
decided that she must be going mad. What did these men
mean? Of course, that was it. They were mad – or else she was
the victim of some terrible misunderstanding. Charles! –
Charles! Oh God! How could they confuse him with the adven-
turer who held all Europe under his heel? He was so kind and
gentle! They did not know him. They could not know him. He
was just an ordinary man – God, how her head hurt!

Marianne became aware of the rim of a glass pressed to her
lips.

'Drink this,' the Chevalier ordered. 'Then we will try and get
to the bottom of this.'

'Charles!' she moaned. 'Charles Denis. You cannot know—'

'Drink, I tell you. You are green.'

She drank. The wine was strong and heady. Its warmth ran
quickly through her chilled body, reviving a little spark of life.
Pushing the glass away with her hand, she stared at the Chevalier with such a lost expression that he nodded with a trace of
pity.

'So young and yet so depraved?' he murmured under his
breath.

'There is no age in women's depravity!' There was no pity in
Morvan's voice.

'I have asked you to let me sort this out, Monsieur the
Wrecker,' Bruslart retorted, without looking round. 'Stand
back a little, gentlemen, you are upsetting her.'

The Baron de Saint-Hubert gave a sardonic crack of laughter.

'One of these days, Chevalier, your incorrigible weakness for
women will make you do something stupid. I am not sure that
day has not come.'

'If it has come, then I am old enough to see that without

your help. For the present, I should like to question this one without interruptions from you.'

'Very well, question her! But we are here. We are listening.'

The Riders of the Shadows withdrew to the far end of the chamber, a black wall against the grey wall of the crypt. Marianne and Bruslart were left alone by the table.

'Last night,' he began patiently, 'you were taken to the pavilion of Butard at La Celle Saint Cloud?'

'That was the name I was told, certainly.'

'Who took you there?'

'The Prince of Benevento. He told me the house belonged to a friend of his, a bourgeois named Monsieur Charles Denis, a man who had recently suffered a cruel bereavement. My singing was to be a comfort to him.'

'And you were not surprised that such a man as Talleyrand should take the trouble to escort you, in person, to the house of a mere bourgeois?'

'Yes. But the Prince told me that they were friends of long standing. I thought – I thought the Prince might have known him perhaps in the Revolution, or that the name might be a cloak for some foreign conspirator—'

'We will come to that later. Who met you at Butard? A servant?'

'No. I think he was a friend of M. Denis. He was called Duroc. And I saw a manservant as well.'

'A manservant by the name of Constant, was it?'

'Yes – yes, I think so!'

The Chevalier's deep voice became suddenly very gentle. He bent over Marianne and looked hard into her eyes.

'This M. Denis – you love him?'

'Yes! Yes, I love him. I think I loved him from the very first. I saw him and then—'

'And then,' Bruslart finished for her quietly, 'you found yourself in his arms. He attracted you, hypnotized you, bewitched you – they say he can talk love like no one else and write it better still.'

Marianne stared at him wide-eyed.

'But then — you know him? He is a man who leads a secret life, is he not, a conspirator, like yourself? I knew he was in danger!'

For the first time, Bruslart smiled briefly.

'Yes, I know him. As for secrecy, it may well be, for it is true that he is often in danger. Shall I show you your Monsieur Denis?'

'Yes — yes, of course. Is he here?' she cried, carried away by a sudden wonderful hope.

'He is everywhere,' the Chevalier said with a shrug. 'Here, look here.'

Taking a gold coin from his pocket he placed it in Marianne's hand. She stared at it in bewilderment.

'The face,' Bruslart persisted. 'Don't you recognize it?'

Marianne looked. A wave of colour mounted her face. She stood up, mechanically, staring with eyes grown suddenly huge at the fine profile stamped on the gold, a profile she recognized only too well.

'Charles!' she stammered helplessly.

'No,' the Chevalier corrected her grimly. 'Napoleon! It was to him that old fox Talleyrand delivered you tonight, you little fool.'

The gold coin slipped from Marianne's fingers and rolled away over the ancient flagstones. She felt the floor heave under her feet. The walls were performing a wild dance around her. Marianne gave one cry and fell headlong, like a felled sapling.

When she came to herself again, she was lying on some straw in a dark place lit by a flickering brazier. A strange individual holding a candle was bending over her sympathetically. With his pointed face, receding hair, large ears and bristling whiskers, he looked like a mouse wearing a goatee. His black eyes, which were round and very bright, strengthened this resemblance. When he saw Marianne open her eyes, he gave a broad smile which split his face in two.

'Ah, that's right! We're coming round! Are we feeling better?'

Marianne made an effort to sit up and managed to prop
herself on one elbow, though not without a groan. Her head
ached horribly and her body felt bruised, as though she had
been beaten.

'I — yes, thank you. I do feel a little better. But what happened to me? Where are we?'

The stranger with the large ears set his candle down on the
ground and sat himself beside her, arms clasped about his
skinny knees, carefully lifting the skirts of his coat before he
did so. His blue coat and nut-brown pantaloons were of good
cloth and well cut. They must have been elegant before the
prison — there was no other name for the place in which they
were, a kind of cavern shut off by iron bars — had worked
irreparable harm on the tasteful garments.

'As to what has happened to you,' he said calmly, 'I cannot
tell you. The Chevalier de Bruslart, who uses these cellars as
a meeting place when he is in Paris, brought you in a short
while ago with the help of some of his friends. I believe I
gathered that you were to take up residence in this charming
spot while the gentlemen examined your case further. They did
not seem able to agree. One was for putting you in the Seine to
cool off, with a good, big stone, but the Chevalier, a true
gentleman indeed, declared roundly that he would kill anyone
who dispatched you without his express permission. As for our
present place of residence—' the little man made an all-embracing gesture taking in the rough-hewn chalky cavern around
them '—I am able to inform you, gracious lady, that we are in
the old quarries of Chaillot which have been disused now for
many years. If it were not for these bars, I could show you the
old lime kiln still in very good order.'

'Quarries?' Marianne said, 'I was in some kind of crypt when
I fainted.'

'It opens off these quarries. It is all that is left of the old
convent of the Dames de la Visitation where the gentle Louise
de la Vallière once sought refuge from the adulterous passions
of Louis XIV, where Bossuet pronounced his funeral oration
over Henrietta of England, where—'

This singular individual was clearly a most cultivated person but just at that moment French history was very far from Marianne's thoughts. She was amazed, and even a little disappointed, to find herself still alive. How much simpler it would all have been if the Riders of the Shadows had killed her while she was unconscious! Then there would not have been this waking with its train of heartache and bitter memories. If only they had thrown her straight into the Seine when they took her from her carriage! She would have had her moment of agony and nameless horror but it would have been comparatively brief and by now it would have been all over. She would be dead, taking with her the sweet and wonderful memory of the night she had just passed. She would have died with Charles' kisses warm on her lips, in the full, dazzling glory of love's dawn. She could have kept that, at least. But now, now that she had learned who he was and knew herself to have been no more than a plaything for an Emperor's whim, now her whole life was in ruins indeed.

She had believed that when he took her in his arms, Charles had been mastered by the same attraction, had suffered the same irresistible revelation as she had herself. But no, she had merely served to distract a selfish man who, for the sake of establishing a dynasty, had just cast down from the throne the woman he had placed there, the companion of his youth, the wife whom the Pope himself had crowned in Notre Dame with such splendid ceremony that day in December. Marianne had given herself gladly to Charles Denis because that Charles Denis had needed love and tenderness but it made her sick with grief and horror to think that she had been simply a toy for Napoleon.

She understood it all now: the care with which Talleyrand had taken her there and also what the Minister, at present out of favour, hoped to gain from making this handsome present to his master.

She understood the flurry caused by the so-called M. Denis' arrival and also the slight Mediterranean accent, and the Italian words of love. The Corsican! It was to the Corsican that she had given herself so trustingly, on the spur of the moment, simply because she had been drawn to him as she had never been to any man before. The memory of their kisses and caresses which, only a few hours before, had been so sweet now burned her life like a red-hot iron. Utterly overcome with shame, she buried her head in her drawn-up knees and began to cry as though her heart would break.

A gentle, clumsy hand pushed aside the tumbled hair that hung over her face and began mopping her tear-stained cheeks with a handkerchief that smelled strongly of orris and a brotherly arm was put round her shoulders.

'There, there, you must not cry like that! You're not dead yet! And if you'll take my word for it, you aren't going to die. The Chevalier de Bruslart has never killed a woman yet and if he decides to protect you—'

'I don't care if he does kill me!' Marianne cried miserably. 'I ask nothing better! Let him kill me and let me have done with this stupid life once and for all!'

'You want to die? You? With that face, those eyes—'

'If you dare tell me I am beautiful, I shall scream!' Marianne burst out passionately. 'I wish I were ugly, hideous, deformed! Then I should not be where I am! Then I should have been no one's wretched plaything! You cannot know what they have done to me, how I have been degraded, ruined, dishonoured—'

The words were pouring out now in a broken, incoherent stream as her control gave way at last. But the little man with the big ears did not seem to care. He got up and going to a pitcher of water which stood in one corner, dipped his handkerchief in it and set himself conscientiously to cleaning up his companion's dirty, tear-stained face. The cold water had a calming effect on Marianne. In a little while, she fell silent and let him wash her like a baby.

'There,' he said with satisfaction when the sobs and crying had dwindled to no more than some slight hiccupping. 'It does you good to cry but, my dear child, when you are my age, which must be about twice yours, you will know that there is nothing in the world to compare with simply being alive and that for someone who looks like you to say they want to die is not merely a wicked sin, it also shows extreme bad taste and ingratitude. You may have much to complain of in this base world but you must agree with me that Dame Nature has shown herself more than generous towards you even if you have suffered a bit just recently. There's nothing more comforting, when things seem to be going wrong, than to confide in someone. So tell your troubles to Uncle Arcadius. He knows some wonderful ways of getting out of the most hopeless situations!'

'Uncle Arcadius?' Marianne said in astonishment.

'Oh the devil! Have I omitted to present myself? That would be an unpardonable lapse of manners!'

He was on his feet in an instant, and, whirling round, favoured his companion with a bow in the best swashbuckling tradition. The only thing lacking was a feathered hat.

'The Vicomte Arcadius de Jolival, at your service, former revolutionary out of step with the times, very present and genuine admirer of his glorious Majesty the Emperor Napoleon, artist and man of letters – and a Greek prince into the bargain!'

'A Greek prince?' Marianne said, stunned by this flow of speech from the little man. She could not help being diverted by it and he had succeeded in distracting her from her own sorrows.

'My mother was a Comnena. Through her, I am related, though distantly it's true, to the wife of the Governor of Paris, the talented Duchess of Abrantes – very distantly, perhaps I should say.'

Marianne recalled suddenly the little dark woman, looking so elegant in the set of enormous rubies, whom she had seen chatting to Countess Metternich in Talleyrand's salon. It was extraordinary how all these French people seemed to know one another. In Paris, one could discover common acquaintances even in a dungeon. Trying to shake off the numbness which chilled her to the heart, she too rose and went to hold her hands out to the warmth of the brazier. Her head still ached but her back felt less painful now. She noticed that this strange little man had declared himself roundly for the Emperor but could she in all honesty blame him for that when she had herself fallen a victim so quickly to the pretended Charles Denis?

'What are you doing here?' she asked suddenly. 'Is it because of your sympathies for — the régime?'

Arcadius de Jolival shrugged.

'If Bruslart set out to imprison everyone who sympathized with the régime, as you put it, he'd need somewhere a great deal bigger than the quarries of Chaillot. Ten provinces would not be enough. No, I am here for debt!'

'For debt? To whom?'

'To the Dame Desormeaux, known as Fanchon-Fleur-de-lis. I dare say you must have met that remarkable lady on the upper floors of this desirable paradise?'

'That horrible old woman in rags? You owe her money?' Marianne cried, feeling more and more bewildered.

'Well, yes.'

Jolival settled himself more comfortably and smoothed out a crease in his pantaloons before continuing in a conversational tone:

'You must not take Fanchon's rags too seriously. She dresses as occasion demands. Believe me, I've seen her dressed like an empress.'

'She is horrible!'

'Morally, I grant you. One could not find worse, but, physically, she was once a great beauty. Do you know how she got her name?'

'How should I know?' Marianne said with a shrug. 'I saw her only a short time ago for the first time.'

'She's had her ups and downs. In her prime, Fanchon was as beautiful as a lily and was done the honours of the Parc-aux-Cerfs. She was one of the does that great huntsman and man of taste, King Louis XV, pursued. She even had a daughter by him, Manette, as lovely as her mother and, even from the first, lavishly endowed. But Fanchon's ambitions for her daughter had no end. She had her brought up like a princess which, in part, she was, under a false name — and in this very convent of which we occupy the ruins. Meanwhile, her mother was indulging in a host of activities which were all highly lucrative but frowned on by good society to such an extent that one fine morning, she found herself kneeling before the Paris executioner and having a fleur-de-lis branded on her right shoulder. But far from being ashamed of it, she actually boasted. After all, she knew all about fleurs-de-lis from the King's bed. At all events, it was that flower which enabled her to survive the Revolution without a scratch and even to enlarge what was already the beginning of a pretty fortune. Unfortunately Manette, after being brought up as a great lady and serving in the household of another great lady, found it quite natural to act as a great lady to the end. On the day her daughter's head fell, Fanchon swore war to the death on the Revolution and all that followed from it. To this day, the King has no more faithful servant and, naturally, she hates the Emperor to the same extent.'

'It is a strange story,' Marianne said, having listened to it with the same rapt attention she had been used to give to her beloved novels. 'But where do your debts come in?'

'Among other wordly goods, Fanchon owns an illegal gaming house, attached, incidentally, to a house of ill-fame. I lost everything I possessed there, as well as a good deal I did not. I'd literally nothing left but my shirt, and only that by some last remaining shred of modesty. But Fanchon had me taken out by her men and clapped in here and here I stay until I pay her what I owe her.'

This did not appear to disturb him unduly and Marianne, distracted from her own troubles in spite of herself, could not help smiling.

'But if she keeps you prisoner here, how can she ever expect you to pay?'

'Oh, that's quite simple,' Arcadius said with an apologetic grin. 'It's marriage she wants!'

'She wants – to marry you?' Marianne exclaimed with horror.

'No, not quite that. She has a niece, much uglier than herself though rather younger. It is this frightful hag I have had the misfortune to please. I do not leave here until the ring is on my finger.'

The misfortunes of the 'Greek Prince' had worked a miracle. Marianne found herself wanting to laugh and instantly her grief seemed lessened. She was discovering that a companion in trouble, especially one like this, was the best of all comforts because he was the kind of person who took even the worst disasters philosophically.

'And – have you been here long?' she asked.

'A fortnight. But I can hold out a bit longer – especially with such pleasant company. The gentle Philomène is really rather too plain!'

There was a silence, employed by the man of letters in cleaning his nails with a piece of straw. Then, looking up, he saw that Marianne, who was still standing by the brazier, had lapsed once more into her own bitter thoughts. He coughed.

'Ahem – if I might – why don't you come and sit here by me and tell me your story. I can have some quite good ideas, I promise you, and besides, it's a relief to share one's burden. I have an idea that your young shoulders are carrying one that's much too heavy for them. Come here – I – I really should like to help you.'

Quite suddenly, he had dropped his careless pose and slightly ironical tone. Marianne saw in his comical face nothing but immense kindness and real sympathy. She moved slowly to sit by him on the straw.

'Thank you,' she said in a small voice. 'You are right. I'll tell you all about it.'

When Marianne had finished her story, she saw that Arcadius was looking at her with eyes that shone with admiration. He had not said a word all the time that she had been speaking except for occasional sympathetic noises at the most tragical parts, but when at last she sighed and fell silent, all he said was:

'You spent more than half the night with the Emperor – and yet you wish you were dead?'

Marianne was left speechless. For him to be a warm admirer of the usurper was one thing but that he should regard what had happened to her as the most wonderful good fortune, seemed to her rather excessive.

'You think I should be glad to have been made a pastime for the master of the hour?'

'I think chiefly that you have a very wrong idea of what has happened to you. It is not so easy to attract Napoleon.'

'And you think—'

'That you attracted him as much as he appealed to you? I'd lay my life on it. To begin with, you possess the thing above all others that he adores: a fine voice. Remember, he kept la Grassini for months when she was as stupid as an owl, and even when he still loved Josephine. And, besides that – but haven't you forbidden me to speak of your beauty? I think you know nothing of the man you love! And yet, he is worth knowing, you know.'

Marianne was beginning to find this conversation quite surprisingly enjoyable but it was rudely interrupted. Candlelight wavered on the chalky walls of the passage that opened off their prison cave and they stopped talking abruptly. Dragging footsteps sounded and a moment later Fanchon-Fleur-de-lis appeared leaning on her cane. After her came the man they had called Requin who carried a large parcel under his arm. Opening the gate in the bars with a large key, he stood back to allow the old woman to enter and then followed himself.

Fanchon hobbled forward to the brazier and gazed at the two prisoners malevolently. She pointed with her cane to Marianne.

'Get up,' she ordered. 'And take your clothes off!'

Marianne did not move. 'You cannot be serious, I imagine?' she said.

'I am so serious that unless you do as you're told at once, you shall taste my stick and Requin shall wield it. Now! Take off those things! Such garments were not made to be dragged in the dirt and I can sell them for a good price. Ho, don't worry,' she sneered, 'I have brought you others. It is no part of my plan for you to freeze to death.'

'And did the Chevalier order you to take her clothes?' Arcadius interrupted. 'It would surprise me. If I were you, my lady, I would go and ask him first—'

'To do that, little gentleman, I should have to gallop after him. He was obliged to set off in haste for Normandy with the Riders. A friend of his, a lady, is in peril at Valognes. In such matters he does not need telling twice! He will be away for several days and, in the meantime, has entrusted this little ewe-lamb to my tender care. He wants her back unharmed so that he can come to a decision about her. And I shall make sure she's returned unharmed because it is my hope he'll give her to me. But come now, quickly—'

Requin had dropped the bundle of clothes on Marianne's knees. She stared unhappily at the three people round her.

'Leave her alone,' Arcadius said angrily. 'What an old miser you are! You'd shave an egg, wouldn't you, Fanchon?'

'And you'd better keep quiet yourself, my little fellow, or Requin will teach you to mind your manners. He's a head taller than you are. You'd come out of it badly,' the old woman retorted, brandishing her cane.

'Please,' Marianne broke in. 'It is no good. I will give her my clothes. All I ask is to be allowed to change in peace.'

Neither Fanchon nor Requin moved. The man actually came and stood directly before Marianne, his hands in his pockets and a gleam in his eyes.

'If that man does not go away,' Marianne said sharply, 'I shall complain to the Chevalier!'

She had scored a hit. The threat worked. Apparently Bruslart had left strong instructions regarding her. She did not relish staying in this underground dungeon until he should return but at least it would give her some respite and from her point of view, to gain time was all important. Talleyrand might institute a search for her. For the present, the only thing that mattered was that the Chevalier de Bruslart had ordered that no harm should come to her. She meant to use that precious knowledge for all it was worth. Moreover, Fanchon-Fleur-de-lis instantly proved her right.

'Out, Requin!' she ordered.

The man growled but obeyed and Arcadius turned his face to the wall while Marianne hurriedly took off her pink dress and cloak, although it made her sad to do so. In a moment, the fairy-tale dress was clutched in the old woman's skinny grasp and Marianne, with an assumption of indifference, put on the thick skirt and bodice and the heavy woollen stockings which had been brought for her, and wrapped herself in the big black shawl.

The clothes were not new or particularly clean but they were warm and all things considered rather more suitable for living in a quarry filled with nothing but straw and chalk dust.

Fanchon, satisfied with her loot, was now ready to go back upstairs but before leaving the cave she had something more to say.

'You'll get some food later, at the same time as this stubborn mule here! Still nothing to say to me, then, eh, handsome? Philomène is getting impatient, you know.'

'Then let her. I am not yet ready to become one of the family.'

'Think, my lad, think carefully! If within a week you have not decided, Philomène may be a widow before she's a wife! My patience has limits.'

'Precisely,' Arcadius retorted smoothly, 'and mine has not.'

When the old woman and her bodyguard had gone, Marianne's new friend returned to her side and began piling up armfuls of straw to make a more comfortable bed.

'You should lie down and try to sleep,' he said kindly. 'I have no means of knowing the time because that gracious lady had my watch off me long ago but it cannot be long till daylight. Not that we'll see it, of course, but at least we shall be left in peace. Our charming Fanchon's little cabaret, the Iron Man, is almost deserted by day. By night, on the other hand, there is generally plenty going on. Go to sleep, you are so pale and there are shadows round your eyes. Besides, there's nothing else you can do.'

Marianne accepted the improvised bed which her companion had made for her while he went over to the brazier and threw on some logs of which there was fortunately a good supply in one corner. Curled up in her shawl, she watched him gratefully. He had been friendly and restored her courage, but above all, he was there. Marianne dared not think what her feelings would have been had she been left all alone in the dark in the depths of this abandoned quarry, a prey to all the phantoms of terror and despair. Now, she would be able to sleep a little and seek, in rest, an answer to all the questions which just at present she did not want to ask. How could she face admitting to herself, without the risk of going out of her mind, that she was thoroughly in love with the very man who, ever since childhood, she had learned to fear and hate above all others? She was utterly exhausted. Her mind refused to function. She must sleep and sleep might bring her counsel. Tomorrow, she would seek some way of escape.

CHAPTER THREE

Greece, Rome and Carthage seek an Ally

Marianne woke from a fitful sleep broken by nightmares, shivering with fever in spite of all the straw which the kindly, anxious Arcadius had heaped over her. Her throat hurt and in a little while she had begun to cough.

'You have certainly caught cold,' her new friend lamented. 'You were frozen when they brought you here. You need proper care!'

Consequently, when the bearer of their food, Requin, arrived, Arcadius set up a vigorous demand for tisanes, blankets and a soothing draught for the cough.

'I've no orders,' the man said roughly. 'Makes no difference to me if she catches her death!'

'But Fanchon will make a difference to you if anything happens to her, for the excellent reason that she will have to answer for her to the Chevalier. If you have no orders, then go and get some!'

Requin dragged away reluctantly, without hurrying, but returned much more quickly carrying a heap of old blankets which he dropped carelessly on top of Marianne. After that he took a flask from his pocket.

'Medicine,' he said.

'I asked for a hot tisane!'

'It's coming—'

He stood for a moment apparently engaged in some kind of inner struggle. At length with a massive sigh he took out a second flask and handed it to Arcadius with the agonized look of one parting from a beloved friend.

'Rum,' he growled.

Arcadius held the flask up to the light and laughed.

'It's not full! Helped yourself to your share, have you? Well, I'll say nothing if you'll bring me everything I want for her.'

'Let her die,' the other muttered in an ugly voice.

'You said that before. It is of no interest to me. Now, be off with you, and do what I ask, or I shall tell Fanchon!'

Like a mother, Arcadius de Jolival set himself to make the invalid swallow a little of the medicine. Then he wrapped her snugly in the blankets. She let him do it. Her mind was a blank and she was tired to death, yet on the verge of tears. She had been ill so little in her life that she had no resources of patience or endurance with which to face this sudden weakness. Her illness only increased her longing to escape and get out of this cavern that was so depressingly like a tomb. She did not want to die there, like a rat in a hole. The moment of despair which had prostrated her the night before had vanished and nothing was left but the commanding instinct of self-preservation.

With the fever, her brain worked more frantically than ever. She cast about desperately for some source of salvation, because although she had gathered that Bruslart did not mean to kill her, she was much less sure of Morvan. He was determined not to let her escape his vengeance even if he had to stand up to the Chevalier himself. Unless, that was, he would consider himself sufficiently revenged were old Fanchon to succeed in reducing Marianne to the kind of ignoble slavery she had threatened. For the present, Morvan had gone with Bruslart and the other Riders of the Shadows, but he would return and who could tell whether he would not by that time have succeeded in persuading the Chevalier that she must die? He had a substantial ally in the Baron de Saint-Hubert whose contempt for Marianne was overwhelming. Day after day, while the prisoner pined in her dungeon, they could be pleading their cause, wearing down Bruslart's resistance. The more she thought of it, the more Marianne was convinced that it would come down to a choice between the Seine and the house at Ranelagh. She had to escape first. But how?

'Stop worrying your head so,' Jolival's voice broke soothingly into her thoughts. 'You think too much, my dear. The man whose regard you won last night is all powerful, surely he will seek you out?'

'If he wished for me tonight, I would have a chance, but he did not conceal from me that it might be several days before he could send for me again. Supposing he ever does—'

'You underestimate yourself. I am sure he thinks of you.'

'You are a kind friend. You are trying to comfort me but is it possible that for him I was anything more than a moment's pleasure? Is there no other woman in his life? I heard in the Prince of Benevento's house of a certain Polish countess—'

'Walewska? It is true, she loved him passionately. She gave up everything to follow him – and it was even the fact that she was pregnant that determined him to give up Josephine.'

'You see,' Marianne sighed.

'Countess Walewska has left him. Not very long ago, but she has left.'

'Because he must remarry and because she would not suffer! Why should I be more fortunate than she? They called her his "Polish wife" – and she is young, lovely, noble – and yet he let her go. What can I hope for more than this one night?'

This time, Arcadius de Jolival had no answer. He knows, Marianne thought, that I am right but he does not like to admit it. He fears that I shall give way to despair.

A desperate fit of coughing almost choked her. Jolival hastily made her drink some medicine and then tried to get her to drink a little of the soup which Requin had brought. But Marianne was not hungry. The mere smell of the food, which was certainly not very appetizing, made her feel sick.

'I'm thirsty,' she said. 'Just dreadfully thirsty.'

He nodded anxiously and made her drink a little water which he had warmed slightly over the brazier, then he wrapped the covers well around her and sat down beside her bed to wait. As she lay there in the silence and exhaustion of the fever, Marianne thought for the first time of Jason Beaufort. She was sorry now that she had not accepted his offer. Dazzled by the glittering, unreal prospect of a brilliant future in the theatre, she had refused to understand his warning. And yet, he had been right. The danger he had foretold had come to pass and now there was nothing he could do for her. When Bruslart and his band returned, the American would be already on the high seas. To be sure, he had spoken of a friend, a man called Paterson, the American Consul at Nantes, but to the prisoner in the quarries of Chaillot, Nantes was as far away as Mars. Marianne closed her eyes and tried to force herself not to think. Thinking was painful, it only increased her fever and she wanted desperately to be better.

Hour upon unending hour, days and nights blending into one another with nothing to tell them apart. Hours that were like days, even weeks. Time dragged so slowly, broken for Marianne into periods of tense, anxious waking and heavy sleep from which she would sometimes wake trembling and drenched with sweat from the grip of a nightmare. During all this time, Arcadius' friendship and concern were inexhaustible. He did not spare himself in his efforts to make the invalid take a little food, making her swallow the endless potions and tisanes which he demanded from Requin. Once a day, old Fanchon came to see how matters stood. There was no solicitude or pity in her manner, nothing but the cold calculation of a horse dealer who sees his stock in trade likely to perish.

'She watches over you like a market gardener when the frost is on his lettuces,' Arcadius would say, attempting to laugh. But his laughter quickly died away, unable to withstand the oppressive atmosphere of the cavern. At other times, the prisoner's wants were supplied by Requin who was as gruff and unapproachable as ever. Even if she had possessed any money, Marianne would not have risked trying to bribe him. He served Fanchon-Fleur-de-lis like a dog and was not the kind of watch-dog to be won over by a bone.

And yet, little by little, she recovered. The bouts of coughing became further apart, the fever diminished and her cracked voice recovered normal tones. There came a time when Marianne was able to smile at her faithful companion:

'I think I'm better — but for you I am sure that I could never have recovered.'

'You are very young. I have merely helped nature. You would have got over it very well without me.'

She shook her head and looked thoughtful for a moment.

'No,' she murmured. 'Because if you had not been here, I should have had no wish to live.'

For the first time since her capture, she fell into a real sleep of the kind that is more restorative than any medicine on earth. She was dreaming that the black cab was taking her back to a Butard of fantasy, shining like a great star under a dazzling blanket of snow, when an unusual sound made her start up wide awake. She sat up and saw that Arcadius, in his own corner, was also awake and listening. Their eyes met in the gloom.

'What is it?' Marianne whispered.

'It sounded like a fall of rock. Listen! There it is again. It comes from somewhere back in the quarry.'

Jolival had already explained to Marianne that the passage outside their prison cave ended a little farther on in a blank wall.

Now they could hear a scratching sound followed by a muffled but unmistakable oath. Arcadius was on his feet in an instant. There was a glimmer of candlelight in the passage, wavering on the chalky walls as it came nearer. By now, Marianne, too, had got nervously to her feet and moved closer to her companion. Someone was coming, beyond a doubt, but who could it be, and where had they come from?

'They must have dug through the wall,' Jolival said in a whisper. 'It's easy enough to pierce the chalk with good tools. But who—'

He did not finish. The light was coming nearer. They heard cautious footsteps, light but real. A shadow loomed up along the wall and, despite herself, Marianne pressed closer to Arcadius. Then, suddenly, she bit back a cry of amazement. Even in the distorting light of the candle he held, she recognized the features and the mop of red hair belonging to Gracchus-Hannibal Pioche, the errand boy who had warned her about the black cab. A sigh of relief escaped her.

'He is a friend,' she said to Jolival.

Gracchus-Hannibal had already spotted the barred recess, illumined faintly by the brazier. He made his way close up to the bars and his anxious face broke into a broad grin.

'So I've found you at last, Mademoiselle Marianne! You've certainly given me a run for it.'

'What? Have you been looking for me? How did you know I had disappeared?'

Her hopes rose suddenly. If the humble Gracchus had had his suspicions, then surely such a remarkable man as Talleyrand could not have failed to have them too.

'Oh, that's easy! The black cab followed you and I followed the black cab. Daytimes, at least. I mostly sleep at night.'

'The Devil!' Arcadius broke in. 'You must have a strong pair of legs to follow a cab—'

'They never go very fast in Paris, especially when they are following someone. But it's true, I have got strong legs. Where was I? Oh, – one morning, a week ago, it was, when I went to find the cab, it wasn't there. Nor did I see you go out. That struck me as odd. So I got into conversation with Joris, the porter at the Hôtel Talleyrand. I swept away the snow on the pavement outside, and so we got talking. I went back later to give him a hand and took a bottle with me. There's nothing like a bottle for making a man's tongue wag. In two days I'd become his bosom pal! He told me you'd gone out one night with the Prince and not come back. There was even some rumour going about the house that you'd been taken up by someone very grand. But that cab's being gone worried me – especially since I knew where it lived and I'd seen the man who was inside it several times going in and out of a bar called the Iron Man. That didn't seem to fit at all with any tale about a grand person. And so, I started making inquiries.'

'But how did you get here?' Marianne said, filled with admiration for the young man's shrewdness.

Gracchus-Hannibal laughed.

'I've known the old quarries a long time. Used to play here as a kid with my pals and had some rare old times before the people from the Iron Man blocked up this gallery which runs into the old crypt of the Visitation. There were a good many hid here during the Terror, as there were in the quarries at Montmartre. But I know them all, like the back of my hand.'

'But this passage is a dead end,' Jolival broke in. 'How did you get into it without going through the crypt? I thought I heard some kind of avalanche.'

'It was a bit like that. Beyond the dead end, the galleries run on for quite a way but the main right bank sewer joins up with them and that runs into the Seine quite close to here. Besides, they're not all that well built. There are cracks and I heard voices last night. That gave me the idea of looking here. I came back with a pickaxe – and here I am! And am I glad to see you still alive, Mam'zelle Marianne! To be quite honest, I'd been none too sure—'

'Why? Do you know these people?—'

Gracchus shrugged and gave Marianne a pitying look.

'The old woman with the fleur-de-lis? Is there anyone in Paris doesn't know her! Or ain't scared to death of her! I think she frightens even Citizen Fouché! At any rate, he needs to pay his men well enough to show their noses in the rue des Bonhommes after sunset! They don't like going near the Homme de Fer either, or its twin in the boulevard du Temple, the Episcié. And those that do, generally vanish without trace. And both those places belong to Desormeaux. Oh, she's a character, all right! A sort of queen of the underworld!'

Marianne had been listening to the boy's words with undisguised fascination but Jolival was beginning to show signs of impatience.

'This is all very well, my lad,' he said at last, 'but I don't suppose you've come all this way just to sing Fanchon's praises? You'd be better employed getting us out of here! I suppose this hole you've dug is big enough to let a young lady through?'

'The hole, yes,' Gracchus said. 'But how am I going to get you out from behind those bars? Those aren't just a little bit of wire! Look at them – thick as a baby's wrist!'

'Look here, my lad, if you don't put a brake on your enthusiasm for our prison and our jailers, I shall personally insert my adult arm between these baby ones and push your face in!

Can't you see the young lady is ill and must be got out of here as soon as possible?'

'Oh, don't be hard on him,' Marianne begged. 'I am sure he will find a way.'

'Why would I have taken all this trouble else?' Gracchus-Hannibal replied in a surly voice. 'All the same, there's nothing to be done tonight. It's too late. It can't be far off five o'clock, though it don't feel like it. And I'll have to get hold of some proper tools. A good file might do — unless we try and get out one or two of the bars—'

'Or knock down the wall!' Arcadius scoffed. 'It seems that you're no locksmith. Find me some good locksmith's tools and come back tomorrow night, if you can. You are right, it's too late now.'

Marianne did her best to hide her disappointment. When she saw the boy appear, she had thought that freedom was within her reach, but now they had to wait another whole day. Gracchus-Hannibal was scratching his head under the blue cap.

'Locksmith's tools?' he said. 'Yes, it could be — but where from?'

'Listen,' Marianne said suddenly as an idea occurred to her. 'If you need help, there may be someone who can give it — at least, if he is still in Paris.'

'Tell us, mam'zelle.'

'Go to the Hôtel de l'Empire and ask for Monsieur Jason Beaufort, he is an American. Will you remember that? Jason Beaufort.'

The boy pulled paper and pencil out of his cap. 'Wait a moment,' he said. 'I'll put it down. There — that's it. What shall I tell him?'

'That you come from Marianne — that she needs help. Then tell him where I am.'

'And if he's gone?'

'Then say nothing to anyone,' she said sadly. 'Just come and tell me, that's all.'

'You don't want me to tell them in the rue de Varennes?'

'No! No — not at present. We'll see if M. Beaufort has gone—'

Marianne could not have said what made her call on Beaufort for help. He had wounded her deeply and even now she did not altogether trust him. But he represented her one chance of escaping from the trouble which had dogged her ever since her marriage to Francis Cranmere. Only with Beaufort did the word 'escape' bear its full meaning. If she succeeded in escaping with him, when his ship left the coast of France it would break all the chains that bound her. No more Fouché, no more reports, no more Talleyrand with his cunning plots, his brilliant ideas and his subtle diplomacy. Above all, and more than all, she would put an ocean like an impassable barrier between herself and the man she could not help loving. She could have devoted her life to Charles Denis, but what was the love of a mere girl like herself to Napoleon I, Emperor of the French? In a week, less perhaps, he would have forgotten her, might indeed have done so already. By now, all his thoughts would surely have turned to that Arch-Duchess of Austria he meant to marry. It was better to go away and never see him again rather than risk yielding a second time. And then, over there, she would try and get over it.

To keep her spirits up, she told herself that she would accept from Beaufort only such aid as she was obliged to and that she would try and support herself by singing. There must be theatres in that far-away country, and concert halls—

'You mean to go to America?' Jolival's voice spoke quietly beside her.

Marianne came down to earth and saw that Gracchus-Hannibal had gone. From the far end of the passage, came the sound of stones being moved. He must be making a rough attempt to cover the hole by which he had entered.

'I think it is the best thing I can do,' she answered.

'Maybe. You do not wish to see him again?'

'No. It is best for me, and for him. I must not see him again at any price.'

'Why?'

The brief question shook Marianne. It forced her to reply as simply, to give the real reason for her longing to escape and it came home to her more sharply as she said it.

'Because I'm afraid,' she said in a low voice.

'You are afraid,' Jolival finished for her calmly, 'because you realize that you love Napoleon as much as Charles Denis, perhaps more. Whatever you may think, a halo of glory never does any harm to one we love – even if our politics are not quite the same. The glory is still there. And – do you think you will forget more easily if you put an ocean between you?'

'I hope so! Someone, I can't remember who, once said that the greatest victory in love was flight.'

Arcadius de Jolival roared with laughter.

'Look no further. He said it. Napoleon has a great belief in the merits of flight where love is concerned. It still remains to be seen whether there is any truth in that pretty phrase. I promise you, he has not often tried it.'

'Well I shall! You see, Arcadius, I should suffer too much if I stayed. He is to remarry again soon, is he not?'

'What then? A marriage of convenience, a dynastic marriage? No such union ever kept a man from his true love.'

'But I am not his true love! I am only a brief interlude in his life. Can't you understand that?'

'Even so. With his help you might become in a few days what you have dreamed of being, a great singer. But you prefer to set off, like Christopher Columbus, to discover America. It may be as well but remember what I say, even at the other end of the world, you will not forget the Emperor.'

'The Emperor . . .'

For the first time, she realized the splendour of that title. The man she loved bore the loftiest of all crowns. He was the greatest warrior of any age since Caesar and Alexander. Nearly all Europe bowed before him. As though it were child's play, he had won victory after victory, conquered vast territories. As though it were child's play, he had conquered her, had made her bow beneath a love too great for her romantic little soul, a love without even the legendary wings to help her bear the crushing weight of history.

When she spoke her voice was drained of all expression.

'Why do you think that I shall not forget him?'

Jolival sighed gustily, stretched and settled himself back on the straw. He gave a great yawn and then said placidly:

'Because it is not possible. I've tried.'

The hours that followed were, for Marianne, the most agonizing she had ever lived. The absence of a clock made itself cruelly felt because time seemed to her endless when she had no means of measuring it. Jolival did try asking Requin when he brought their one meal of the day but all he got for answer was:

'What difference does it make to you?'

They were forced, therefore, to rely on guesswork. Jolival attempted to soothe his companion's nerves by observing that darkness fell early in winter but nothing and no one could calm Marianne's nerves. So many obstacles lay between her and freedom. Would Beaufort be still there even? Would the boy manage to come back at all or would he be so overcome by the difficulties before him that he would abandon the whole plan altogether? A host of possibilities, each more desperate than the last, occurred to Marianne's fevered mind. There were times when she actually believed she must have dreamed that Gracchus-Hannibal Pioche was there. But for Jolival and his imperturbable calm, she would never have been able to control herself. But the man of letters appeared so calm and relaxed that it was almost irritating. Marianne would have preferred him to share her terrors and her cloudy suppositions instead of simply peacefully awaiting the outcome of events. But then, she reflected, he had little to fear beyond a disagreeable marriage.

Marianne had just returned for the hundredth time to striding up and down their prison when a whisper from Arcadius stopped her in her tracks.

'Someone's coming!' he said. 'Our red-headed saviour can't be far off – if my calculations are correct it must be getting on for nine o'clock.'

Someone was certainly approaching but not from the dead end of the passage. The figure who rose suddenly before Marianne's horrified eyes was that of Morvan. He was enveloped in a great black cloak with drops of water shining wetly on it and his scarred face was without its mask. Marianne could not hold

back a cry of terror as he loomed up out of the shadows and
her terror was increased at the thought that any moment they
might hear Gracchus' pick working away at the loose stones in
the wall. The Riders of the Shadows would have no mercy on a
lad who to them would be no more than a spy and therefore a
potential danger. Marianne's eyes sought Jolival's and read in
them the reflection of her own thoughts. He was already standing close beside the bars and suddenly he spoke in a voice
much louder than his normal tones.

'It seems we have a visitor! We certainly looked for none, or
not of this quality!'

Marianne understood at once that by talking so loudly he
hoped to make Gracchus, supposing he were already on the
other side of the wall, hear and be on his guard and she too
spoke as loudly as she could.

'I take no pleasure in such a visit. What is your business
here, sir plunderer of wrecks?'

Morvan's twisted lips curved in an unpleasant smile.

'To see how you are, my beauty! In truth, since we were
obliged to part so abruptly, I have thought of you almost constantly — and talked of you too! Your ears must have been
burning, we have argued so much about you, the Chevalier, the
Baron and myself—'

'I do not know what you may have said and I do not wish to
know, or not from you. The Chevalier de Bruslart will no doubt
repeat to me the gist of your remarks and from him they are
more likely to come correctly.'

Morvan scowled and drew back a pace.

'Do you have to shout like that? I am not deaf! You are
almost bursting my eardrums!'

'I am sorry,' Marianne said without lowering her voice. 'But I
have been ill and my voice is only audible if I shout.'

'Shout as much as you like, before long you will shout to
another tune! This little journey was quite providential. Our
dear Chevalier has always had an eye for a pretty woman and
he was showing signs of quite unnecessary kindness and clem-
ency towards you. He is a simple, tender-hearted soul in whom
the old principles of chivalry are still regrettably alive. For-

tunately, I had plenty of time to provide him with some detailed information concerning you which, I think, has prevailed upon him.'

Marianne felt her heart quake. It had happened exactly as she had feared. Morvan had turned the Chevalier against her. No doubt he had come now to give himself the gruesome pleasure of informing her of her imminent death. But not for anything in the world would she have shown this man the gnawing fear within her. Instead, she turned her back on him with a disdainful shrug.

'My congratulations, if you have succeeded in persuading the Chevalier de Bruslart to abandon his sacred principles and murder a defenceless woman in cold blood. You should have made yourself a career in diplomacy! It would have been more honourable than your chosen occupation – although less lucrative perhaps!'

Her words caught Morvan on the raw. He made an angry movement as though he would have thrown himself against the bars but then thought better of it. When he spoke, his voice was light enough but his smile was evil.

'Who mentioned murder? That principle is one of which the Chevalier de Bruslart admits no compromise but none the less, you shall be punished as you deserve. I have managed to persuade him to hand you over to our dear Fanchon who seems to take in my view a quite excessive interest in you. She will find you employment for which you are well fitted. And she will also be grateful to the man who can renounce his own vengeance for her profit, and his own.'

'I wonder at the Chevalier's scruples,' Marianne retorted, sick at heart, 'that he spares a woman's life and yet dishonours her in a baser fashion!'

'Dishonours? A fine word, coming from you! The Chevalier's scruples yielded somewhat after I had told him of your exploits in my barn with that spy of Bonaparte's who was your so-called servant – and also that I found you on the shore clad in the most rudimentary fashion and attempting to seduce two of my men. One of whom, moreover, you murdered not long afterwards. No, after this very circumstantial account, the Chevalier had no more hesitation. Especially since he hopes to be your first customer.'

Speechless with horror at this display of cruelty and duplicity, Marianne could find no answer. In her disgust she even forgot Gracchus and his danger but Arcadius Jolival intervened.

'I think that will do, monsieur,' he said, his fingers playing nervously with his moustache. 'You have played your foul part to perfection and now I must ask you to leave this lady in peace. As to the worth of Bruslart's scruples, if he accepts the base assertions of a wrecker I can say nothing, but I can tell you what you are at once. You are a first-class scoundrel!'

Morvan's face paled and Marianne saw his jaw tighten. But before he could reply, the Chevalier's voice called from the hollow crypt nearby.

'Ho there! Kérivoas! Come here and leave the prisoners alone. We'll settle that afterwards. For the present, we have more urgent business.'

The distant gleam of torchlight was now dancing on the walls and there was a hum of voices not far off. Morvan, who had seemed about to hurl himself bodily at the bars, stopped short and turned on his heel with a shrug.

'I'll come back later to slice off those big ears of yours, little man! Don't worry, you'll lose nothing by waiting.'

He went away to join the others and Marianne went disconsolately back to her straw bed where she sat down with her arms around her knees and her head with its long, tumbled mane of hair resting on her arms.

'This is the end,' she murmured. 'We are finished. And if that poor boy comes now he will be finished with us.'

'Be patient. We shouted loud enough to warn him! He may be on the other side of the wall—'

'What should he wait for? He cannot get near us! The conspirators are still in the crypt and we cannot tell how long they will be there – you can hear them—'

'Ssh! Listen!' Jolival said sharply. He went and pressed himself up against the bars as near as possible to the confused voices coming from the crypt.

'They are having a meeting,' he whispered.

'And – can you make out anything?'

He nodded and touched his big ears with a meaning smile. Marianne was silent, watching her companion's mobile features as they grew at first grave and then thoroughly alarmed. She heard a gruff voice which she recognized as belonging to the Chevalier de Bruslart but was unable to make out a word of what he said. The leader of the band was speaking. He seemed to be explaining something. From time to time another voice would interrupt but the main burden always returned to Bruslart. And, gradually, the look on Jolival's face became so tragic that Marianne laid her hand on his arm and whispered urgently: 'What is it? You are frightening me! Are they talking about us?'

He shook his head and muttered swiftly under his breath:

'No – in fact, they're going away. Be patient a little longer.'

He listened again but the council seemed to be breaking up. There was a noise of seats being scraped on the floor, and a clatter of booted feet. All the voices began speaking at once, then Bruslart's rose above the rest.

'To horse, gentlemen! For God and for the King! Tonight, at last, fortune is with us!'

This time, it was beyond a doubt. They were going. The footsteps died away, the voices faded and the lights vanished. In a few moments, Marianne and Arcadius found themselves once more alone with the heavy silence and the dim, ruddy light of their dungeon. Jolival left his post by the bars and went over to the brazier. Marianne saw that he was avoiding her eyes.

'You heard what they were saying?' she asked.

He nodded affirmatively but did not open his mouth. He seemed to be deep in thought. However, Marianne was too anxious to respect his silence.

'Where are they going?' she asked with a touch of irritation. 'Why is fortune on their side tonight? What are they going to do?'

Jolival looked at her at last. His mouse-like face, usually so cheerful, was overcast as though by some distressing thought.

He seemed to hesitate for a moment then, as Marianne came and clutched his arm anxiously, he said at last:

'I am in two minds whether to tell you but whether or not they are successful you will hear anyway. They have learned from one of their spies in the palace that the Emperor goes tonight to Malmaison. The former Empress is unwell. She has also learned that the Emperor's choice of a wife has fallen definitely on the Austrian Arch-Duchess and the news has affected her badly. The Emperor's decision to go was taken only an hour ago.'

'And?' Marianne felt her heart beat faster at the mention of the word 'Emperor', only to contract painfully at the news of his impending marriage.

'And they mean to carry out the old plan of Caboudal and Hyde de Neuville, the old plan which ever since the Consulate, Bruslart has always failed to carry off. They will set a trap for Napoleon when he leaves Malmaison, probably very late, stop his carriage, overcome his guard and then carry him off and—'

'Kill him!' Marianne almost screamed.

'Bruslart said no. He wants only to carry off the Emperor, get him across the Channel and deliver him bound hand and foot to England – unless he will consent to fight a duel. A duel with Napoleon has always been the Chevalier's great dream.'

'Is he mad?'

'No. He is a paladin, in his way. He believes only in fair fight and you could say that he only became a conspirator because there was nothing else for him to do and because there was no longer a royalist army. But Bruslart might be killed in such a duel or, if there is not one, the others may force the Chevalier's hand. The stake is high, this time, and there are some, I know – your friend Morvan among them – who want Napoleon's head at all costs.'

'Why?'

Jolival chuckled cynically.

'It's very simple. The Duke of Medina-Coeli, the richest of all the Grandees of Spain, has offered half his vast fortune to whoever kills Napoleon and brings proof of his death.'

In the silence that followed, Marianne was able to gauge the depth of her feelings. Her heart was beating uncontrollably. She was trembling in every limb but she forced herself to be calm.

'Why did they say fortune was with them?'

'Because the journey was decided very quickly. There will be only a small escort to avoid attracting attention. And tonight, the conspirators number twenty-five at least.'

'But Fouché? Fouché knows all, sees all. Can Fouché not prevent this plot like all the others?'

'Fouché will be taken by surprise. Besides which, it must be admitted that for some time now Fouché seems to have been relaxing his care a little. Deliberately, no doubt, because he is a man who does nothing without a reason. My dear child – it is very possible that in a short while we shall have the great honour of sharing our dungeon with his Majesty our Emperor and King, which will give me both the greatest possible joy and at the same time the utmost regret.'

Marianne bravely thrust away the sweet yet agonizing picture he conjured up of her love, in fetters, joining her in her dungeon.

'But we have to stop it! We must! I know Morvan. He will not let Bruslart bring him here. In the dark, in a struggle, a pistol shot is soon fired. Oh my God! I must go to him! I cannot stand by and see him murdered. Not him! These villains are going to kill him! I tell you, they are going to kill him!'

She had flung herself blindly on the bars, gripping them with both hands and trying to shake them loose by sheer force but they did not so much as quiver. The rusty iron skinned her hands but she did not feel the pain, any more than she saw the prison around her. What she saw was a road at night, in the snow, a carriage halted, perhaps overturned, the horses struggling in the grip of masked men, figures stretched out in the snow which was already turning red, an unarmed man held by the conspirators and Morvan laughing evilly as he held a pistol to the head of that man, the man she loved.

'I won't let them,' she screamed desperately, resisting with all her strength Jolival's attempts to prise her away from her lacerating grip on the bars. 'I won't let them kill him! I love him! Napoleon!'

In the confusion of her mind, she cried aloud for the first time the name which had haunted her ever since she had learned the truth and which she had murmured to herself many times in her fever. Arcadius had to gag her with his hand to silence her, and with a supreme effort he managed at last to tear her away from the bars.

'You will rouse the whole rat's nest!' he scolded. 'Have you forgotten we are waiting for someone?'

It was true. She had forgotten Gracchus-Hannibal Pioche. But her hysterical panic was over in an instant and Marianne crumpled on to the ground, put her head in her hands and wept.

'He will not come now. He must have heard those men and realized that there was no chance tonight. Even supposing he came at all—'

'And why shouldn't he have come?' Jolival said roughly. 'Myself, I trust that lad! He's got honest eyes. He'll do all he can to get you out of here.'

'Maybe. But not tonight. He won't come back tonight. And, oh my God, the Riders must be on the road to Malmaison by now—'

As though to shut out the sound of galloping hoofbeats ringing in her head Marianne put her hands over her ears and closed her eyes. Never in her whole life had she so longed for oblivion as in that moment. Consequently, she did not see Arcadius go quickly to the bars and grip them in his turn as, from the depths of the underground cavern, came the sound of a stone falling. It was followed by another.

In a flash, Arcadius was on her, shaking her unmercifully by the shoulders.

'Listen! Only listen! He's coming! He is breaking down the wall again.'

Marianne jerked upright, eyes wide, and gripping Arcadius' hand in her own, she listened with all her soul. It was true, someone was coming down the blind passage. Hardly daring to breathe, she followed the boy's progress. There was the sound of someone running and all at once, she saw Gracchus-Hannibal burst out of the passage. Hard on his heels was the much taller figure of a man and, the next moment, Jason Beaufort's large frame was towering on the other side of the bars. Marianne gave a cry of joy.

'You! God be praised, you have come! You had not left!'

She saw the blue eyes laughing in his tanned face and felt her cold hands folded in the American's warm ones as he reached through the bars to hold and clasp them.

'Not quite!' he said gaily. 'I leave tomorrow but no power on earth would have prevented me from getting you out of this new pickle you've got yourself into, you little fool! Come now, don't cry. We'll have you out of there in a trice. Look there,' he added, turning to Gracchus-Hannibal who, armed with a file almost bigger than himself, was bravely attacking one of the bars with Arcadius' help, explaining as he worked that they had been forced to wait for the conspirators to go away.

'I was up top,' he said, 'and Monsieur Beaufort down below.'

'Hurry!' Marianne begged. 'We must get out of here quickly! Or, no—'

Another thought came to her. What did her own fate matter if Napoleon were safe.

'Leave us here and go and warn him!'

'Warn who?' Beaufort exclaimed in surprise. 'You are madder than I thought. Let us get on with our work.'

'No, please, listen to me – it is too important.'

She explained in a few short sentences the plot that was afoot and the Emperor's mortal danger. He listened with a frown, not pausing in his work but when she had finished he threw down the file with an exasperated shrug.

'We are not leaving here without you. Much as I admire Napoleon, I will not leave you any longer in the hands of these savages. Especially if they come back thwarted. We'll not do it that way, kid.' The last part of this speech was addressed to Gracchus-Hannibal who was bending to pick up the file. Glancing at Arcadius, Jason went on abruptly: 'If you shout, can they hear you up there?'

'Yes. I've summoned the lackeys in this charming hotel before now by bellowing like a bull at need.'

'Then shout, my friend, shout as loud as you can, but get your jailer down here! I'll take care of the rest. Go on now, and do your best!'

Jolival opened his mouth and let out a sustained yell of such power that Marianne jumped. Beaufort, meanwhile, hid out of sight round the corner of the blind passage. His lean, muscular form, moulded into some kind of seaman's sweater and tight black breeches, merged so completely into the shadows of the passage that after a moment even Marianne could not see him. She did not understand what he meant to do but Arcadius was still yelling with complete conviction. She would never have believed that he could own such a powerful voice. It rolled among the dripping vaults until the whole place rang with it. When at last he stopped for breath, they could hear the sound of running footsteps followed by the angry voice of Requin.

'What's up with you, yelling yer 'ead off like that? I'll make you shut up!'

As the ruffian came in sight, Jolival flung himself on the ground and began rolling about like someone writhing in extreme agony, shouting once more at the top of his voice.

'Hurry,' Marianne cried urgently, having finally understood what was happening. 'He's ill! I don't know what's the matter.'

Requin swore violently as he struggled to open the gate. Before he could do so, Jason was on him. With a spring like a wild beast, the American leapt for his back and bore him down beneath his weight, at the same time locking his left arm under the man's chin, abruptly choking him. Requin gave a strangled gasp and lost consciousness. Jason gave him a swinging blow with his fist for good measure then, taking possession of the bunch of keys, he opened the gate and made straight for Marianne, sweeping her up in his arms like a feather.

'Let's get out of here,' he said kicking aside the recumbent Requin who blocked his way. 'Stow that behind bars and lock him in, then give me the key. We'll drop it in the sewer. This rat will be coming round in ten minutes and we must make the most of them.'

'What if we was to strangle him?' Gracchus-Hannibal suggested sweetly. 'It'd be no great loss and make things easier for us.'

Jason laughed.

'I should have done so a moment ago, but as I didn't, let him be. I can't kill an unconscious man.'

Still carrying Marianne, who had slid her arms instinctively round his neck, he made for the hole in the wall. He had to put her down to pass through it because the crack was only a small one. Behind him came Arcadius, endeavouring to recover some of the spring in legs rusty with captivity. Gracchus-Hannibal brought up the rear, taking the trouble to put back the displaced stones when he had passed through.

'You never know,' he remarked prudently.

Jolival laughed.

'Are you hoping to have business here again?' he said, clapping the boy affectionately on the back. 'You certainly came to our rescue, son, and I hope one day that I'll be able to repay you. I owe you more than my life!'

'Go on,' the boy muttered awkwardly, 'it wasn't worth mentioning.'

'You think not? I think so!' Jolival said meaningfully.

On the other side of the wall was a short passage and then the sewer. Marianne's nostrils were filled with the foul stench. Jason had taken her up in his arms again, remarking that in a moment they would have to go through the water and there was no need for two of them to get wet.

For a short distance, they followed the narrow ledge which ran alongside the black waters. Arcadius went first to light the way, armed with a torch which he had thrust into the brazier before leaving the prison, but following directions given him by the American. The cold, which had been not unbearable in the underground caverns, grew more biting as they went towards the outside world, but Marianne did not feel it. Clinging to Jason's neck, she no longer felt any of her old loathing and distrust of him. What he had done that night had wiped out at one go all the accumulated hatred and bitterness she thought she had felt for him and instead, there was a warm feeling of trust which made her for a moment forget her terrors. If it had not been for the threat hanging over the man she loved, she would have felt a simple, almost child-like happiness in the feeling of being carried in those strong arms, which could never know weakness.

Jason had now plunged into the evil-smelling water right up to his waist and was holding her as high as he could to keep her abové the stream. She saw his tanned seaman's face close to her own, with its fierce profile and the stern lips with their mocking twist. From time to time, he looked at her and smiled as if to encourage her, with a gentleness that relaxed all his features. In spite of the unpleasant stench all around them, he still gave off a faint agreeable scent of tobacco, of good leather and eau-de-Cologne which Marianne found comforting.

'Be brave,' he said at last. 'We're nearly there.'

Then they were out in the main sewer and he was able to get up again on to the narrow footway. A strong current of icy air blew in on them from a black opening beyond which gleamed the river. Jason set Marianne gently on her feet and bent to take the torch from Arcadius' chilled fingers and help him climb on to the ledge. Young Gracchus was up already. A few more steps and they were out in the open. Jolival breathed in with rapture.

'Ah! How good it is!' he said joyfully. 'I had not realized how much I missed the air of Paris!'

He was soaking wet and frozen and his teeth were chattering, but he did not seem to notice it.

Marianne, however, had no time to waste on savouring the joys of her recovered freedom. Time was short. The Riders of the Shadows had a long start and if by ill-luck the Emperor should leave Malmaison too early – she dared not frame the rest of her thoughts in words but clung to Jason's arm.

'Can you find me a carriage! Quickly – very quickly.'

'I have one waiting a little way off, at the quai de Billy, near the place de la Conférence.[1] Where do you want to go?'

[1] The present place de l'Alma.

'I must go to Malmaison, of course!'

He made a movement of protest.

'Not that again! The Emperor is well guarded. It will take more than a few fanatics to put him in danger. I mean to take you somewhere safe – and dry! And tomorrow, I will take you away—'

'Tomorrow, yes, I will go with you, but tonight, I implore you to let me save him! I know – I can feel that he is in danger.'

She felt the American's wet arms stiffen under her hand. He drew himself up and his eyes moved away from her to the darkly moving waters of the Seine.

'He—' he said with a rather bitter emphasis, 'how you speak of him! I thought you hated him?'

'I do not hate him any more. No more than I hate you any more now. You have acted like a friend, a true friend and that wipes out everything. Tomorrow, I tell you I will go with you because I shall have nothing more to do here and because I am tired of being continually in what you call all kinds of impossible scrapes. Perhaps, in your country, I may find peace.'

'I shall do everything in the world to help you,' he said gently. 'If it is in my power, you shall be happy.'

'Then if you really want my happiness,' she said eagerly, 'do as I ask you, Jason. Let me go to Malmaison. But quickly, I implore you, quickly! We are wasting so much time and every minute counts.'

A tremor ran through him when she spoke his name for the first time and Marianne's woman's intuition told her she had touched him. She was about to return to the attack when he suddenly bent over her and laying his hands on her shoulders, looked deep into her eyes.

'Tomorrow,' he said earnestly, 'you will go with me? You promise?'

'Yes. I promise.'

'Come then. I will take you there myself. We'll drive the horses into the ground, if need be, but we'll get there. Follow us, gentlemen. We'll talk as we go. There are dry clothes in the carriage.'

His voice rang suddenly joyful. Seizing Marianne by the hand, he ran with her along the dark river bank. Arcadius and young Pioche followed hard on their heels without further questions. They passed the buildings of the soap works and then those of the Dépôt des Marbres and then, as they came to the place de la Conférence, the shape of a carriage rose before them against the faint light of a lantern hung outside the shed where the fire-wagon was kept. It was then Arcadius leaned towards the boy who was running steadily beside him. He was chilled to the bone in his wet clothes but had lost none of his usual good humour for all that.

'Your name is really Gracchus-Hannibal?'

'Yes, monsieur, why?'

'Because my name is Arcadius!' was the apparently illogical answer. 'Do you know that together we represent Athens, Rome and Carthage? My boy, we have just created an alliance that not even the maddest historian ever dreamed of. And when you add to that the collaboration of America, you must admit the world has never seen a league like ours.'

'Yes, monsieur,' Gracchus-Hannibal said meekly, making no attempt to understand. 'But perhaps we'd better hurry on a bit. They're waving to us—'

'Quite right,' Arcadius said cheerfully. 'We have still to set the seal on our glory by saving the new Caesar! And a Corsican Caesar into the bargain!'

CHAPTER FOUR

Malmaison

Once past the vineyards of the Côte de Saint-Cloud, the road to Malmaison stretched on, dreary and all but deserted and bounded on either side only by waste ground and disused quarries. The snow had dwindled to a few isolated patches, like spilt milk on the dark landscape. Shortly before the bridge, they had come down the route de la Reine to the Boulogne crossroads and there they had parted from Gracchus-Hannibal who declared his intention of going to spend the night with his grandmother, a washerwoman in the route de la Révolte.

'Come and see me tomorrow at my hotel,' Jason Beaufort had called down to him from the box. 'We must have a talk together, you and I. About eleven.'

'Very well monsieur! I'll be there.'

He was about to leap out with a cheery goodnight to those whose saviour he had been when Marianne suddenly pulled him back and kissed him warmly on both cheeks.

'Thank you, Gracchus. We are friends for ever now.'

The darkness hid the deep blush which spread over the boy's face but as they moved on, Marianne heard him singing at the top of his voice.

> *I know not whence this feeling comes*
> *That grips me when I look at you—'*

'Amazing!' Jolival remarked. 'He sings Mozart though he surely does not know it!'

The man of letters was settled comfortably in the carriage beside Marianne, but while she was tense with anxiety and trying vainly to control her fears, Arcadius was thoroughly enjoying the comfort of the vehicle and the dry clothes he had found there. Beaufort's aforethought had provided some for young Gracchus also. Marianne had been obliged to bury her head in the cushions while her companions changed, which was by no means easy owing to the fact that Beaufort had not delayed an instant for such formality.

Regardless of his wet clothes, Jason had climbed on to the box and settled himself beside the coachman. He had merely emptied his boots and wrapped himself in a great black cloak, remarking that there had been many worse times at sea. From time to time, Marianne could hear his clipped voice telling the coachman to press his horses harder.

Even so, it seemed to Marianne that they were barely moving. She sat, tense and strained, watching the trees go by. They had in fact come to a broken wooded stretch where it was difficult to go fast. Suddenly, Marianne turned to her companions.

'Did you manage to hear where they meant to attack the Emperor's carriage?'

Jolival nodded. 'They meant to hide at a place called Fond-Louvet,' he said, 'not far from the Château de Rueil—'

'Near where the Empress lives? They are bold.'

'The Château de Rueil is not Malmaison, my dear child. It belongs to Marshal Massena, Duke of Rivoli, but the Marshal has just been made Prince of Essling and Thourars and has gone to visit his new lands. Besides, Massena is loyal to the dethroned Empress and has no wish to be involved in any of the Emperor's marriage plans. He prefers to be away at such a time.'

Marianne regarded her companion curiously.

'How do you know all this? To hear you, one would think you were familiar with the court?'

'And seeing my splendid appearance, you find that hard to believe, I daresay,' he said with a comical grin. 'My dear Marianne, you cannot imagine how much gossip one picks up in gaming houses. I am one of the best informed people in Paris, don't forget that.'

'Then, if that is so, answer me one question. How are we going to get into Malmaison and obtain a hearing?'

'To be quite frank with you, that's just what I was thinking. One doesn't just walk into Malmaison. Perhaps we should have thought of that earlier.'

'We must get in, Arcadius. We must warn the Emperor. Is the château well guarded?'

'Like an imperial palace,' Jolival said gloomily. He shrugged. 'A detachment of the guard stationed at Rueil in the former barracks of the Swiss Guard are generally responsible for the former Empress' safety. I don't think we'll find it easy to persuade them to let us see Josephine, especially when we look like this!'

'Shall we be there soon?'

Arcadius leaned out of the window and glanced at the high wall past which the carriage was travelling at that moment.

'We are nearly there already,' he said as he threw himself back into his seat. 'This is the wall of the Château de Rueil. Malmaison is a little farther along, on the left.'

'But then — we must have gone right past the place where they are waiting for the Emperor? But we saw nothing?'

'Did you think they would show themselves? What an innocent you are. They are waiting off the road in an old quarry and they will not come out until the moment is right. But don't imagine they have missed our passing. The only thing to fear will be the watch they must have placed between the gates of Malmaison and Fond-Louvet.'

Suddenly, the carriage picked up speed. They were passing a pair of great gilded gates flanked by lodges with triangular pediments and square pilasters. Great bronze lanterns suspended from wrought-iron brackets shone on the golden lances of the gates and on the tricolor sentry boxes, by which were soldiers dressed in buff uniforms with green fronts and tall black shakos with yellow cockades.

'The Corsican Tirailleurs!' Jolival said. 'There is a world of affection in the choice of that regiment.'

Marianne said nothing. For the first time, this reference to Josephine, haloed in the great love Napoleon had borne her, awoke her jealousy. It was true Josphine must be suffering now, seeing herself put aside to make room for another, but had

not the best part of the Emperor's heart been hers? Compared
with those long years lived side by side, Marianne thought
bitterly that the hours at Butard were pitifully short.

At the end of a broad avenue, she had caught a glimpse of a
small, lighted château. A berlin stood outside, a berlin and a
number of horsemen dressed in red and green with flowing
cloaks and tall red-plumed busbies. Jolival had clutched her
arm in an excited grip.

'You saw? The Emperor is still there!'

'That is his carriage, are you sure?'

'Those were certainly the mounted chasseurs of the Imperial
Guard. I don't know who else they could be waiting for. They
are fine lads, Prince Eugène's cavalry. They are not many but I
wonder if we should not let them deal with the conspirators.'

'Are you mad? They are a dozen at the most—'

'But equal to thirty! Never mind, you are right. A surprise
attack can come suddenly – ah, and I think we too have come.'

The carriage was indeed slowing down. Some little way past
the gates of the château the road made a slight bend and
there they could leave the carriage without risk of being seen.
Jason sprang down from the box to open the door and help
Marianne out. They stood in a road enclosed between high
walls overhung with trees. The bare branches were etched as
though in Indian ink against a sky that was hardly lighter,
while the sides of the road and the tops of the walls were
lightly outlined in snow.

'We must be quick,' the American said, leading her to the
left-hand wall. 'The Emperor's coach is still outside but it is not
far off midnight and he will surely be leaving soon.'

'Why did you come past the château? You should have
stopped before—'

'So that the watch which the conspirators will certainly have
posted could oversee our movements? One can tell you are not
used to this kind of thing. Now, we have to get inside—'

Marianne thought privately that he, apparently, was quite
used to this kind of thing but she said nothing and only asked:
'How are we going to do that? Do you think the guards will let
us past?'

She saw the American's white teeth gleam for an instant in the darkness and heard his stifled laugh.

'We shan't try. It would be so much waste of time. You, sweet Marianne, are going to show me how a well-brought-up young lady can climb walls. After that, we can only pray to God we don't meet a patrol before we reach the house – at which point we can relax and get ourselves arrested.'

'Arrested! What do you mean?'

'That the only way of attracting the Emperor's attention will be to make as much noise as possible. Once outside the château we'll kick up such a rumpus that someone is bound to ask questions. Those splendid horsemen kicking their heels in the snow so quietly will be only too delighted to have it out with us.'

It was wholly insane but, as put by Jason, the audacious plan sounded simplicity itself. After all, all that Marianne wanted to do was warn Napoleon of the danger lying in wait for him. After that, she did not care if they did send them to prison, her and Beaufort – even to St Lazare.

'You are wonderful!' she said and meant it. 'Let's go!'

'Excuse me,' Jolival's voice said politely, 'but what is my part in all this?'

'The ladder, my friend. If you feel strong enough to bear me. After that, keep our coachman company. It will be best to have someone on watch outside.'

'By the by, the coachman, are you sure of him?'

'As sure as one can be of anyone who has been well paid. It was young Pioche who found him for me. He's as deaf as a post. I'm afraid you won't have a very chatty time, Jolival, although he can lip-read quite well. But we've wasted enough time. Quick now. And I'd as soon he didn't see us get over the wall. He might start wondering.'

Without answering, Arcadius set his back against the wall, clasped his hands and waited. Setting the toe of his boot in the clasped hand, Jason moved with cat-like agility. The next instant he was sitting astride the top of the wall.

'Now you, Marianne,' he called softly. 'Unless you'd rather let me go alone?'

'Not for all the tea in China!'

Her ascent was a matter of infinitely less ease than his had been. Weakened by her recent illness and hampered by her dress, she found herself a lot less agile than she had been in those days when she used to climb the great trees of Selton like a squirrel. But she was also lighter than the American and, half pushed by Jolival and half pulled by Jason from above, she found herself on top of the wall at last.

'If we have not returned in two hours,' the American called down to Arcadius in a low voice, 'go back to Paris. Where do you live?'

'Nowhere. I had been evicted from my lodgings when Fanchon-Fleur-de-lis took me under her wing.'

'Then go and wait for me in my room at the Hôtel de l'Empire. The coachman has been paid.'

'One way or another,' Jolival muttered, 'you'd better get out. I prefer to wait. Good luck!'

For answer, Jason jumped down into the park and held out his arms to Marianne.

'Jump! Don't be afraid, I'll catch you.'

She closed her eyes, took a deep breath and jumped. She landed in Beaufort's arms and, for a second, before he let her slip gently to the ground, he held her against him, perhaps to feel for a moment longer the kiss of her loose hair against his face.

'Marianne,' he whispered in a voice he could not altogether control, 'you will go with me tomorrow, truly?'

She freed herself, not roughly, but with some impatience.

'I have already told you so. And now is not the time to talk of that. We must run! He may be leaving—'

All her agony of mind was in those words. The park was well wooded at this point and a thick belt of trees hid the château. Only a few lights shone twinkling between the trunks of the leafless oaks.

'Make as little noise as you can,' Jason breathed.

Hand in hand, like two lost children, they began to run towards the pinpoints of light that showed where the château

lay. Wet branches smacked their faces and their feet sank
deeply into a slush of rotten leaves and melted snow. Marianne's were soon frozen but she was unconscious alike of the
icy water and the scratching branches.

The curtain of trees thinned out and Marianne and Jason
came out abruptly into the open. Before them rose the
château, gleaming white under its steep tiled roofs. In the
centre of the building, a glazed entry porch was lit up like a
huge lantern. The coach was still there but a curt command
had just sent the troops of chasseurs into the saddle.

'The Emperor is coming out,' Jason breathed. 'Quickly—'

Between them and the house lay a large garden in the English style, laid out in lawns and flowerbeds. Even as Jason spoke
they could see figures moving in the porch, one of which made
Marianne's heart beat faster. That grey form in the midst of all
the colourful dresses and resplendent uniforms, that must be
him.

But scarcely had the two of them left the heavy shadow
of the trees and started running towards the brilliantly
lit château than a command came sharply from behind
them.

'Halt! Halt or we fire!'

At the same time, the dogs began barking furiously behind
the château.

Marianne turned and saw some soldiers who must have been
patrolling along the edge of the wood and recognized the
yellow plumes of the Corsican Tirailleurs. She let out a wail of
despair. They were still a long way from the house. She gripped
Jason's hand tightly. Ahead of them, the horses were stamping restlessly. Lackeys in powdered wigs were opening the
doors of the berlin. There were people outside, men and women
muffled in thick cloaks.

'Run!' She gasped. 'Never mind if they fire!'

'Marianne, this is madness!'

She did not listen to him. She was already racing forward.
Jason followed.

They had hesitated barely an instant. With one accord, they

began to run on. Behind them they could hear the click of weapons being cocked.

'Halt!' The voice commanded once again. 'Stop, by thunder, will you!'

There was a shot, quickly followed by another. Marianne felt fear in the pit of her stomach and commended her soul to God. She saw nothing but the lighted château coming rapidly nearer. She felt nothing but Jason's hand supporting her. The horsemen around the berlin had dismounted hurriedly and now formed a barrier blocking their way. At the top of his voice, that powerful voice which could rise above the storm on board his ship, Jason shouted:

'The Emperor! Save the Emperor!'

More shots rang out but, hampered perhaps by the darkness and by the speed at which their quarry moved, the riflemen fired raggedly. Even so, one bullet must have hit Jason because he gave a muffled curse and let his hand slip from Marianne's. But the chasseurs were already surrounding them. Rough hands seized them and they were subjected to a barrage of questions:

'Who are you? What do you want? Are you conspirators?'

'The Emperor,' Marianne gasped. 'For the love of heaven, take us to the Emperor – he is in danger.'

'A woman? What are you doing here? How did you get in?'

This time it was the officer in command of the troop, a splendid tall fellow, moustaches bristling under the plumed fur busby. He was already separating Marianne from her wounded companion but she had eyes only for the brilliant group of men and women rushing excitedly out of the porch, all talking at once. A man had emerged from their midst, a man in a grey coat holding a wide cocked hat under his arm. At the sound of his curt voice, Marianne's heart almost stopped beating for happiness.

'Captain Trebriant! What is going on there?'

The handsome chasseur had no time to reply. He was still coming smartly to attention, when Marianne wriggled away and flung herself headlong at the Emperor's feet.

'Sire, for pity's sake, listen to me! They mean to kill you! There are men lying in wait for you at Fond-Louvet! There are many of them and your escort is small.'

A low growl of disapproval gave Marianne a clear notion of what the chasseurs of the Guard thought of their own worth. However, Napoleon's eyes had widened a little at the sight of the dirty, dishevelled woman in her tattered, mud-stained garments raising to his face a pair of luminous green eyes he knew.

'What's this? You – and in this condition?' he said, unable to conceal his surprise. 'Where have you sprung from?'

Before Marianne could answer, a tall, fair young woman, in a dress and cloak of violet-coloured velvet sewn with seed pearls, with a simple diadem on her golden hair, broke in.

'Sire, be careful,' she said nervously. 'This woman may be dangerous – or mad!'

Napoleon gave a brief smile which never reached his eyes but in which Marianne, desperate and overawed, saw Charles Denis restored to her for an instant.

'No, no, Hortense, I know her. She is not mad in the least. As for being dangerous—'

'The man who came with her is unconscious, Sire,' Captain Trebriant volunteered. 'He is wounded. One of the shots must have hit him.'

'Jason! He is hurt! Oh God—'

Marianne would have sprung to her feet in terror and run to him but the Emperor's iron hand held her fast.

'One moment,' he said sternly. 'Who is this man?'

'Jason Beaufort, an American, Sire. He rescued me and brought me here to warn you. He is a brave man. Have his hurts seen to, I implore you, and do not send him to prison.'

'As to that, we shall see. For the present—'

'Sire,' the young woman he had addressed as Hortense spoke again, 'is it necessary to continue this out here? It is very cold—'

'A Queen of Holland feels the cold here!' the Emperor scoffed. 'Whoever saw the like?'

'Maybe, but my mother wishes to see this woman. She is very anxious. You know how sensitive she has always been to rumours of conspiracy.'

'Very well, we'll go in. Duroc, look after this American the heavens have dropped on us and send a patrol to see what is going on at Fond-Louvet. Make it a strong one!' He turned to Marianne. 'How many are these men?'

'About thirty, I think.'

Marianne saw Duroc, her host of Butard, detach himself from the group of ladies and uniformed men but now he was dressed in splendid blue with gold braid. He, too, threw her a glance of stupefaction, but it was only for an instant, then he turned and went to Jason who was being supported in the arms of two chasseurs.

'This way,' Napoleon said, guiding Marianne none too gently into a marble-floored entrance hall adorned with antique busts. The brilliant crowd of onlookers parted before them, out of respect for the Emperor and from obvious disgust at his companion. Marianne, her mind in a ferment, could only think that they must make a strange couple. But she heard his voice whisper in her ear.

'Take care you make no allusion to the other night. I will not have the Emp – her caused the slightest pain. I have given her enough already.'

Marianne's heart throbbed with a sudden ache of mingled jealousy and pain. The curt words, the hard grip on her arm all told her that her estimate of her own part in the life of the supposed Charles Denis had been all too correct. She was a plaything, a passing fancy, a momentary distraction, soon forgotten – while she felt her love for him keener than ever. He was treating her almost as a criminal when she had risked her life to save him, when Jason had been shot by his guards. She asked nothing now except to be allowed to go away. She would go with Jason whenever he decided. She knew that she could never live in the same land with him, close to him, without the right even to be near him.

'Your garden is full of odd surprises, Josephine,' he said with assumed lightness, 'look what I have found! The guards found this young person who merely seems to have climbed your wall in company with an American, who has been wounded by a shot.'

Brought back to earth by Napoleon's voice, Marianne saw that she was in a long room decorated in pale green, a music room to judge by its furnishings. A rather plump woman dressed in white cashmere and a great deal of filmy lace was reclining on a sofa done up in light red silk with black trimmings like the rest of the room.

'Bonaparte, please, do not make a joke of it. They told me of a conspiracy—' said the woman, who was none other than the former Empress herself.

She held out trembling hands to him. He took them and gripped them warmly.

'If there is a conspiracy, we shall soon know all about it. Don't upset yourself. Nothing will happen. Which reminds me,' he turned to Marianne who stood speechless, hardly daring to breathe, 'can you tell me who is their leader?'

'Yes, Sire. The Chevalier de Bruslart.'

'Him again!' Josephine cried and the Emperor frowned.

'Come here, mademoiselle, and tell us what you know. Here, sit here—'

She pointed to a low chair but Marianne did not even see it. She was fascinated by the still lovely woman with her pale, transparent skin, heavy mahogany-coloured hair and huge Creole eyes, at present red with weeping. But all this was nothing without the truly inimitable grace which made Josephine someone quite exceptional. Every glance, every look on her face showed her love for the husband who had rejected her, so that Marianne forgot her jealousy and felt drawn to her by a sympathy as spontaneous as it was unconscious. Both of them loved the same man, both feared for him. That was a much stronger bond between them than the distant tie of blood by which they were united.

'Come,' the former Empress said again. 'Come and sit here.'

Marianne made a faultless court curtsy. 'Madame,' she murmured, 'I dare not. Your Majesty sees how I am dressed – and the harm I might do to these pretty chairs.'

'No matter,' Josephine cried airily with the sudden play-fulness which was so much a part of her charming, unpre-dictable nature. 'I want to talk to you, I want to find out who you are! The truth is, you are a mystery to me. You are certainly dressed like a vagabond but your curtsy is like a great lady's and your voice goes with it. Who are you?'

'Just a second,' Napoleon broke in. 'Here's another! It seems the conspirators were not the only ones on the road.'

It was indeed Duroc once more, accompanied this time by a thin figure muffled in a furred driving coat in whom Marianne was disconcerted to recognize Fouché. The Minister of Police was paler than ever except for a somewhat red and swollen nose due partly to the cold outside and partly to a magnificent cold in the head which thickened his voice and obliged him to be constantly using his handkerchief. The two men halted side by side and bowed. The Grand Marshal of the Palace spoke first.

'There was indeed a conspiracy, Sire. I found his Grace the Duke of Otranto on the spot, very busy unravelling it.'

'I see.' The Emperor stood with his hands behind his back regarding his two officials in turn. 'How is it, Fouché, that I was not warned?'

'I was not warned myself, Sire, until the last moment. But, as your Majesty sees, I left my bed at once although my state of health should have kept me there — besides, your Majesty's accusation is unjust. You were warned, Sire. Is that not Mad-emoiselle Mallerousse I see there, beside her Majesty the Empress? She is one of my most loyal and valued agents.'

Marianne opened her mouth but no words came. Fouché's presence of mind was stupefying. That he should dare to claim the credit for what she had done and take it all to himself, when, but for Gracchus-Hannibal Pioche, she might have stayed in the underground cavern of Chaillot for ever!

But Napoleon's blue eye was turned on her and she felt her heart shrink at its hardness.

'One of Fouché's agents, eh? That's news — what have you to say to that, Duroc?'

The words were a threat. The Duc de Frioul reddened and

groped for a reply but Fouché gave him no time. Smiling, very much at his ease, he dabbed delicately at his nose and purred. 'Indeed yes, one of the best. I even christened her The Star. Mademoiselle Mallerousse is at present reader to the Princess of Benevento. A charming girl! Utterly devoted to your Majesty as your Majesty no doubt – er, appreciates.'

The Emperor made an angry movement.

'Talleyrand, now?' He turned to Marianne who was terrified by this sudden anger. 'It seems to me, mademoiselle, that there are some explanations you must give me. I had heard of a Demoiselle Mallerousse, a pupil of Gossec's, with a charming voice, but nothing more! I perceive now that your talents are not confined to singing – that you have more than one string to your bow. You are a consummate actress certainly – a great artist, truly! A very great artist! It is true that to be a star with Fouché requires a variety of talents – and a heart to match!'

His voice shook with anger and the harsh Corsican accent became more striking. He was striding furiously up and down the music room as he launched this flood of bitter insults at Marianne's head. Josephine uttered an alarmed protest.

'Bonaparte! Don't forget she may have saved your life!'

The frenzied pacing stopped short and Marianne was crushed beneath a glance so heavy with contempt she felt the tears come into her eyes.

'That is so! I will see to it that you are rewarded, mademoiselle, according to your deserts! His Grace the Duke of Otranto will arrange for a proper sum—'

'No! No – not that!'

This was more than Marianne could bear. It had been cruel enough to be compelled to give up her dream of love and make up her mind to go away from him for ever. No one could ask her to endure his contempt as well, to let him treat her like some low servant, a common spy! She was willing to go but not to let him spoil the wonderful memory of their night of love. That, at least, she meant to keep intact to feed her dreams on for the rest of her life. In her indignation, she had sprung to her feet and now stood facing Napoleon, the tears rolling down her scratched and dirty face but with her head held high and her green eyes flashing defiance at the angry Caesar.

'If I tried to save your life, Sire, it was not to have you throw money in my face as though I were a servant you had dismissed – it was for love of you! And because I am indeed your servant, though not as you would have it! Is it a crime that I have worked for your police? I do not think I am the only one to do that!' She hurried on regardless of the mortified looks of Josephine who had herself supplied the inquisitive Minister of Police with information about her husband's actions on more than one occasion. 'But I did so,' Marianne went on, too well away for Fouché's warning glance to stop her now, 'I did so only because I was forced to do it. Because I had no choice—'

'Why not?'

The abruptness of the question and the harsh voice in which it was uttered made Marianne's heart miss a beat. He was observing her ruthlessly. This was the end. She had lost him now for ever. If that was so, she might as well complete the ruin with her own hands and tell him everything. Afterwards, he could do with her what he liked, throw her into prison, send her back to the gallows in England – what did it matter! She slid wretchedly to her knees.

'Sire,' she said in a low voice, 'let me tell you the whole story and then you can judge fairly—'

Fouché, clearly anxious at the turn events were taking, made an attempt to intervene.

'All this is ridiculous,' he began but a sharp, 'Silence!' from the Emperor cut him short. Marianne went on.

'My name is Marianne d'Asselnat de Villeneuve. My parents died under the guillotine and I was brought up in England by my aunt, Lady Selton. A few months ago, I was married to a man whom, I believed then, I loved. It was a terrible mistake. On the very night of my wedding, my husband, Francis Cranmere, staked everything I possessed at cards and lost. He staked my honour also. And so – I killed him!'

'Killed him?' Josephine's horrified exclamation was not altogether unadmiring.

'Yes, madame – killed him in a duel. I know it may seem strange for a woman to fight a duel, but I was brought up like a

boy – and had no one left but myself to defend my name and
my honour. My aunt had died a week earlier. After that, I was
obliged to flee. I had to leave England where I had nothing to
look forward to but the hangman's noose. I managed to make
my way to France by means of a smuggling vessel – and there,
to save me from the laws against returning émigrés, his Grace
the Duke of Otranto offered me a post as reader to Madame de
Talleyrand and at the same time—'

'To render some small services to himself!' the Emperor
finished for her. 'It does not surprise me. Never do anything for
nothing, do you, Fouché? I think you had better tell me how
you came to be offering your protection to an émigrée returning
to the country illegally.'

Fouché's faint sigh of relief had not escaped Marianne. 'It is
very simple, Sire,' he began. 'It happened this way—'

'Later, later—'

The Emperor had resumed his pacing up and down but much
more slowly now. With his hands clasped behind him and his
head sunk forward on his chest, he seemed to be thinking. The
kindly Josephine took advantage of this to raise Marianne from
her knees and make her sit down once more. She wiped the
girl's tear-drenched eyes with her own handkerchief and, calling her daughter Hortense who, alone of her entourage, had
been present at the scene, asked her to send for a warm drink
for Marianne.

'Tell them to prepare a bath and dry clothes, and a room – I
am keeping Mam'zelle d'Asselnat with me!'

'Your Majesty is very kind,' Marianne said with a sad little
smile, 'but I should prefer to go. I should like to rejoin my
wounded companion. We were to leave together, tomorrow,
for America. His ship waits for him at Nantes.'

'You will do as you are told, mademoiselle,' Napoleon told
her shortly. 'Your fate, I think, is not in your own hands. We
have not yet done with you. Before you leave for America, you
shall have some more explaining to do.'

Explain what, my God? Marianne thought. What a fool she
had been to plunge into this wasps' nest in order to save him,
or rather, to see him, even for an instant, because she still

hoped for something, though for what she could not have said. Perhaps for some return of the other night's tenderness? No, that hard, clipped voice told her all too clearly that she had never meant anything real to him. He was cold and heartless! But then, why did he have to have such a hold on her?

'I am your Majesty's to command,' she murmured with death in her heart. 'Command me, Sire, and I will obey.'

'I should hope so. Accept the clothes and hot water her Majesty is good enough to offer you, but hurry! You must be ready to go with me to Paris within the hour.'

'Sire,' Fouché offered graciously, 'I can easily take charge of mademoiselle. I am returning to Paris and I can set her down in the rue de Varenne.'

His willingness to oblige earned the Duke of Otranto a swift, angry glare.

'When I need your advice, Fouché, I shall ask for it. Off you go, mademoiselle, and be quick.'

'May I at least know what has become of my companion?' she asked with a measure of determination.

'In the Emperor's presence, mademoiselle,' Napoleon retorted, 'you need concern yourself with no one but yourself. Matters are already sufficiently black for you. Do not make them worse.'

But it would take much more than Napoleon's anger to make Marianne desert a friend.

'Sire,' she said in a tired voice, 'even one under sentence of death has the right to care about a friend. Jason Beaufort was hurt trying to save you and—'

'And in your view my behaviour is thoroughly ungrateful? Don't worry, mademoiselle, your American friend is not seriously hurt. A ball in the arm, and I daresay not the first. Captain Trebriant is at this moment looking for the carriage he says he left on the road. After which, he will go quietly back to Paris.'

'In that case, I want to see him!'

Napoleon's fist smashed down on a fragile lemonwood table with such force that it broke beneath the blow.

'Who dares to say "I want" to me! Enough! You will see this

man only with my permission and when I think fit! Fouché, since you are so keen on acting as escort, you may see to this Beaufort—'

The Minister of Police bowed and with an ironical glance, accompanied by a discreet shrug of the shoulders, he took leave and withdrew.

She watched him as he went through the door, round-shouldered and beaten. It was a sight that should have given her pleasure but the man whose anger she had just witnessed was too far removed from the charming Charles Denis. She understood now why they called him the Corsican ogre! But, for all her present fury, Marianne could not pretend to herself that she did not like that masterful tone.

Josephine had watched this scene without interfering. But when Fouché had gone she rose and took Marianne's arm where she stood rooted to the spot.

'Obey, child. One must never cross the Emperor – whatever his commands.'

Marianne's eyes, still flaming with revolt, met Josephine's sad, gentle ones. Despite her own love for Napoleon, she could not help feeling drawn to this lonely woman who was so kind to her and seemed to give no thought to the strangeness of her situation. She did her best to smile and then, bending quickly, placed her lips on the pale hand of the dethroned Empress.

'I obey you, madame.'

The Emperor gave no sign of hearing this final piece of defiance. He stood with his back to the two women, staring out of the window and twisting the fringe of a gleaming watered silk curtain nervously between his fingers. Without another word, Marianne dropped a curtsy to Josephine and followed the maid summoned by Queen Hortense. As she went, she wondered if there would ever come a time when she would be able to choose her own clothes and not be obliged to borrow from all and sundry.

Half an hour later, wearing a dress and coat belonging to Madame de Rémusat, the former Empress' lady-in-waiting who was more or less the same size as herself, Marianne took her place with drooping head and heavy heart in the imperial berlin. She was not even conscious of the amazing honour done her. For her, it meant nothing because she cared not whether the ill-humoured little man who sat next to her were Emperor or not. Since he did not love her, she would a hundred times have preferred any stranger. The burning memories of Butard lay between them — a source of hideous anguish now, which only increased her pain and wretchedness. The man she loved had changed suddenly into some kind of judge, as icy and indifferent as justice itself. Any fears she might have of the journey which lay ahead were because she knew what power this ruthless man possessed to make her suffer.

She had said her thanks and farewells to Josephine and the gentle Creole had made her promise to come and visit her again while, at the same time, casting an appealing glance at the Emperor which he pretended not to see. But even this evidence of kindness had failed to comfort Marianne. This, she did not doubt, was the last stage in her ordeal. Tomorrow, she would try and find Jason and go away with him at last. But for tonight, she did not even wonder what Napoleon meant to do with her.

Just before the door closed, Duroc's head was poked into the carriage.

'To — the Trianon, Sire?'

'Don't be a fool! Not the Trianon, or Saint Cloud. To the Tuileries! And send a messenger ahead to say I'm coming!'

'As your Majesty commands.'

The door banged shut and the coach moved off towards the lighted gate. All around were the rhythmic hoofbeats of the escort of chasseurs. Marianne had noted that, in suggesting the Emperor's possible destination, Duroc had taken good care to say nothing about Butard. That was no doubt a name which must never, never be uttered again. It could not be other than highly disagreeable to the Master of Europe even to remember what had passed between himself and one of Fouché's spies.

Once through the gate amid the clatter of arms being presented, the road stretched before them. Marianne closed her

eyes, partly to hold back the tears that would come and partly
to breathe in the smell of Spanish jasmine and snuff which
filled the carriage. The green velvet cushions were impregnated
with it and she breathed in almost furtively, like a thief, because it alone had power to conjure up the sweet, tormenting
memories she so longed to forget. Even the smell of him was a
tiny fragment of happiness.

Suddenly, she heard him speak.

'This American, what is he to you? Your lover?'

She answered without looking at him, trying to hide her
pain.

'Only a friend – a faithful friend. Tonight, he rescued me
from the prison where I had been held ever since—' her voice
died away. Then, all at once her fighting instinct revived, she
felt the need to give back blow for blow and turned on him.
'You have asked me a great many questions about my past life,
Sire, why have you not asked what I have been doing this past
week and more?'

'No need. I know.'

'You know? How?'

'While you were being cleaned up, I asked a few questions. I
am grieved at what has happened – but that is beside the point.
Where did you meet this American?'

Marianne was revolted by the monstrous egotism this per-
sistence revealed. She flung the words at him like a challenge,
unable to control herself any longer.

'He was the man to whom Francis Cranmere lost all that I
had brought him – myself included!'

'So, I was right. He is your lover.'

'Because you suppose me capable of fulfilling such a bargain? Because you think it possible that when someone comes
to a young girl on her wedding night and says: "Your husband
is not coming. I am going to take his place. I won you at cards",
she will instantly open her arms and her bed to him? I believe I
told you I had killed Lord Cranmere.'

'But you have not, to my knowledge, killed Jason Beaufort?'

'He had already gone. I threw him out. It was only long

afterwards that I met him again — here, in fact, in the house of the Prince of Benevento. Oh — anyway, does all this really matter? How can my life interest you, past, present or future? You have an Empire, subjects, as many women as you want—'

It gave her a kind of awful joy to hurl the inmost feelings of her heart in wild confusion at the feet of this unfeeling man before whom all trembled. Only she was not afraid because not even if the fancy took him to put her to death could he hurt her more than he had done already. She actively enjoyed trying to provoke him and make him angry. Yet, oddly enough, Napoleon did not seem to have heard. His splendid profile was turned away, towards the road and he murmured absently, as though thinking aloud:

'I'd like to know who that devil Talleyrand doesn't know in this world.'

Then, before the choking Marianne could say another word, he turned to her suddenly.

'You know,' he said, in a voice full of laughter, 'that it is treason to argue with the Emperor?'

'Argue? Me? — I—'

'Unless you wish to be punished as you deserve, you'd better hurry up and beg my pardon.'

With a quick movement he snapped down the blinds. But, not until Napoleon's lips sought her own, did Marianne realize that he had taken her in his arms.

CHAPTER FIVE

Once a 'Merveilleuse' . . .

Marianne lay with her head hanging slightly over the edge of the bed, gazing up at the shining bronze gilt eagle with outstretched wings which, high above, surmounted the crown on the great, circular baldachin. In spite of the exhausting and fantastic adventures of the night, and the long love-making which had followed, she was not sleepy. She would sleep later, she was not quite sure when but she did know very well that she would never sleep in this impressive bed. The great curtains of purple velvet fringed with gold, the winged victories, their bronze feet treading globes of lapis lazuli, even the dais on which the imperial bed was placed, all helped to make her feel that she might as well be sleeping on the throne of France itself. It was simultaneously impressive, flattering and – rather funny. Napoleon, accustomed to it, slept with his head resting on Marianne's shoulder. The glow from a night-light of silver gilt threw a gentleness over his wilful features, relaxed now in sleep, bringing back a little of the child he had once been. Overcome by a vast tenderness, Marianne could not take her eyes off him. She wanted to savour this night's happiness to the last drop.

Between the bed and the windows opposite, the great carpeted expanse was dotted with a series of strange islands, her own clothes, ripped off impatiently and scattered to the winds, and his, which he was in the habit of leaving where they dropped as he got out of them. Outside, the freezing night was almost over and the regular footsteps of the sentries reminded Marianne that she was in the Tuileries. But the room in the apartment on the first floor which had belonged to the unhappy Louis XVI, was warm and safe, still vibrant with their kisses and their words and sounds of love. How he had loved

her, in those two hours from the time when he had led her in
by the small, private door leading directly to his apartment! It
was as though he could never have enough of her. He had made
her promise she would never leave him, that she would stay
with him, and be all his own. And when, timidly, she had mentioned his approaching marriage of which everyone was talking, he had roared with laughter.

'I'm marrying a brood mare!' he had told her crudely, like
the soldier he was. 'I need an heir for my throne — but you, you
will give me what no other woman can ever give me.'

She had discovered then how hard it was to love an Emperor. Jealousy, the need she had to know everything about
him, brought a host of questions to her lips which she dared
not ask aloud. How could she speak to him of all those women
whose names she had heard linked with his? How could she
speak of the Polish Countess who had gone away to the snows
of her own country to give birth to his child? She sensed that
he would not endure curiosity from her. So many things that
would be possible with an ordinary man were not so with him.

When the thought of that unknown woman he was to marry
had made her pensive, Napoleon had drawn her into his arms
again, softly and slowly caressing her bare skin with that inti-
mate knowledge which never failed to arouse her. Then, with
her heart beating wildly, she had forgotten everything but the
furious pumping of her blood, and he had crushed her to him
hard.

'I love you and only you,' he told her fiercely. 'That must be
enough for you.'

'It will be enough as long as you go on loving me. But I fear it
may not be possible. If I must return to my place with Madame
Talleyrand—'

'Impossibility is a bugbear for cowards and a refuge for
fools! As for going back to that old cow! I have better things
in store for you — my sweet, beautiful — wonderful singing
bird!'

He had said no more because at that point neither of them
had been able to hold out any longer against the demands of
their bodies and beyond that point there was no room for

anything but silence. And now he was asleep, leaving her to enjoy these moments of warm, full happiness all by herself, counting them out as a miser counts his treasure. She knew she could not stay here in the palace, that soon she would have to go, but she did not even begin to wonder where to. She left everything to him, he was all-powerful and he was the man she had chosen for her master. Whatever he decided would be right.

A clock from a nearby church struck seven. From the palace courtyard came sharp commands, the click of heels, the clatter of horses' hoofs on cobblestones, the distant call of a trumpet. Marianne sighed. The fantastic night which had begun in the quarries of Chaillot and ended, by the strange twist of fate, in the imperial bed, was over.

The door was opened softly. A man entered on tiptoe. Quickly, Marianne pulled the sheet up to her chin. It was Constant, the Emperor's valet, and the man she had already seen that night at Butard. In one hand, he carried a branch of lighted candles, in the other a small tray on which were two steaming cups. Both these, he set down on a small side table, then quickly gathered up the scattered garments and placed them carefully on a chair according to their owners. Marianne watched from between half-closed lids that quick, familiar certainty of his movements. Not until he had finished did he approach the bed.

'Sire,' he said loudly, 'it is seven o'clock. I have the honour to wake your Majesty.'

As though he had only been waiting for the signal, Napoleon stirred, sat up and gave a light yawn.

'Already?' he said. 'A short night, Constant. What is the weather like?'

'Much warmer, Sire, than yesterday. It is raining. May I ask how your Majesty is feeling?'

'Wonderful! Ah, tea! Come on, lazybones, wake up—'

The concluding remarks were addressed to Marianne who had been covering her embarrassment by pretending sleep. Seizing her by the shoulders, Napoleon shook her vigorously and bundled her up in the sheets, laughing like a child at the same time.

'Come on! Open your eyes! Here, drink this! I always begin the day with a cup of tea or orange! Give it to her, Constant.'

The valet obeyed with a smile after first greeting Marianne pleasantly with: 'I hope madame has slept well?'

She thanked him with a smile and then carried the steaming beverage to her lips before remarking wickedly:

'I did not know that you had English habits, Sire?'

'And you know them, don't you? The English have some good ones, you know. One must be their enemy, as I am, to admit it honestly. Any news, Constant?'

'The lady sent for by your Majesty awaits your Majesty's pleasure in the antechamber.'

'Ah, splendid! Take her into my office and ask her to wait. I'm coming. Give me my dressing-gown and slippers and find one for this young lady. Quick now!'

As Constant withdrew, Napoleon leapt out of bed regardless of his nakedness and ripped away the sheet which Marianne had drawn up under her arms.

'Let me look at you a moment more before I go off to work! You know you are lovely enough to damn an Emperor? I cannot make you an Empress, alas, but I shall make you a queen, a queen of beauty and of talent — I'll lay my Empire at your feet.'

He filled both hands with the sumptuous mass of hair that fell around her, cradling her face in it. He swept her joyously into his arms and hugged her, then, just as suddenly, dropped her back on to the bed and heaped the sheets and covers over her.

'Now cover yourself, siren! Not even Constant is privileged to see my treasures.'

By the time the valet returned, the Emperor was dressed in trousers and a white flannel dressing-gown and was putting on his slippers.

'Your Majesty has not put on a neckcloth?' Constant said, earning himself a black look from his master who, however, merely replied:

'My bath in fifteen minutes. Tell Corvisart that I am quite

well and have no need of him this morning. See that mademoiselle has everything she needs. I am going to see Madame
Hamelin.'

Marianne had no time to ask any questions about this early
morning visitor. Napoleon had gone. Instead, she got up and
made her way into the Emperor's dressing-room, thrown open
to her by Constant. As though it were perfectly natural, he
gave her everything she might need, including a large bottle of
eau-de-Cologne.

'His Majesty gets through vast quantities of it,' he observed
with a smile. Marianne thought she liked this confidential servant. He had a frank, open face, immediately likeable, the face
of one belonging to the north. On the other hand, she also had
the feeling that Constant liked her, a feeling partly due to the
many little attentions he showed her without in the least ap-
pearing to do so.

When, after ten minutes or so, Napoleon returned, she was
already dressed in the soft blue woollen gown given her by
Madame de Rémusat.

'Bravo!' he cried. 'I like women who don't dawdle over their
toilet. You'd make a good soldier! Come now, I'm going to
present you to the lady I've decided shall have charge of you
until I find you a house worthy of you.'

'Is she this – Madame Hamelin?' Marianne said with a slight
hesitation. 'I know the name and I believe I may already have
seen the lady.'

'You will certainly have seen her at Talleyrand's. She is a
great friend of his but the only difference is that I trust her,
which is more than I do our dear Prince of Benevento. His
house is no place for the woman I love.'

'Is she then a very virtuous lady?' Marianne hazarded, thinking of Madame Fouché and seeing herself already shut up in a
household of grim respectability.

Napoleon's shout of laughter reassured her instantly.

'She, Fortunée? She has been called the giddiest creature in
France. Oh, no, she is by no means a prude. She was one of the
most spectacular *merveilleuses* in the time of the Directory and
since then has lost count of the number of her lovers. But

though her virtue may be only a distant memory, she has other much more solid and reliable qualities, such as an honest, sincere heart, unfailing loyalty and a strong belief in friendship. Do you know, she even went on her knees to beg me not to divorce my wife? Yes, she's a good friend. Her house, her belongings and her sharp tongue are always at the service of those she likes — and I want her to like you. You will never find a better bastion against the malice of the fashionable world, which she knows as no one else does. Besides which, she lives in a delightful house not far from Montmartre, and sufficiently discreet for nocturnal visitors to pass unnoticed and to make it possible to hide someone there.'

'Hide someone? Who is to hide there—'

'You, *mio dolce amore!* I have decided to hide you until the time, don't worry, it will not be long, when you shall burst on the world. Didn't I tell you I wanted to put Paris, Rome, Milan and Brussels at your feet? No. No questions. You'll see. Now come.'

The Emperor's office was a plain room, dominated by tall mahogany bookcases. Marianne remembered the woman waiting there at once. How could she ever forget that dark, fascinating Creole face? Fortunée Hamelin's style of beauty was frankly exotic and, at thirty-four, she was still a remarkably attractive woman with magnificent black hair, teeth that were very white and pointed, and red lips with a very slight thickness that betrayed perhaps a touch of Negro blood. With all this went an island grace which only Josephine could rival. The one came from Martinique, the other from Saint Domingo but they had always been firm friends. Marianne liked Madame Hamelin's steady, smiling eyes and even the strong scent of roses which enveloped her like a cloud.

As soon as Marianne appeared, looking somewhat stiff and uncomfortable, Fortunée leapt up from the little green and gold striped satin sofa on which she had been sitting amid a great mass of furs, and came forward eagerly to embrace her, exclaiming as she did so in her musical Creole voice:

'My dear, dear girl, you cannot conceive how happy it makes

me to take you under my wing. For ages I've been longing to steal you from that great stupid Princess! How did you manage to dig her out, Sire? Our dear Talleyrand watched over her like Jason with the Golden Fleece—'

'To be honest, it was not so very hard. The old rogue was hoist with his own petard! But I shall not prevent you telling him that I have given her into your keeping – on condition he keeps his mouth shut. I don't want her talked of for the moment. He will have to make up some story when he knows what has become of her.' Napoleon smiled wickedly. 'I have an idea,' he went on, 'he must be beginning to feel a little anxious about her! Now, run away, both of you. It is nearly time for my levee. Your carriage is at the side gate, Fortunée?'

'Yes, Sire. It is waiting.'

'Excellent. I'll come to your house tonight, about eleven. Now be off with you. As for you, my singing bird, take care of yourself but think only of me.'

He was in a hurry now, fiddling nervously with the heaps of papers and portfolios in red morocco which littered his enormous desk. But Marianne herself was too lost in thought to feel offended. Madame Hamelin's reference to the Golden Fleece had reminded her of the companion of her adventures and the recollection was not a pleasant one. He had been hurt, he might be waiting for her and she would have to break the word she had given him. It was an uncomfortable thought. But then, she was so happy. She could not help preferring that slight sense of guilt to the regret that would have been hers had she left France. Jason would soon forget the girl he had won at cards in one night's madness.

Napoleon tweaked her ear. 'You might at least kiss me instead of standing there dreaming,' he reproached her. 'The time will go slowly for me, until tonight. But I must send you away.'

Fortunée had gone discreetly to look out of a window but even so Marianne was conscious of her presence and gave herself to his embrace with some timidity. Napoleon, though still in his dressing-gown, was Emperor once more. She slipped from his arms and swept him a deep curtsy.

'Your Majesty's to command and, more than ever, his faithful servant.'

He laughed. 'I love you when you put on your court airs,' he told her. Then, in a different voice, he called out: 'Rustan!'

On the instant, the mameluke appeared, dressed in a splendid costume of red velvet embroidered with gold and a white turban. He was a Georgian of great size, formerly sold as a slave by the Turks and brought home by General Bonaparte with a hundred others from his Egyptian campaign. Although he slept each night across the Emperor's door, he had been married for two years to the daughter of an usher at the palace, Alexandrine Douville. No one could have had a more peaceable nature but Rustan, with his brown skin, his turban and his great, curved scimitar, was an impressive figure, although it was his exotic character which most impressed Marianne.

Napoleon now told him to conduct the two ladies to their carriage and, with a final curtsy, Marianne and Fortunée left the imperial presence.

As they went down the little private staircase behind Rustan, Madame Hamelin slipped her arm through her new friend's, enveloping her in the scent of roses.

'I predict that you will be all the rage,' she said gaily, 'that is unless his Majesty enjoys playing sultan and keeps you shut up too long. Are you fond of men?'

'I – I am of one man,' Marianne said in astonishment.

Fortunée Hamelin laughed. She had a warm, open infectious laugh that showed a gleam of sharp, white teeth between her red lips.

'No, no, you don't understand! You do not love a man, you love the Emperor! You might as well say you love the Pantheon or the new triumphal arch at the Carrousel!'

'You think it is the same thing? I don't. He is not so imposing, you know. He is—' She paused, hunting for the word that would best express her happiness but, finding nothing strong enough, she simply sighed: 'He is wonderful!'

'I know that,' the Creole exclaimed. 'And I know, too, how attractive he can make himself; when he wishes to take the trouble, that is, because when he cares to be disagreeble—'

'Can he be?' Marianne cried, genuinely astonished.

'You wait until you have heard him tell a woman in the middle of a ball room: "Your dress is dirty! Why do you always wear the same gown? I have seen this one twenty times!"'

'Oh no! It cannot be true!'

'Oh yes, it is, and if you want me to tell you what I really think, it is that which makes his charm. What woman is there who is truly a woman who does not long to know what this boorish Emperor with his eagle look and boyish smile is like in bed? What woman hasn't at some time or other dreamed of playing Omphale to his Hercules?'

'Even – you?' Marianne asked, a trifle wickedly. But Fortunée answered with perfect sincerity.

'Yes, I admit it – for a while at least. I got over it very quickly.'

'Why was that?'

Once again that irresistible laugh rang through the palace corridors and out to the steps.

'Because I am too fond of men! And believe me, I have good reasons. As for his Majesty the Emperor and King, I think that what I have given him is worth as much as love.'

'What is that? Friendship.'

'I wish,' the other woman said in a voice grown suddenly thoughtful, 'I wish I could be really his friend! Besides, he knows I am fond of him – and more than that, that I admire him. Yes,' she added with sudden fervour, 'I admire him more than anyone in the world! I am not sure if, in my heart of hearts, God does not take second place to him.'

The sun was just rising, painting the Venetian horses on the new triumphal arch a delicate pink. It was going to be a lovely day.

Madame Hamelin lived in the rue de la Tour d'Auvergne, between the former barrière de Porcherons and the new barrière des Martyrs, cut in the wall of the Fermiers Généraux, in a charming house with a courtyard at the front and a garden at the back where, before the Revolution, the Countess de Genlis had brought up the children of the Duke d'Orléans. For neighbour, she had the Inspector of the Imperial Hunts and opposite, a dancer from the Opéra, Margueritte Vadé de l'Isle, the mistress of a financier. The house itself had been built in the previous century and recalled the clean lines of the Petit Trianon, although with substantial outbuildings. Although the wintry garden was silent and melancholy, there was a fountain singing in a pool in the courtyard. Marianne liked it at once, and especially because the sloping street lay a little out of the common way. Even at this hour of the morning, with servants going to and fro about their work and the cries from the streets as Paris woke once more, there was something quiet and restful about Fortunée's white-walled house which made her feel much happier than all the luxurious splendours of the Hôtel Matignon.

Fortunée conducted her guest to a delightful room done up in pink and white pekin silk with a bedstead of pale wood hung with full white muslin curtains. This room, which was close to her own, belonged to her daughter Léontine, then away boarding at Madame Campan's famous school for girls at St-Germain. And suddenly, Marianne realized that the Creole's vagueness was only apparent and that she was, on the contrary, a person of great energy. In no time at all, Marianne found herself presented in succession with a flowing robe of lace and batiste, a pair of green velvet mules, a lady's maid all to herself (all these being possessions of Léontine Hamelin) and a substantial breakfast. To this last, she was very soon sitting down by a good bright fire in company with her hostess, who had also shed her walking dress. Marianne was amused to see that the former *merveilleuse*, who had once dared to appear in public in the Champs Elysées stark naked underneath her muslin gown, happily reverted to her old ways in the privacy of her own apartments. Her filmy draperies, in spite of an abundance of delicately-coloured ribbons, did little to conceal her perfect figure and served, in fact, to bring out something of the primitive, Southern quality of her dark beauty.

The two young women set to with enthusiasm to consume new bread, butter, preserves and fresh fruit, washed down with quantities of tea drunk very hot and strong with milk in the English fashion, all served on an exquisite pink service of exotic pattern. When they had eaten, Fortunée sighed contentedly.

'Now,' she said, 'let us talk. What would you like to do now? Bathe? Sleep? Read? For myself, I mean to write a note to Monsieur de Talleyrand to let him know what has become of you.'

'If you please,' Marianne broke in earnestly, 'there is something which seems to me still more urgent. One of my friends, the man who rescued me yesterday from the quarries of Chaillot, was hurt. He is an American, a sea captain and a most remarkable man, and I do not know what has become of him. The Emperor—'

'—who, like most Corsicans, is subject to terrible fits of jealousy, refused to answer your question! But tell me about this American. I have always adored people from his country because I was born not far away myself. There is a breath of adventure and eccentricity about them I find fascinating. Besides, the Emperor has told me very little about what has happened to you. It sounds just like a novel. You must tell me all about it, for I adore novels!'

'So do I,' Marianne said with a smile. 'But I did not enjoy this one very much.'

Fortunée's eyes sparkled as she listened with rapt attention to all that had happened since the evening of the twenty-first of January when Marianne had left the house in the rue de Varennes to go to Butard. Marianne told her about Bruslart and Morvan, of whose fate she was still ignorant, about her friend Jolival, who must also be in some anxiety on her account, about Gracchus-Hannibal Pioche and, finally, about Jason Beaufort in whose company she should have been setting out for America that very day.

'I would have gone with him without hesitation,' she finished, 'if the Emperor had not made me promise to stay.'

'You would really have gone with him — even after what happened last night at the Tuileries?'

Marianne thought for a moment and then sighed.

'Yes. If I had not been made to promise that I would remain, if I had not been assured that I was needed, I should have gone today without a moment's hesitation.'

'But – why?'

'Because I love him. Now that I know who he is and what must happen in the months ahead, this – this marriage to the Arch-Duchess, I am frightened of being hurt. Whatever he may say or do, I know I shall be hurt because I can't help being jealous of her. That is why it would have been better for me to go, even more so after those hours of love. Then I should have taken away with me a wonderful memory. And even at this moment, while I am talking to you, I am still sorry I have stayed because I am afraid of what lies in store for me. I even wonder if it would not be better to go against his will. I don't even know what he means to do with me, what kind of life I shall have!'

'In your place, I should trust him and have a little patience. As for running away, you cannot do that,' Fortunée said seriously. 'He would not let you go. He would have you pursued, caught, brought back to him willy-nilly. Napoleon has never let go anything he wanted. You belong to him! And, sooner or later, you must be prepared for him to bring you suffering, even if it is not by his own will. It is no easy task to love a man like that. But if you take it on, you will have to do all you can to make the best of it and not suffer more than you can help. That was why I asked you, just now, if you liked men. With more than one to think about, their power to make us suffer is that much less. For myself, I'd rather make two men happy than one miserable.'

'Love more than one man?' Marianne exclaimed, genuinely shocked. 'But I could never do that!'

Fortunée rose, stretched her long, supple golden body in its white gauzes and bestowed on Marianne a smile part-friendly and part-quizzical.

'You are too young to understand. We'll talk about it again another time. But now, write a few lines quickly to your American and invite him to come and call on you. Where does he stay?'

'At the Hôtel de l'Empire in the rue Cerutti.'

'Not very far. I'll send a man round at once. Here, there are writing materials on this table.'

A few minutes later, the side gate banged behind Fortunée's messenger and Marianne went to perform a toilet somewhat more complete than that which had been possible at the Tuileries. Without being altogether willing to admit it, she was glad to think of seeing Jason again with Jolival and Gracchus, whom she had asked him to bring with him. All three had now assumed a special place in her heart because they had shown her what true friendship could be. Once the letter had been written and entrusted to a servant, Fortunée had asked her suddenly whether Jason was in love with her and Marianne had answered quite sincerely:

'No, not really. He believes he owes me a great debt and being an honest fellow, I see that now, he wants to give back what he has taken from me. He'll be disappointed that I do not go with him but nothing more.'

'Has he never claimed – your part in your husband's wager?'

'Oh no. Oh, I think he finds me attractive, but there is nothing in it. He is a strange person, you know. What he loves more than anything is the sea, his ship and his crew. There is not much room for love in such a life.'

Fortunée had not insisted. She had merely shrugged and smiled indulgently. But when, an hour later, the doorbell rang announcing a visitor, she reappeared in the salon, fully dressed, as though by magic. Clearly, the American had piqued her curiosity. But it was not Jason who appeared. As the two young women came in through one door, Arcadius de Jolival was making his entrance through the other. He was dressed like a fashion plate, radiating elegance and cheerfulness. Marianne stared at him with a mixture of amusement and disappointment as he made a bow with all the elaborate grace of a past age.

'You behold me, ladies, bursting with pride and happiness at the privilege of laying my homage at your charming feet!'

Fortunée was looking at the new arrival with frank curiosity. 'Who is it?' she asked.

'My Greek Prince of whom I told you, Arcadius de Jolival,' Marianne replied absently. 'But where is Jason, my friend? Why is he not with you?'

The happy smile faded from Jolival's face.

'But he is, my dear child, he is! Only, in the form of a letter which I have here. I could not persuade him to come. He said it could do no good. And as I left to accompany your servant, madame, he was on the point of setting out for Nantes.'

'He has gone? Without seeing me, without saying good-bye?'

The sudden break in Marianne's voice brought Fortuneé's observant eyes upon her. It suggested something very like distress. Arcadius came forward slowly, taking a letter from inside his snuff-brown coat and slipped it into Marianne's hand.

'I think he says goodbye in this,' he said gently. 'He believed there was no more for him to do here. His ship and his business called for him.'

'But, his wound?'

'A small matter for a man like him. The Emperor sent him his personal physician this morning with expressions of his gratitude – and a memento. Besides, there is nothing like sea air for an invalid. Wounds are well known to heal far quicker at sea than on land. That, at least, is the opinion of the Emperor's physician. He expressed it more than once. But–' the man of letters spoke with some hesitation, '–did you, then, still mean to go with him?'

'N-no–' Marianne said doubtfully. 'No, of course not! That cannot be now.'

She had not missed the reference to the imperial physician. Certainly Napoleon left nothing to chance.

'Well then. Read his letter, it will certainly tell you more than I can.'

Quickly, Marianne broke the black seal with its simple device of a ship in full sail, unfolded the paper and read the few words Jason had written in a large, bold hand.

'Why did you not tell me what you were to him? It might have stopped me making a fool of myself. I realize it is not possible for you to come and live in my country. But did you really, honestly, wish to? I wish you all the happiness in the world, but if, some day, that happiness seems to you to leave a bitter taste, then remember me – and that I owe a debt to you –

for the danger of which I told you is not yet past. But it is true that in future you will have a much better defence than any I could give you. Be happy. Jason.'

Marianne held out the letter to Fortunée with trembling fingers. But a cloud had come over her happiness less on account of this new mention of the mysterious danger which hung over her than because he had gone making no attempt to see her, giving her no chance to explain, or even to ask his forgiveness, and tell him of her gratitude and friendship. The sharpness of her disappointment took her by surprise. God alone knew what she had been hoping for. Perhaps that Jason's wound would oblige him to stay longer in Paris so that they might have had time to see one another, to talk and get to know each other better. It would have made her so happy to establish their hitherto stormy relationship on a basis of real friendship. But then, she dared say, Jason did not want her friendship maybe because she was the Emperor's mistress and had not told him of it. The tone of his letter suggested that his masculine pride was injured. He could not have known how much he had come to matter to Marianne, to be someone dear whose absence could be a source of grief.

She looked up and met Jolival's eye and it seemed to her that she read some pity in it. But just at that moment in her life, pity was one thing she could not endure. She threw up her chin, gripped her hands tightly together and forced herself to smile and speak of something else, no matter what, so long as it hid her feelings.

'You are looking splendid,' she said to fill the silence which had fallen. 'What has happened to you? But please, won't you sit down?'

Jolival sat, carefully smoothing the pale blue pantaloons over his bony knees where they fitted snugly into his elegantly pointed boots.

'Our friend Beaufort lent me a little money with which I was able to recover my wardrobe and my room on the Montagne Sainte Geneviève. But none the less, I shall have to find some situation by which to earn my living. Gaming has few attractions for me and besides, I am not anxious to come up against

Fanchon-Fleur-de-lis and her Philomène a second time.'

'Do you think we have anything more to fear from her?' Marianne asked with sudden horror at mention of the dreadful old woman and remembering the danger of which Jason had still spoken.

'For the present I do not think so. So long as we do not venture into her territorial waters, she will not sail into ours. And I cannot see that we should have much to do at the Episcié or the Homme de Fer. Besides, Bruslart and Saint-Hubert managed to escape but the rest of the conspirators were arrested. Our friend Morvan is under lock and key. And I think there was a raid on the cabaret in the rue des Bonhommes, although Fanchon is certainly too clever to be caught like that.'

At this point, Fortunée, who had finished reading the letter and had for a moment or two been looking rather pensive, gave it back to her friend.

'What is this danger he speaks of?'

'Truly, I do not know. He has always talked of it and then said he can tell me no more in my own interests. But, apart from that, what do you think of his letter?'

'If this man does not love you, I'll be hanged,' Madame Hamelin answered simply. 'For myself, I am very sorry he has gone. I should have liked to meet him.'

'What for?'

'Shall we say—' the Creole gave her teasing smile, 'I like his handwriting. I have always told you I was fond of men. Something tells me this one is a man. Should he come back, you must present him to me without fail.' She turned to Jolival. 'But did he say anything to you about this mysterious danger?'

'Yes,' said the man of letters. 'I know what it is but it is best that Marianne should not. One never knows. It may not come to anything. So why worry? Forget it. And, should our American come back one day, I shall make it my personal business to present him to you, gracious lady!' he finished gallantly.

Deliberately rejecting the possible notion of Jason and Fortunée's becoming one day attached to one another, Marianne launched into a grandiose account of what she hoped to do for those who had helped her and promised Jolival to do what she could on his behalf. She would speak to the Emperor, who would certainly find some employment for the varied talents of such an inveterate idler.

'I wish I could do something for you,' he said with a sigh. 'Have you given up the idea of a singing career?'

'It is not for me to say,' she answered, blushing with mingled pleasure and embarrassment at this proclamation of her dependence.

'Well, if you should come back to it, remember me. I have all the makings of a quite outstanding impresario.'

Meanwhile, since it was by now almost dinner time. Fortunée invited Jolival to share it with herself and her new friend. She had a fondness for original characters and he had taken her fancy. In spite of the shadow thrown on Marianne's spirits by Jason's departure, the meal was a very cheerful one. Fortunée and Arcadius occupied themselves in thinking up a host of plans for their young friend, nearly all of which were centred on the theatre. Fortunée, like all Creoles, adored the theatre and music and her delight at finding out that Marianne was the possessor of an exceptional voice was almost childlike.

'The Emperor must let her sing!' she cried, filling Jolival's glass up with champagne for the fifth time. 'If necessary, I shall tell him myself.'

Marianne scarcely listened. It was as though all this did not concern her. She was still dazed by this sudden turn her life had taken. She was not yet used to the idea that a power quite out of the ordinary had taken charge of her life. Everyone was saying what she ought to do but surely she herself had some say in the matter. While the others talked, she was making her own decision.

'I will sing,' she told herself fiercely. 'I will sing and he will have to let me! That is the one thing that would make it possible for me to live in his shadow without too much suffering. He has his glory — I shall have mine!'

Late that afternoon, she was surprised when they received a visit from Talleyrand himself. Dressed with his usual dark elegance and leaning on his gold-headed cane, the Prince bowed over Madame Hamelin's hand and then kissed Marianne on the forehead with a fatherly warmth that took her by surprise.

'Nice to see you again, my child,' he said, for all the world as though they had parted the night before. 'The Princess sends you her warmest regards and Madame de Périgord, who has been very anxious on your account, commands me to tell you how glad she is to know that you are safe and sound.'

'My Lord,' Marianne said in some confusion, 'your Highness is too kind, I feared you might be offended—'

'How? By seeing our lovely bird spread its wings and fly away into the sky to sing? But, my dear, it is what I have always wished. Why do you think I took you to – Monsieur Denis? I had foreseen, and am delighted by, everything that has happened, except of course the interlude at Chaillot! Let us keep your friendship, that is all we ask. And while I think of it, my dear friend,' he added, turning to Fortunée, 'have your people take out the boxes which are in my carriage. The Princess insisted that this child must have all her things at once.'

Marianne's cheeks flushed with happiness. 'There is no end to the Princess' goodness, my Lord!' she exclaimed. 'Will your Highness be so good as to convey to her my gratitude and tell her that I remain her servant as in the past?'

'I will tell her. Did you know, my dear, that I had a letter from Cazimir this morning? He sends you a host of compliments.'

'Could he not have sent them to me directly,' Fortunée said tartly, half jesting, half angry, 'or are the Dutch women keeping him so busy that he has no time to write to me?'

'Believe me, he is far more occupied with money than with women.'

Cazimir de Montrond, Talleyrand's closest friend, was also Fortunée's favourite of all her lovers. Attractive, witty, and as wicked as sin but a great lord to his fingertips, he was a born gambler with an inordinate love of money and had a finger in a host of financial pies, not all of which would have had the approval of the authorities. Fortunée adored this scapegrace who Talleyrand had nicknamed 'Hell's Infant Jesus', but, as a faithful subject of the Emperor, she had made no protest when he exiled her turbulent lover to Anvers on the grounds that virtue was impossible with him at court.

'The truth is,' she explained to Marianne a little later when Talleyrand had departed after his brief visit, 'that poor Cazimir was unlucky. At the end of last year, there was a duel in the rue Cerutti. The fight took place at dawn in Queen Hortense's garden. Charles de Flahaut and Auguste de Colbert crossed swords over her *beaux yeux* and Cazimir got drawn in because he lived nearby. Napoleon could not take it out on Hortense or Flahaut and so he satisfied himself with sending Auguste de Colbert to get himself killed in Spain and dispatching Montrond to Anvers with orders not to stir.'

'Wasn't that rather harsh?'

'I told you the Emperor was not easy. But I must admit that was not the whole of it. Before that, in the summer, that wretch Cazimir went to Cauterets where the Duchess of Abrantes was weeping because Metternich had left her and, so they say, helped to console her somewhat. On the whole, Napoleon acted wisely. And, in one way, he was doing Montrond a service because otherwise he might have been mixed up in the Abrantes scandal as well.'

'What scandal?'

'My dear, where have you been?'

'In the quarries of Chaillot, as you know quite well.'

'Oh, yes, of course! So you were! Well, you must know that last month, after Count Marescalchi's ball, Junot, who everyone knows deceives his wife quite shockingly, threw a frightful scene in the course of which he half killed her with a pair of scissors in a fit of jealousy. If Madame de Metternich had not intervened, I really think he would have killed her. The Emperor was furious. He sent Junot back to Spain and his wife with him, to force them to make it up. To my mind, he would have done as well to punish that cat Caroline as well!'

'Caroline?'

'Her sister, Madame Murat, Grand Duchess of Berg and Queen of Naples for the last year and a half. A gorgeous, dimpled blonde, as pink and luscious as a bon-bon – and the greatest bitch ever born! It was she who told Junot about poor

Laure d'Abrantes — when he had actually been her own lover!'

This brief glimpse into the habits of the great ones of the court made Marianne open her eyes wide, much to Fortunée's delight.

'You had no idea such things went on, I daresay? But, while I am about it, let me give you some advice. Love the Emperor as much as you like, but take care with his noble family. Apart from his mother, the inaccessible Madame Laetitia, who remains as stiff-necked and Corsican as ever, and Lucien, who has chosen exile for love, the others have made themselves into a kind of nest of vipers, a collection of people as arrogant and greedy and as vain as peacocks and altogether, to my way of thinking, not fit to be with. Avoid them like the plague, for they will hate you as much as the Emperor loves you.'

Marianne took good note of her advice but she had no desire to come to blows with the imperial family, or even to be known to them. She wanted to love Napoleon in the shadows, without drawing attention to herself, because it was only away from the light and noise of the crowd that such a love as theirs could blossom fully.

As the day wore on, her mood became more and more abstracted, so that she listened to Fortunée's gossip with only half an ear. Her eyes kept going back more frequently to the bronze gilt clock with its representation of the sleeping Psyche. Never had she been so glad to see night fall because the night would bring him back to her. A fever began to run in her veins when she thought of the hours of love ahead. Already, she had so much to tell him! And yet the hours seemed to go more and more slowly.

Fortunée, having barred her doors to all her friends on the excuse of a headache, had yawned at least thirty times before ten o'clock sounded from the church of Notre-Dame-de-Lorette.[1] The last stroke had just died away when they heard the rumble of a carriage. It slowed down and entered the gates which the porter had been told to leave open, then stopped in

[1] Not the present church, which dates only from 1836. When the old church of Notre-Dame-de-Lorette was destroyed, its name was given to the Chapel of St-Jean-Port-Latine at the Cimetière des Porcherons.

the deliberately darkened courtyard. Marianne ran to the window with her heart beating wildly while Fortunée rose, intending to withdraw to her own room. But she had no time. In an instant, Napoleon was there.

'Don't run away, madame,' he said as his hostess sank into a curtsy at the door of the salon. 'I have only a moment—'

Flinging his hat on to a sofa, he caught Marianne in his arms and kissed her while she said protestingly:

'What, only a moment?'

'An Emperor cannot often do as he likes, *mio dolce amore*. I have to go back to the Tuileries. There are important dispatches waiting for me and someone I must see, so I have not much time. But there were a number of things I had to tell you which would not wait. This first.'

From a pocket in his coat, he drew a roll of papers sealed with a great red seal which he placed in her hands.

'I promised you a house,' he said, smiling. 'I am giving you this one. I think you will like it.'

Marianne unrolled the papers but before she had read more than the first words of the deed the colour fled from her face. There were tears in her eyes as she flung herself into his arms.

'Thank you – oh, thank you!' she gasped, hugging to her breast the wonderful deeds which told her that the Hôtel d'Asselnat in the rue de Lille, her family's house where her parents had been arrested and where she herself had been found abandoned by the Abbé de Chazay, was now her own.

Gently, Napoleon stroked the heavy crown of dark hair.

'Don't cry. More than anything, I want you to be happy. I have already given orders. Tomorrow morning, Percier and Fontaine will go to the rue de Lille to begin on the necessary repairs, for the house has stood empty since 1793. Fortunée will go with you and you can order it all as you like. There now, don't cry. I have something else to tell you,' he added with affectionate roughness.

She made an effort and dried her eyes.

'I am not crying—'

'Liar! Never mind, I shall go on. Tomorrow, Gossec will

come here. He has orders to prepare you for an audition with
the director of the Opéra. Within a month, all Paris shall ac-
claim a new idol. Maria Stella. You have a wonderful voice and
it shall be your glory!'

'Maria Stella?' she was too surprised now to feel any wish to
cry.

'That is the name I have chosen for you. You cannot appear
in the theatre under your real name and as for your adopted
one of Mallerousse, that is hideous. Besides, the public will
dote on an Italian. You can have no idea of the snobbery of
Parisians! They may not take readily to one of their own
countrywomen, but an Italian will be sure of their support. So
there you are, established as a singer from Italy. Where should
you prefer? Venice, Rome, Florence?'

He offered a choice of cities as easily as a choice of gowns.

'Venice!' Marianne cried rapturously. 'I should so love to
know Venice.'

'You shall go there! You shall sing in Venice, my whole
Empire will be fighting for you – so, we'll give you a Venetian
passport.'

Vast prospects were suddenly opening up before Marianne,
but these prospects involved so many separations. Yet they
were inevitable separations. When he could not have her with
him, it would be better for her to travel, to be far away. And
with her music, everything would be easy.

'Maria Stella!' she murmured as though engraving her new
name on her mind.

'It was not I who gave you that name, it was Fouché, star
you were, and star you shall remain – but in a very different
sky. One more thing. A great singer needs someone to be a kind
of impresario for her, to deal with contracts, arrange her pro-
gramme and protect her against unwelcome intruders. I think I
have found what you need. What do you say to the little man
with the big ears we found kicking his heels on the road outside Malmaison last night in company with a deaf coachman? I
have had a suitable report on him during the day. He seems an
odd fellow, but I think he'll do the business. And, if I have
understood correctly, you owe him something—'

'But—' Marianne was almost speechless. 'How do you know all this? In so short a time?'

'Didn't you know? I have excellent police. And Fouché stands in some need of forgiveness.' He smiled so wickedly that Marianne could not help laughing. Dazed by the unexpected avalanche which had fallen on her, she had sunk on to a sofa but now he bent forward quickly and tweaked her ear to draw her back to him.

'Happy?'

'How could I help it? I don't know what to say. All this is so sudden, so unexpected – it's almost frightening!'

'I told you I had a heap of things to tell you. Now kiss me and then get some sleep. You need it. And there's nothing like a good night's rest after a deal of excitement. I must go.'

Urgent to be gone now, he kissed her somewhat absently, picked up his hat and was striding to the door when, just as he reached it, he stopped and clapped his hand impatiently to his forehead.

'Fool that I am! I nearly forgot!'

Turning back to Marianne who still stood rooted to the spot, he put into her hands a large green morocco jewel case, stamped with the imperial arms, which he produced as though by magic from yet another of his enormous pockets.

'Here,' he said. 'Wear these on the night of your first appearance! Then I shall know you are thinking of me.'

As though in a dream, Marianne opened the case. Lying on a bed of black velvet, gleaming and flashing in the candlelight, was a fabulous set of emeralds and diamonds. Not even at Talleyrand's had she ever seen anything so splendid. But when she looked up with dazzled eyes, she saw that Napoleon was already back at the door.

'Don't tell me they won't suit you. They are the same green as your eyes. Goodbye, my heart.'

When, a little later, Madame Hamelin, growing anxious at the continued silence in the salon, entered cautiously, she found Marianne sitting on the floor by the fire with her hands full of documents and a cascade of fabulous jewels on her knees, crying as though her heart would break.

CHAPTER SIX

The Phantom of the rue de Lille

In the grey, rain-swept light of a new day, beneath a sky that held no promise of sunshine, the great entrance portico framed by dilapidated walls, with here and there a stone missing, presented a dismal sight. Dead weeds sprouted from the gaps in the stonework where their seed had been carried by the wind, and the paving stones before the door, with its sad, flaking green paint, gaped to make way for a mass of brown and soggy vegetation.

Marianne stood leaning on Fortunée's arm and her eyes behind the heavy veil which hid her face filled with tears as she looked at the old house where her life had begun, from which her father and mother had gone out hand in hand to meet their deaths. She had wanted to visit it alone, before the architects took possession of it, because it seemed to her that she alone had the right to break the silence which had enveloped the Hôtel d'Asselnat for so many years. She wanted to see it in all its loneliness and neglect, before the magic wand was waved that would give it a new life, but he found now that this neglect was painful to her. So much lay behind it.

But for the Terror, all her youth would have been passed in this splendid old dwelling, its noble proportions and the cracked stone trophies over the porch still telling of the splendours of the reign of the Sun King, or else in the old château in Auvergne which now she might never see. Instead, she would have a different life, but would it be any happier? Who could tell what Marianne d'Asselnat de Villeneuve might have been at this moment if – but there was no end to it.

Behind her, Marianne heard Arcadius de Jolival telling the coachman to wait. She walked a few steps towards the house, strangely unwilling to make use of the keys which had been handed to her on waking. Opposite the silent entrance, a splendid, luxurious mansion was just awaking to a spate of furious activity contrasting strongly with its neglected neighbour. The staff were going about their morning tasks, and the place was alive with servants sweeping out courtyards and pavements, polishing brass and beating carpets. People were coming and going, many of them men in Army uniform on foot or on horseback, entering or leaving a vast forecourt at the far end of which rose an impressive building in the Egyptian style. Seeing Marianne turn to look, disturbed by the noise breaking in on her thoughts, Arcadius frowned.

'You're going to have noisy neighbours, when they are in Paris, at least. That is the Hôtel de Beauharnais. Prince Eugène, the Viceroy of Italy, is there at present. And yesterday, there was a ball and a reception. Prince Eugène likes entertaining and the Emperor was there. But it means hard work for the servants this morning. That's why they are so busy. But when he is back in Milan it will be quieter. The Emperor is very fond of him,' he added, knowing that this would be the best way of soothing his young friend's irritation. He was quite right. She smiled.

'Oh well, if the Emperor is fond of him. Come, shall we go in? It is freezing out here!'

She proffered the great keys which she had been carrying in her muff. Arcadius took them and went up to the little postern gate beside the main one.

'It will probably be very stiff,' he said. 'If this gate has not been opened for years, the wood frame will have warped and we'll have trouble from rusty hinges.'

He inserted the key and leaned against the door, prepared to push with all his strength as he tried to turn it. But the key turned smoothly in the lock and the door opened without the least resistance.

'Someone seems to have taken the trouble of oiling the lock,' he said in surprise. 'And the door opens as though it were used every day. Who can come here?'

'I don't know,' Marianne answered in some alarm. 'Let's go in.'

The forecourt lay before them in all its desolation. Ahead,
framed in moss-grown outbuildings, the noble, classical
façade displayed black windows with broken panes and stonework smeared with green stains and chipped, here and there,
by bullet holes. A number of steps were missing from the imposing perron and the stone lions which had formerly guarded
it lay headless among the weeds in the courtyard. The ground
was strewn with debris of all kinds and over on the right some
blackened walls and pillars told of the beginnings of a fire,
probably the same the Abbé de Chazay had put out before he
fled. A riot of vegetation had sprung up everywhere, as though
trying to draw a veil over the poor, gutted house. A thin trail of
ivy had begun climbing tentatively up the carved oak door, as
though nature were trying to comfort the mutilated stones
with this fragile ornament. A black cat sprang suddenly
through the twisted ironwork of the cellar grille and streaked
away to disappear through the gaping doorway of an old stable.

Like a good, superstitious Creole, Fortunée Hamelin
shivered and clutched Marianne's arm a little tighter. She
sighed.

'Percier and Fontaine will have their work cut out. What a
ruin! I am beginning to think the Emperor has given you an odd
present!'

'But none that could have given me greater pleasure,' Marianne said fiercely. 'Even the emeralds are nothing beside this
sick old house.'

'It is not as bad as that,' Arcadius said comfortingly. 'With a
little care and work all this can soon be repaired. The damage
is more superficial than really serious. Let's look inside.'

He gave his hand to Marianne to help her up the few wobbly
steps that remained of the perron and then returned to perform the same service for Madame Hamelin who followed.

The carved door opened as easily as the one in the street
had done. Arcadius frowned.

'Who troubles to look after the locks in a ruined house?' he
mumbled. But Marianne was not listening. She stepped forward
with a thudding heart into the huge, deserted entrance hall.
Not a stick of furniture remained. The coloured marble which

had clothed the walls and surrounded the doors lay shattered on the cracked black marble floor. The exquisitely painted doors had been torn from their hinges, allowing the eye to penetrate unhindered into the recesses of the house where everything showed the same traces of blind vandalism.

In the dining-room with its tattered hangings, the bare sideboards, tall cabinets and furnishings too heavy to be carried away showed shattered panels rotten with damp. The mutilated remnants of King Louis XIV's profile still showed on a large cartouche above the red marble fireplace, and the grate was full of ashes in which were small bright scraps of gilt bronze from the furniture burnt there.

In the salon which came next, the ravages were still more terrible. Not one piece of furniture was left standing. The once exquisitely polished harpsichord lay in a heap of rubbish, among which one carved foot and a few ivory keys were still distinguishable. The pale silk hangings were only filthy, blackened rags hanging from bits of wood that still showed traces of gilding. Only the scrolled panelling – but suddenly Marianne gave a start. Her eyes widened, staring. Over the mantelpiece, lonely, splendid and wholly unexpected, the portrait of a man reigned over this scene of devastation. It was a fine piece of work. The face beneath the powdered hair was dark, with proud features and fierce, brooding eyes. He stood, hand on hip, proud and arrogant in his handsome colonel's uniform, against the smoky background of some battle scene. The painter's model must have been a man of rare charm and Fortunée, coming up behind Marianne, exclaimed in wonder.

'Oh!— What a splendid man!'

'It is my father,' Marianne said tonelessly.

All three stood motionless, their feet in the dust, their eyes riveted on the portrait which gazed back at them mockingly, with eyes that were extraordinarily alive. For Marianne, there was a great poignancy in this confrontation. Until this moment, her father had been to her only a rather faded miniature in a frame of seed pearls, the picture of an elegant, sardonically smiling man, a little world-weary, almost effete, whom she had regarded with the same kind of vague fondness she might have felt for any attractive portrait or for the hero of a novel. But the arrogant young soldier portrayed here touched her in the deepest fibres of her being, because in each of those bold features she recognized herself. He was so like her. The high cheekbones, the challenging look in those mocking, slightly upward-curving eyes, the wide, sensual mouth, betraying the stubbornness of that strong, square jaw. He was all at once very close to her, this father she had never really known.

It was Jolival who broke the spell.

'You are his daughter all right,' he said pensively. 'He cannot have been much older than you when that picture was painted. I have never seen a man more handsome, or more virile. But who could have hung it there? Look—' Jolival brushed the gilded frame with one pale kid-gloved finger, 'not a speck of dust! While everything else—'

An expressive movement of his arm embraced the desolation around them. Then he paused, his arm still in mid-air, as from somewhere upstairs a floorboard cracked sharply, as though under someone's feet.

'But – is there someone here?' Marianne said softly.

'I'll go and see,' Arcadius told her.

He ran quickly to the staircase, whose broad sweep could be seen through a gaping doorway, and leapt up two at a time with the lightness of a dancer. Left alone in the salon, the two women looked at each other, neither anxious to break the silence. Marianne had a strange feeling that this empty, desolate house, where the one portrait hung in state, was none the less alive, with a dim, underground life of its own. She was torn between two contradictory urges, to sit down right there on the dusty ground and wait for God knew what, or to run away, shut fast the doors that had opened with such suspicious ease, and never return. The thought that very soon workmen would come and break the silence of this peculiar shrine with all their clamour troubled her, as though there was something wrong about it. And yet, no one had more right than she to cross this threshold, and to awaken the sleeping echoes of the old house. The house to which, even yesterday, she had not given a thought, had now become part of her flesh and she knew that she could never tear it from her again without leaving a wound. Her eyes returned to those of the portrait which seemed to follow her wherever she went and she spoke to it, a silent, earnest prayer from her heart.

'Is it your wish, tell me, is it your wish that I should come back here, to our house? Already, I love it so! I will restore it to its past splendours, and once again you shall preside over a setting worthy of you.'

Then, as though the house were trying to answer her, the one remaining whole window in the room, its fastening perhaps broken or ill-latched, was caught suddenly by a gust of wind and flew open. Marianne moved across to shut it and in doing so saw that it gave, like the rest, on to a small garden laid out around a green and stagnant pool. Beside the pool a stone cupid with a blackened nose stood dreaming with his arms around a large dolphin that had long since ceased to spout water. And just at that very moment, the rain-filled clouds parted to make way for a pale, timid ray of sunshine which caressed the cupid's cheek, revealing his enigmatic smile. And, without quite knowing why, Marianne felt comforted and accepted. Just then, Arcadius came back.

'There's no one there. It must have been a rat.'

'Or just the woodwork creaking,' Fortunée added, shivering in her furs. 'It is so dank in here! Are you sure you want to live here, Marianne?'

'Quite sure,' Marianne answered on a note of sudden happiness, 'and the sooner the better. I shall ask the architects to work as quickly as possible! I think they will be here soon.'

For the first time, she had spoken out loud, as though officially taking possession of the silence. The warm notes of her voice rang through the empty rooms triumphantly. She smiled at Fortunée.

'Let's go,' she said. 'You are almost dead with cold. It's as draughty here as in the street.'

'You don't want to see upstairs,' Jolival said. 'I can tell you, there is nothing there. Apart from the walls, which could not be stolen, and the charred remains in the fireplaces, absolutely nothing is left.'

'Then I had rather not see. It is too sad. I want this house to find its soul again—'

She stopped, her eyes on the portrait, with the sensation of having said something foolish. The soul of the house was there, before her, smiling arrogantly against an apocalyptic background. What she had to do was to restore its body, by re-creating the past.

Outside, they could hear the horses blowing and stamping on the cobblestones. The cry of a water-carrier rang out, waking the echoes of what had been formerly the rue de Bourbon. It was the voice of life, of the here and now which held so much appeal for Mariannne. With Napoleon's love to protect her, she would live here as sole mistress, free to act as she pleased. Free! It was a fine word when, at that very moment, she might have been buried alive in the heart of the English countryside by the will of a tyrannical husband, with boredom and regret her only companions. For the first time, it occurred to her that after all she might have been lucky.

Slipping her arm affectionately through Fortunée's, she walked back with her to the hall, though not without one last affectionate look of farewell at the handsome portrait.

'Come,' she said gaily. 'Let's go and have a big, scalding hot cup of coffee. That's the only thing I really want at present. Close the doors carefully, my friend, won't you?'

The 'Greek Prince' grinned. 'Don't worry,' he said. 'It would be too bad if so much as a single draught escaped.'

In a cheerful mood, they left the house, re-entered the carriage and were driven back to Madame Hamelin's.

Charles Percier and Léonard Fontaine might have been called the heavenly twins of decoration under the Empire. For years, they had worked together in such close collaboration that beside them, Castor and Pollux, Orestes and Pylades might have seemed mortal enemies. They had met first in the studios of their common master, Peyre, but then, when Percier won the Grand Prix de Rome in 1785 and Fontaine the second Grand Prix in 1786, they came together again beneath the umbrella pines of the Villa Medici and had remained together ever since. Between them, they had undertaken to re-design Paris in the Napoleonic style, and there was nothing good of Percier's that did not show the hand of Fontaine and no proper Fontaine without a touch of Percier. And being the same age, within a year or two, one born in Paris the other at Pontois, they were generally regarded in everyday life as inseparable brethren.

It was this pair, so eminently representative of French art under the Empire who, late that afternoon, stepped through the doors of Fortunée's salon. That salon had never been so empty of company, but since this was Napoleon's wish, that amiable lady uttered no word of protest. Except for Gossec, not a soul had crossed her threshold all that day.

The two architects, after bowing politely to the ladies, gave Marianne to understand that they had paid a preliminary visit to the house in the rue de Lille earlier that afternoon.

'His Majesty the Emperor,' Charles Percier added, 'has intimated to us that the work should be so carried out that you, mademoiselle, may take possession of your house with the least possible delay. We have therefore no time to waste. To be sure, the house has suffered a good deal of damage.'

'But we feel,' Fontaine went on, 'that we shall very soon be able to remove all traces of the ravages worked by time and men.'

'We have therefore,' Percier took him up, 'taken the liberty of bringing along with us some designs we happened to have by us, simply one or two ideas sketched for our own pleasure, but which seem perfectly suited to this old house.'

Marianne's eyes, which throughout this well-orchestrated dialogue had been swivelling between the two men, from the short Percier to the tall Fontaine, came to rest at last on the roll of papers which the first named was already unrolling on a table. She caught a glimpse of Roman-style furnishing, Pompeian friezes, alabaster figures, gilded eagles, swans and victories.

'Gentlemen,' she said quietly, taking some pains to stress the slight foreign accent with which she spoke French so as to lend substance to her supposed Venetian origin, 'can you answer me one question?'

'What is that?'

'Are there in existence any plans indicating what the Hôtel d'Asselnat was like before the Revolution?'

The two architects looked at one another with barely concealed alarm. They had known they were to work for an Italian singer, as yet unknown, but destined for great fame, a singer who was quite certainly the Emperor's latest fancy. They were expecting a creature of whims and caprices who might not be easy to please and this start to the interview seemed to prove them right. Percier cleared his throat with a little cough.

'For the outside, no doubt we can find plans, but for the interior — but why should you wish to have these plans, mademoiselle?'

Marianne understood perfectly the meaning behind the question. Why should a daughter of Italy be interested in the original appearance of a house in France? She smiled encouragingly.

'Because I should like my house, as far as possible, restored to the state in which it was before the troubles. All this you have shown me is very fine, very attractive, but it is not what I desire. I want the house to be as it was and nothing more.'

Percier and Fontaine raised their arms to heaven in unison, as though performing a well-drilled ballet.

'In the style of Louis XIV or Louis XV? But, mademoiselle, permit me to remind you that is no longer the fashion,' Fontaine said reproachfully. 'No one has anything like that nowadays, it is quite outdated, not at all the thing. His Majesty the Emperor himself—'

'His Majesty will wish first and foremost for me to have what I want,' Marianne interrupted sweetly. 'I realize of course that it will not be possible to reconstruct the interior decorations exactly as they were, since we do not know what they were like. But I think it will do very well if you will carry out everything to suit the style of the house and, especially, the portrait which is in the salon.'

There was a silence so complete that Fortunée stirred in her chair.

'The portrait?' said Fontaine. 'Which portrait—'

'But, the portrait of—' Marianne stopped short. She had been

on the point of saying: 'The portrait of my father', but the
singer Maria Stella could have no connexion with the family of
d'Asselnat. She drew a deep breath and then continued hurriedly: 'A magnificent portrait of a man which I and my friends
saw this morning hanging over the fireplace in the salon. A man
dressed in the uniform of an officer of the old King's—'

'Mademoiselle,' the two architects answered in unison, 'I can
assure you that we saw no portrait—'

'But, I am not going out of my mind!' Marianne cried, losing
patience. She could not understand why these two men refused
to discuss the portrait. She turned in desperation to Madame
Hamelin.

'Oh really, my dear, you saw it too?—'

'Yes,' Fortunée said uneasily, 'I saw it. And do you really say,
gentlemen, that there was no portrait in the salon? I can see it
now: a very handsome man of noble bearing, wearing a
colonel's uniform.'

'We give you our word, madame,' Percier assured her, 'that
we saw no portrait. Had it been otherwise we should certainly
have mentioned it at once. A single portrait left in a devastated
house would have been remarkable enough!'

'And yet it was there,' Marianne persisted stubbornly.

'It was there, certainly.' Jolival's voice spoke from behind
her. 'But just as certainly, it is not there now.'

Arcadius had been missing all afternoon but now, as he
walked farther into the room, Percier and Fontaine, who had
been beginning to wonder if they had fallen among lunatics,
breathed again and turned gratefully to this unlooked-for res-
cuer. But Arcadius, as amiable and unconcerned as ever, was
kissing the fingers of the mistress of the house and Marianne.

'We can only imagine someone has taken it,' he remarked
lightly. 'Well, gentlemen, have you reached an agreement with
the – Signorina Maria Stella—'

'Er – that is – not yet. This business of the portrait—'

'Forget it,' Marianne said tersely. She had realized that Jolival did not wish to speak of it before strangers. Now, much as
she had liked these two in the beginning, she had only one

wish, to see the back of them and be left alone with her friends. With this view, she forced herself to smile and say lightly but firmly:

'Remember only one thing. That my desire to see the house look as it used to remains unaltered.'

'In the style of the last century?' Fontaine murmured with comical dismay. 'Are you quite determined on that?'

'Quite determined. I want nothing else. Do your best to make the Hôtel d'Asselnat look as it used to, gentlemen, and I shall be eternally grateful to you.'

There was nothing more to add. The two men withdrew, assuring her they would do their best. Barely had they gone downstairs before Marianne fell on Arcadius.

'My father's portrait, what do you know about it?'

'That it is no longer where we saw it, my poor child. I went back to the rue de Lille without saying anything to you, after the architects had gone in fact, I watched them leave. I wanted to go over the house from top to bottom because there were a number of things which struck me as odd, those well-oiled locks among other things. It was then I noticed that the portrait had disappeared.'

'But, then what can have happened to it? This is ridiculous! It's unbelievable!'

Marianne was bitterly disappointed. It seemed to her that now she had really lost the father she had never known and had discovered that morning with such joy. This sudden disappearance was very cruel.

'I should not have left it. I was so incredibly lucky to find it, I should have taken it with me, at once. But how could I have guessed that someone would come and move it. For that must be what happened, surely? It has been stolen!'

She was walking up and down the room unhappily as she spoke, wringing her hands together. Arcadius, though outwardly calm, never took his eyes off her.

'Stolen? Perhaps—'

'What do you mean, perhaps?'

'Don't be cross. I am merely thinking that whoever put it in the salon has simply taken it away again. You see, instead of trying to find out who took the portrait, I think we should do better to try and find out who put it there in the midst of all that wreckage. Because it is my belief that when we know that, we shall also know who has the portrait now.'

Marianne said nothing. What Jolival said was true. Instead of grieving, she began to think. She remembered the brightness of the canvas and the frame, how meticulously clean they were in contrast to the squalor around them. There was some mystery there.

'Would you like me to inform the Minister of Police?' Fortunée suggested. 'He will make inquiries, discreet ones if you like, but I'll be prepared to swear that he will find your portrait before very long.'

'No – thank you, I would rather not.'

What, above all, she would rather not see was the astute Fouché dabbling in something which concerned her so closely. She felt that by putting Fouché's men with their dirty fingers on the trail of her father's disappearing image, she would be in some way soiling the beauty of that image which she had so briefly recovered.

'No—' she said again, 'truly I would rather not.' She added: 'I prefer to try and find out myself.'

In that moment her mind was made up.

'Jolival, my dear,' she said calmly, 'tonight, we will go back to the rue de Lille, as unobtrusively as possible.'

'Go back to the rue de Lille tonight,' Fortunée protested. 'You cannot mean it? What for?'

'It would seem that there is a ghost in the old house. Don't ghosts prefer the night time?'

'You think someone comes there?'

'Or hides there.'

An idea was growing in her mind as she spoke. Or rather, a memory which was becoming clearer with every moment. Of a few remarks she had heard as a child. More than once, Aunt Ellis had told her of her adventures as a tiny baby, how the Abbé de Chazay had found her, left all alone in the house after her parents had been taken away. At that time, the Abbé himself had been living in the rue de Lille, in one of those secret hiding places which had been constructed in a great many aristocratic houses in town and country to hide refractory priests. 'That must be it!' she said, finishing her thoughts aloud, 'someone must be hiding in the house.'

'It is impossible,' Jolival answered. 'I have been everywhere, I tell you, from top to bottom.'

But he listened very attentively when she told him the story of the Abbé de Chazay. Unfortunately, she did not know where this hiding place lay. It might be in the cellars, the attic or behind the panelling in one of the rooms. The Abbé himself, whether intentionally or from sheer absentmindedness, had never told her precisely.

'In that case, we may search for a very long time. Some of these hiding places were completely impossible to discover, except by a stroke of luck. We shall have to sound out the walls and ceilings.'

'At all events, no one could live long in one of those hiding places without outside help,' Marianne said. 'They would need food and fresh air and all the other necessities of life.'

Fortunée, who was lying on a blue watered-silk chaise longue, sighed and stretched, then began rearranging the folds of her red cashmere gown, yawning widely as she did so.

'You don't think perhaps you two are romancing a little?' she said. 'I think the house has been empty for so long that some poor homeless wretch took to living in it, and our going in like that, followed by the architects, must have disturbed him, that is all that happened.'

'And the portrait?' Marianne said seriously.

'He must have found it in the house, perhaps in the attics or hidden away in some odd corner, which would explain why it escaped when everything else was wrecked. Because it was the only pretty thing left, he used it to adorn his desert and when we invaded his domain today he simply went away and took with him what he had come to regard as his own property. I sincerely believe, Marianne, that if you want to get your picture back, the only sensible thing to do is to tell Fouché. It can't be easy to wander about Paris with a canvas that size under one's arm. Would you like me to send for him? We are reasonably good friends.'

It began to look as though the charming Fortunée had good friends everywhere, but once again, Marianne refused. Against all the evidence, some instinct was telling her that there was some other explanation, and that the eminently simple and rational theory put forward by her friend was not the right one. She had been conscious of a presence in the house, which she had at first put down to the magnetic power of the portrait, but now she realized that there was something else. She recalled the footfalls they had heard upstairs. Arcadius had decided it must have been a rat, but was it? She could not help thinking that there was some mystery about her ancestral home and she meant to get to the bottom of it, but she would do so alone. Or at least, with only Arcadius to help her. She turned to him now.

'I meant what I said. Will you come with me tonight and see what is going on in my house?'

'Why ask?' Jolival shrugged. 'For one thing, not for anything in the world could I allow you to go alone into that morgue, but for another – I must admit that this peculiar business intrigues me too. We'll leave here at ten o'clock, if that suits you.'

Fortunée sighed. 'And much good may it do you! My dear child, you do seem to be inordinately fond of adventures. For myself, I shall stay quietly at home, with your permission. Firstly because I have not the slightest desire to go and freeze to death in an empty house, and secondly because someone must be here to warn the Emperor in case you are running into another of those traps you seem to have a knack of finding. And I dread to think what he will do to me if anything should happen to you!' she finished with comical alarm.

The remainder of the evening passed supping and in making ready for the intended expedition. For a moment, it did occur to Marianne to think of the mysterious danger against which Jason Beaufort had warned her but she rejected the idea at once. Why should she expect any danger? Surely no one could have foreseen that Napoleon would give her back the house which had been her parents'? No, the Hôtel d'Asselnat could be in no way connected with the American's fears.

But Marianne was not fated to go adventuring with Arcadius that night. The clock had just struck a quarter to ten and she had already risen from her chair to go and put on some more suitable clothes for what lay ahead, when Fortunée's black servant Jonas appeared to announce with his invariable solemnity that 'Monsigneur le Duc de Frioul' requested admittance. Absorbed in their own conversation, neither Marianne, nor Fortunée, nor Arcadius had heard the carriage arrive. They gazed at one another blankly but Fortunée recovered herself at once.

'Show him in,' she said to Jonas. 'The dear Duke must be bringing word from the Tuileries.'

The Grand Marshal of the Palace was doing better than that. Hardly had he entered the room and kissed Fortunée's hand before he said gaily to Marianne:

'I come in search of you, mademoiselle. The Emperor is asking for you.'

'Truly? Oh, I am coming, I am coming at once—'

She was so happy to be going to him that evening when she had been given no reason to hope for it, that for a second she forgot the business of the missing picture. In her haste to go to Napoleon, she hurried away to put on a pretty dress of green velvet braided with silver with a deeply scooped-out neckline and short sleeves trimmed with a froth of lace, snatched up a pair of long white gloves and flung on a great cloak of the same velvet, cut like a flowing domino with a hood trimmed with grey fox. She loved these things and blew a kiss with her fingertips at the radiantly joyful reflection in her mirror before running down to the salon where Duroc was calmly drinking coffee with Fortunée and Arcadius. He was talking at the same time and, as he was talking about the Emperor, Marianne paused in the doorway to listen to the end of what he was saying.

'—and when he had seen the finished column in the place Vendôme, the Emperor went on to inspect the Ourcq Canal. He is never still for a moment!'

'Was he pleased?' Madame Hamelin asked.

'With these works, yes, but the war in Spain remains his greatest anxiety. Things are going badly there. The men are sick, the Emperor's brother, King Joseph, lacks imagination, the marshals are weary and jealous of one another, while the *guerrilleros* harry the Army and are helped by the local population, who are both hostile and cruel. And then Wellington's English are firmly established in the country.'

'How many men have we there?' Arcadius asked in a grave voice.

'Nearly eighty thousand. Soult has replaced Jourdan as Major-General. King Joseph has Sébastiani, Victor and Mortier under him, while Suchet and Augerau are occupying Aragon and Catalonia. At this moment, Massena and Junot are joining forces with Ney and Montbrun ready to march into Portugal—'

Marianne's entry cut short Duroc's military disquisition. He looked up, smiled and set down his empty cup.

'Let us go, then, if you are ready. If I let myself be drawn into Army talk we shall be here all night.'

'All the same, I wish you could go on! It was very interesting.'

'Not for two pretty women. Besides, the Emperor does not like to be kept waiting.'

Marianne felt a brief stab of remorse when she met Jolival's eye and remembered their planned expedition. But after all, there was no danger in the house.

'Another time,' she told him with a smile. 'I am ready, my lord Duke.'

Jolival gave her a sidelong smile while continuing to stir the spoon gravely in his blue Sèvres cup.

'But of course,' he said. 'There is no hurry.'

When the impassive Rustan opened the door of the Emperor's office for Marianne, Napoleon was sitting working at his big desk and did not look up, even when the door was shut. Marianne looked at him in astonishment, uncertain how she should react. The wind was completely taken out of her sails. She had come to him in happy haste, borne up on the wave of joy which the mere thought of her lover awoke in her. She had thought to find him in his own room, or at least waiting for her impatiently. She came, expecting to throw herself into arms wide open to receive her. She had come, in short, hurrying to meet the man she loved — and found the Emperor.

Hiding her disappointment as best she could, she let her knees give and, sinking into a deep curtsy, waited with bent head.

'Get up and sit down, mademoiselle. I will be with you in a moment.'

Oh, that terse, cold, impersonal voice. Marianne's heart contracted as she moved to sit down on the little yellow sofa placed in front of the desk at right angles to the fire where she had seen Fortunée for the first time. There, she sat quite still, not daring to move, practically holding her breath. The silence was so complete that the swift scratching of the imperial pen across the paper seemed to her to make a shattering noise. Napoleon went on writing, eyes down, amid an improbable pile of red folders, open and closed. The room was strewn with papers. A sheaf of rolled-up maps stood in a corner. For the first time, Marianne saw him in uniform. For the first time, the thought came to her of the vast armies he commanded.

He was wearing his favourite olive-green uniform of a colonel of the chasseur of the Guard but instead of the high uniform boots he wore white silk stockings and silver-buckled shoes. As usual, his white kerseymere breeches were ink-stained and showed the marks of his pen. Across his white waistcoat lay the purple ribbon of the Légion d'Honneur, but what struck Marianne most of all were the locks of short brown hair plastered to his forehead by beads of sweat from the heat with which he worked. In spite of her disappointment, in spite of her vague feeling of anxiety, she was suddenly overwhelmed by a warm rush of tenderness. She was suddenly so sharply conscious of her love that she had to make an effort not to throw her arms about his neck. But certainly an emperor was not a man like any other. The impulses which would have been so sweet and natural with an ordinary mortal, must be mastered until it suited his pleasure. No, Marianne thought with childish regret, truly it was not easy to love one of the giants of history.

Suddenly, the 'giant' threw down his pen and looked up. The eyes that met hers were as cold as steel.

'So, mademoiselle,' he said abruptly, 'it seems you dislike the style of my times? From what I hear, you wish to revert to the splendours of the past century?'

For a moment, surprise left her speechless. This was the last thing she had been expecting. But anger soon restored her voice. Did Napoleon, by any chance, mean to dictate every single act of her life, even her likes and dislikes? All the same, well knowing it was dangerous to cross swords with him, she forced herself to be calm and even managed to smile. After all, it was rather funny. Here she came running to him, all throbbing with love, and he was talking about decoration. The thing that seemed to vex him most was her apparent lack of enthusiasm for the style he had adopted as his own.

'I have never said I did not like your style, Sire,' she said sweetly. 'I merely expressed a wish that the Hôtel d'Asselnat should look once more as it used to do—'

'What makes you think that when I gave it to you I desired such a resurrection? The house I gave you must be that of a famous Italian singer, belonging wholly to the present régime. There can be no question of turning it into a temple for your ancestors. Do you forget that you are no longer Marianne d'Asselnat?'

Oh, the tone was merciless and cutting! Why did there have to be two such contradictory natures to this man? Why, oh why did Marianne have to love him so desperately? She rose, white to the lips and shaking with distress.

'Whatever name it may please your Majesty to call me by, it cannot make me other than I am. I have killed a man for the honour of my name, Sire, and you will not prevent my feeling for my parents the love and respect which is their due. For myself, if I belong to you body and soul, which you cannot for an instant doubt, I alone belong to you. My family is my own.'

'And mine too, remember! All Frenchmen, past, present and to come, belong to me, by which I mean they are my subjects.

You are somewhat too apt to forget that I am the Emperor!'

'How could I forget it?' Marianne said bitterly. 'Your Majesty gives me little chance! As for my parents—'

'I have no wish to prevent you mourning them, discreetly, but you must understand that I have little love for the fanatics of the old régime. I have a good mind to take that house back and give you another.'

'I want no other, Sire. Your Majesty may withdraw your architects if it offends them to work in an outmoded style, only leave me the house. I prefer the Hôtel d'Asselnat as it is, ruined, mutilated and pitiful, to the most sumptuous house in Paris! As for the noble subjects of the King — I thought your Majesty had been one of them!'

'Do not be insolent. It will do you no good with me. The reverse, in fact. It seems to me, that you have too much pride of caste to be a loyal subject. I hoped to find more submission and obedience in you. Know that what I value most in a woman is gentleness, a quality in which you seem to be singularly lacking!'

'The life I have led hitherto has scarcely taught me gentleness! I am deeply sorry I must offend your Majesty, but I am as I am. I cannot change my nature!'

'Not even to please me?'

The tension was increasing. What game was Napoleon playing? Why this sarcasm, this attitude almost of hostility? Was he truly such a despot as to demand from her a submission that would make her blind, deaf and dumb? Was it the servile obedience of a slave in a harem that he wanted? If so, it was too bad. Marianne had fought too hard simply to preserve her dignity as a woman to bend now. Even if it meant tearing the heart out of her breast, she would not yield. Her eyes did not fall before that terrible blue gaze as, with infinite gentleness, she said:

'Not even to please you, Sire! And yet, as God is my witness, I have no more earnest desire than to please your Majesty.'

'You are going the wrong way about it,' he said with a sneer.

'But not at the price of my self-respect! If you had deigned, Sire, to tell me that all you looked for in me was a servile creature, a mere consenting slave, going in perpetual terror of your Majesty, then I should have begged you to let me leave France as I had meant to do. Because, for me, to love so is not to love at all.'

He took two steps towards her and with a quick movement untied the velvet ribbons holding her cloak. The heavy folds slid to the ground. He gazed at her for an instant, standing very straight before him. The candlelight fell softly on her beautiful shoulders and on the swell of her bare breasts, gilding them like summer fruits in their basket of white lace. Her face was very pale under the heavy helmet of midnight-coloured hair but her long green eyes were bright with bravely unshed tears. She looked, in that moment, breathtakingly lovely. He had only to make a single movement, to take her in his arms and wipe away the pain from her face. But he was in one of those tyrannical moods when no human power could have made him yield to that desire. She dared to stand up to him and that was enough to rouse in him a cruel determination to break her.

'And what if that is how I wish to be loved?' he said slowly without taking his merciless eyes off her.

'Then I do not believe you! You cannot wish for love that is crawling, terrified, debased – not you!'

He ignored the cry of protest, in spite of all the love it held. His hand was on her breast, hot, ungentle fingers working upwards to the slender column of her neck.

'What I love in you,' he said with brutal sarcasm, 'is your matchless voice and your beauty. You are a wonderful singing bird with the body of a goddess. It is my intention to enjoy both to the full. I am not concerned with feelings. Go and wait for me in my room. Take your clothes off and get into bed. I will come to you in a moment.'

Marianne's cheeks flamed suddenly as though he had hit her. She recoiled instantly, and her two hands flew to her uncovered breasts. Her throat dried suddenly and her eyes burned with shame. All at once, she remembered the gossip overheard in the rue de Varennes. The story of Mademoiselle Dudresnoy whom he had dismissed without so much as a word of explanation after getting her into his bed. The episode of the little girl he was betrothed to in Marseilles, got rid of by a curt letter on the patently false excuse that she had not asked her parents for her own hand. And, finally, the well-known story of the Polish Countess whom he had so maltreated that she became unconscious, of which he then took advantage to rape her, and afterwards sent her back to her native Poland to bear his child. Was it possible that all this could be true? Marianne was beginning to think so. At all events, not at any price, even that of her love, would she consent to be treated so. Love did not give him the right to everything.

'Don't be too sure,' she murmured, clenching her teeth to force back her anger. 'I gave myself to you before I knew you, because, like a fool, I fell in love with you. Oh, how I loved you! I was so happy to belong to you! You could have asked anything of me because I thought you loved me a little! But I am not an Eastern concubine to be caressed when the fancy takes you and then kicked out when your desire is slaked.'

Napoleon drew himself up to his full height, hands clasped behind his back. His jaw was set, his nostrils white with anger.

'You refuse to belong to me? Think carefully! That is a grave insult!'

'And yet — I do refuse,' Marianne said sadly. She felt suddenly very tired. Now there was only one thing she wanted, to escape as soon as possible from this close, quiet room into which she had come so happily a few minutes before and where, since then, she had suffered so much. She knew very well that she had just placed her whole life in jeopardy once again, that his power over her was limitless but not for anything in the world would she have accepted the degrading part that he was trying to force on her. She still loved him too much for that. In a low voice, she said: 'I refuse — more for your sake even than my own — because I want to be able to go on loving you. Besides — what pleasure would it give you to possess a senseless body, made insensible by grief.'

'Don't look for excuses. I had believed myself to possess a greater power over your senses than you grant me.'

'Because there was a love between us then, which you are killing now!'

She almost screamed the words, goaded by the grief that nearly stopped her heart. Now she was trying to find the chink in his armour. He could not be this monster of ruthless pride, this utterly insensitive despot! She could still hear his words of love ringing in her ears.

Abruptly, he turned his back on her, walked over to a bookcase and stood before it, hands clasped behind his back.

'Very well,' he said curtly. 'You may withdraw.'

For a moment she hesitated. They could not part like this, quarrelling over a trifle. It was too hard! Suddenly, she wanted to run to him, tell him that she renounced everything he had given her, that he could take back the Hôtel d'Asselnat and do what he liked with it, only so long as he would keep her with him! Anything, only not to lose him, not to be cut off from the sight and sound of him – she stepped forward.

'Sire—' she began brokenly.

But then, as though the plain front of the bookcase had opened suddenly, she seemed to see before her, with terrifying clarity, the great portrait hanging on the crumbling walls. She saw the proud eyes, the arrogant smile. The daughter of such a man could not demean herself to beg for a love that was denied her. And just then she heard:

'Have you not gone?'

His back was still stubbornly towards her. Slowly, she went and picked up her green cloak and laid it over her arm, then sank into a curtsy so deep that she was almost on her knees.

'Farewell – Sire,' she whispered.

Once out of the room, she walked straight ahead, like a sleep-walker, not even seeing Rustan who looked at her with big, horrified eyes, not even thinking to throw her cloak over her bare shoulders. She was dazed with grief, too numb to feel the full pain. Shock had formed a merciful cushion around her which, as it melted away, would give place to the real suffering, in all its sharpness and cruelty. She did not even think what she was going to do, what would happen now. No. Nothing mattered to her at all, nothing except this dull burning pain within her.

She went down the stairs without so much as seeing them and did not turn, even when a breathless voice called after her. Not until Duroc took the cloak from her to place it round her shoulders was she aware of his presence.

'Where are you off to so fast, mademoiselle? I hope you did not mean to go out by yourself at this hour of night?'

'I? Oh, I do not know. It doesn't matter—'

'How's that? Doesn't matter?'

'I mean — I can easily walk. Don't trouble yourself.'

'Don't talk foolishness! You do not even know the way. You'd get lost — and, here, take this.'

He thrust a handkerchief into her hands but she did not use it. It wasn't until the Grand Marshal of the Palace gently wiped her cheeks that she realized that she was crying. He handed her carefully into the carriage and wrapped a fur rug round her knees, then went to give some orders to the coachman before climbing in beside her.

The coach was on its way before Marianne moved a muscle. She seemed like one thunderstruck. She huddled into the cushions like a hurt animal, seeking only silence and darkness. Her eyes looked out unseeingly at the passing spectacle of Paris by night. For a time, Duroc watched his young companion in silence but then, as the tears began again, running slowly down her cheeks while she made no move to stop them, he began trying clumsily to comfort her.

'You must not upset yourself so,' he murmured gently. 'The Emperor is often harsh, but he is not unkind. You have to understand what it means to have an Empire stretching from Ushant to the Niemen and from Denmark to Gibraltar resting on the shoulders of a single man—'

The words came to Marianne as through a fog. For her, that gigantic Empire had only one meaning. It had made its master into a monster of pride and a ruthless autocrat. However, encouraged perhaps by hearing her sigh, Duroc went on:

'You see, the fifth anniversary of the coronation was celebrated two months ago and a fortnight later, the Emperor
divorced his wife for the sake of assuring the crown, which still
seems to him so precarious. He lives in a state of constant
uneasiness because only the power of his will and his genius
keeps this unlikely mosaic of peoples together. His brothers
and sisters, though he has made them sovereigns, are incompetents, thinking only of their own interests and ignoring those
of the Empire. Think how many victories it has taken to weld
all this together since the Italian campaigns first made him
Emperor of the French! Six great battles since the sun of Austerlitz, and that scarcely four years old, to say nothing of the
endless fighting in Spain . . . Jena, Auerstadt, Eylau, Friedland,
Essling, where he lost his best friend, Marshal Lannes, and then
Wagram where he defeated the man whose daughter he is now
about to marry. If the Empire is to continue, there must be an
heir – even if he has to sacrifice a little of his heart to achieve
it, for he loved his wife. The Emperor is alone against them all,
between the changeable moods of an unstable Tsar and the
hatred of England, hanging like a bulldog to his coat tails. And
so – when there are times when you think you could hate him,
when he rouses feelings of anger and revolt in you, you must
think of all that. He needs to be understood – and it is not
easy.'

He fell silent, exhausted perhaps, with the effort of saying so
much. But his plea, even if it found a way to Marianne's heart,
only added to her grief. Understand Napoleon? She asked
nothing better! But would he let her? He had driven her away,
flung her back into the shadows, into the anonymous and face-
less crowd of his subjects from which, for an instant, he had
plucked her.

She looked at the Grand Marshal who, still bent towards
her, seemed to expect a reply, and nodded sadly, murmuring
the thought that was in her mind.

'I wish I had the right to understand him – but he will not let
me.'

Then she huddled back again in her corner and resumed her
melancholy thoughts. Seeing she was not going to speak again,

Duroc sighed and settling himself as comfortably as possible in his own corner, closed his eyes.

Time must have stood still. Numbed and incapable of thought, Marianne had paid no attention to the route, which was in any case one she did not know. Even so, after the passing of a period of time whose length she had no means of estimating, she did begin to feel that the journey was unusually long. She looked out of the window and saw that the carriage was now travelling through open country. The night was bright enough for her to be in no doubt on this score. She turned to her companion and spoke abruptly.

'If you please? Where are we going?'

Startled awake, the Emperor's confidant sat up with a jerk and glanced wildly at Marianne.

'I – you were saying?'

'I was asking where we were going?'

'Er – well, that is – where I was told to take you.'

This as good as told her that she would get no answer to her question. Perhaps he was cross with her for refusing to talk to him? But, in her heart of hearts, she did not greatly care. Napoleon must have decided to send her away from Paris in order to be thoroughly rid of her. They were probably taking her to some château a long way away, a prison where it would be easier to forget than in Paris. And the Emperor would no doubt feel that a woman who had once received his favours could not be shut up in any common prison. But she had no illusions as to her fate, and not much interest either. Later, when she was not so tired – then she would try and see if she still had any will to fight.

The carriage passed through tall gates and entered what seemed to be a park. They drove along a paved avenue and drew up at last before a lighted entrance. Still half dazed, Marianne caught a glimpse of the pink marble columns of a vast peristyle which had been enclosed with glass windows,[1] the magnificent extent of a large, low palace surmounted by a

[1] The columns of the Grand Trianon were glazed in at this period by the Emperor's order.

marble balustrade, a few splendid rooms, in the best Empire
style, through which she was led by a servant in a powdered
wig, carrying a heavy branched candlestick. Duroc had vanished as soon as they were inside, without her even noticing. A
door opened, revealing a room decorated in beige satin and
deep mauve velvet. And Marianne found herself suddenly face
to face with Napoleon.

He was sitting in a claw-footed armchair by the fire, watching her with a teasing smile, evidently enjoying her bewilderment as she struggled vainly to get her thoughts into
some kind of order. She had a gloomy feeling that she must be
going mad. She felt deathly tired, her body ached and her legs
felt like jelly. It did not occur to her to curtsy, or make the least
polite acknowledgement of his presence. She simply leaned
back against the door post.

'I wish I understood—' she murmured.

'What? How I could be here before you? It's quite simple.
Duroc had orders to take you a long way round before reaching
the Trianon.'

'No – it's you I wish I understood. What, exactly, do you
want of me?'

He stood up at last and came towards her and tried to take
her in his arms but she resisted. Far from being angry now, he
merely smiled briefly.

'A test, Marianne, a simple test. I wanted to know just what
kind of woman you were. Remember, I hardly know you. You
fell from the skies one night like a beautiful meteor, but you
could have been any number of things: a clever adventuress, a
courtesan, an agent of the Princes, an unusually devoted friend
of our dear Talleyrand – and you must admit the last was the
most likely. Hence this test – I had to know just what you
were.'

'A test that could have been the death of me—' Marianne
murmured, still too shaken to feel in the least comforted.

Even so, Duroc's words were gradually coming back to her.
She realized that they had made their way into her mind and
that now she saw this extraordinary man with new eyes and,
more important, according to his true dimensions.

'You are angry with me, aren't you? But that will pass. You must understand that I have the right to know who it is I love.'

'Because — you love me?'

'You don't doubt it for a moment,' he said softly. 'As for me, you can't imagine how many women they try to get into my bed, for their own reasons. Everyone around me is trying to provide me with a mistress so as to have some kind of influence over me. Even my family! Especially my family and especially since I have been obliged to part from the Empress. Only a few weeks ago, my sister Pauline presented me with one of her ladies-in-waiting, a certain Madame de Mathis, a charming girl—'

'And — without success?'

He could not help laughing at that and the odd thing was that it was his laughter, so young and gay, that melted Marianne's resentment more surely than any amount of explanation.

'Oh,' he admitted, 'to be sure, to begin with. But I did not know you then. Now everything is different.'

Very gently, he laid his hands on Marianne's shoulders and drew her to him. This time, she let him do it, though with still a faint trace of rigidity. She was trying, with all her strength, to understand, to catch hold of this quick incisive mind which she admired, even while it frightened her. She knew well enough now that she had not only not stopped loving him but that, on the contrary, her love had emerged from this nightmare stronger than ever. But he had hurt her so! She felt as though she were slowly coming to life again after a long illness. She tried to smile.

'And so,' she murmured, 'Have I passed my examination?'

He tightened his arms around her till they hurt.

'Admirably. You would make a worthy Corsican! Oh no, you have not the soul of a slave, you proud little aristocrat! You are not servile or self-seeking, but clean, open and upright. If you had been what at one moment I feared, you would have given in on all points, but you did not give an inch. And yet — you could not have guessed how I should react. You do not know me either. But I love you, Marianne, you can be sure of that, for all these and many other reasons.'

'Not just my voice and my person?'

'Idiot!'

Then, at last, she gave in. Suddenly, her nerve broke. Shuddering, she pressed herself against him and with her head on his shoulder she began to cry in great tearing sobs, like a little girl who has been punished and forgiven. The tears eased her and tenderly, with patience, Napoleon waited until she should be calm again, holding her with almost brotherly gentleness. Still cradling her close, he led her over to a small sofa and sat her down. When her tears had died away a little, he began murmuring in Italian, the fond words she had loved so much that first time. Little by little, his kisses and caresses calmed her. After a while, she freed herself from the arms that held her and sat up, wiping her eyes with Duroc's hankerchief which he had put into her hand earlier.

'Forgive me,' she said unsteadily. 'I am very stupid—'

'Perhaps, if you really think so – but you are so lovely not even tears can make you ugly.'

He went over to a large silver-gilt wine cooler standing on a small table with some clear glasses and a small cold supper, took out a bottle of champagne and filled two glasses. Then he brought one to Marianne.

'Now, we must set the seal of our reconciliation. We will begin again from the beginning. Only this time, we know who we are and why we love one another. Drink, *mio dolce amore*, to our happiness.'

They drank, gazing into one another's eyes, and then Marianne let her head fall on to the back of the sofa with a little sigh. For the first time, she looked around her at the exquisite fabrics, the gilt bronze and satinwood furnishings, all these strange and magnificent surroundings. What had he told her a moment ago? That this was the Trianon?

'Why here?' she asked. 'Why this journey, all this comedy?'

'There too I have an excellent reason. I am going to give myself a little holiday – comparatively speaking. I remain here a week – and I am keeping you with me.'

'A week?'

'Yes. Do you think it's too long? Don't worry, you will have plenty of time afterwards for your audition with the Director of the Opéra. You are engaged in advance. Rehearsals begin on your return. As for your house—'

He paused and Marianne held her breath, not daring to interrupt. What was he going to say? Surely their stupid argument was not going to begin all over again after all? He looked at her, smiling, and then, dropping a light kiss on the fingertips he had taken in his own, he finished calmly:

'As for your house, Percier and Fontaine do not need you to carry out their work. Don't worry, they have orders to act strictly in accordance with your wishes. Does that make you happy?'

For answer, she offered her lips and dared for the first time to say the words.

'I love you.'

'You've taken your time about saying it—' he observed between kisses.

Much later in the night, a log falling in the fire woke Marianne from a light doze. Lifting herself up on the pillows, she flung back the heavy mass of hair out of her eyes and leaned on her elbow to look at her lover as he slept. He had gone into sleep in an instant after their love-making, and now he lay across the bed as naked as a Greek warrior on the field of battle . . . For the first time, Marianne was struck by the perfection of his body.

Stretched out like that, he looked taller than he really was.[1] The firm muscles showed through the smooth, ivory-coloured skin in the manner of some ancient marble. Napoleon's chest and shoulders were broad, almost hairless, and his arms and legs modelled on the strictest canons. He had excellent hands and took the greatest care of them, as of all his person. Marianne laid her face softly against his shoulder, stroking it with her cheek and breathing in the faint smell of

[1] His actual height was about five feet six inches.

eau-de-Cologne and Spanish jasmine, softly taking care not to wake him.

A great Venetian mirror over the fireplace gave her back their two reflections. She saw herself, pink in the soft candle-light, half shrouded in the gleaming wave of her hair and was pleased with what she saw. It made her glad and triumphant because if she was beautiful tonight it was for him, and because of him. Happiness had given her a glow which she had never had before, and which filled her at the same time with joy and humbleness. There, in that quiet room that still throbbed to their caresses, Marianne offered to the man she loved a more total and absolute submission than any he had asked of her earlier, a submission which she herself perhaps would deny him when daylight came again.

'I'll give you all the love you want,' she whispered softly, 'I'll love you with all my heart, and all my strength – but I will always speak the truth to you. You can ask anything of me, my love, any suffering and sacrifice, anything except lies and ser-vility—'

The fire in the hearth was almost dead. The room which had been warm a moment before was growing chilly. Marianne got up quickly, and opening the white and gold rail that enclosed the bed, ran on bare feet to the hearth and stirred up the glowing embers. Then, piling on a few more logs, she waited for them to catch and burn up again.

She glanced at her naked image in the mirror and smiled to think of the picture she would present should any of the four men who, according to etiquette, slept in the antechamber dare to open the door.[1]

Faithful Constant also slept in a little room close by, ever ready to answer a ring at the bell, and then there was the impressive Rustan, barring the door with his great, sleepy body.

Marianne stood on tiptoe and leaned forward to examine the new woman she had become. It was something to be the mistress of an Emperor! No doubt, the servants and officials,

[1] A page, an aide-de-camp, a sergeant, and a corporal of the Imperial Mews.

like the Grand Marshal of the Palace, would treat her with the greatest respect during her brief stay here, a stay which might well be unique because the new Empress—

She thrust back the unpleasant thought as hard as she could. She had suffered enough for one night. And now, she was going to have him all to herself for a whole week. In a way, she would be Empress herself and she meant to extract every last ounce of happiness from those few days. She did not mean to waste a single second.

She walked with her light step back to the bed and pulled up the covers over the sleeping man. Then with infinite caution, she slipped in beside him, and cuddled up close to him, drawing his warmth into her own shivering body. He turned in sleep and put his arm around her, murmuring something indistinct. With a happy sigh she pressed close against his chest and fell asleep, satisfied with the pact she had concluded with herself and with the sleeping master of Europe.

CHAPTER SEVEN

So Brief a Happiness

The Grand Trianon, a huge, shimmering, translucent soap bubble of crystal and rose-coloured marble set amongst immemorial trees, unreal and splendid as a dream ship anchored to the shores of heaven, was covered in the early hours of the morning by a soft silent mantle of snow. Far more than the remote splendours of the Tuileries or the rather sophisticated charm of le Butard, it came to stand in Marianne's mind first as an ideal and then, afterwards, as the symbol of paradise lost.

She very soon discovered, however, that Napoleon had his own peculiar ideas of what he called a holiday. When the first ray of cold, wintry sunshine struck through the windows of the imperial bedchamber, which faced east, like all the private rooms the Emperor had set aside for his own use in the palace, she found that she was alone in the big bed and that Napoleon was nowhere to be seen. The fire was blazing cheerfully in the hearth, and a frothy lace wrapper lay over the back of a chair but there was no one else in the room.

Alarmed in case Constant or some other servant should come in, Marianne hastily slipped on the nightgown she had left unused the night before. It was the property of the Emperor's sister, Pauline Borghese, who frequently resided at the nearby Petit Trianon. Next, she put on the wrapper, thrust her feet into a pair of pink velvet slippers and throwing back the heavy black masses of her hair, ran to the window like a happy child. As if in her honour, the park was dressed in an immaculate white splendour, enfolding the palace within a casket of silence. It was as if heaven had decided to cut off the Trianon from the rest of the world and halt the vast machine of Empire at the gilded gates of the park.

'All mine!' she thought joyfully. 'I am going to have him all to myself for a week.'

Thinking that he might be at his toilet, she turned and made quickly for the adjoining dressing-room. Just then Constant came out, calm and smiling as ever, and bowed respectfully.

'May I assist mademoiselle?'

'Where is the Emperor? Is he already dressing?'

Constant smiled and, taking a large enamelled watch from his waistcoat pocket, studied it gravely.

'It is nearly nine o'clock mademoiselle. The Emperor has been at work for more than an hour.'

'At work? But I thought—'

'That he was here for a rest? That is so indeed, but mademoiselle is not yet familiar with the Emperor's idea of a rest. It means simply that he will work a little less. Has mademoiselle never heard his favourite description of himself: "I was born and made for work—"?'

'No,' Marianne said, feeling somewhat disconcerted. 'But then, what shall I do meanwhile?'

'Breakfast is served at ten o'clock. Mademoiselle will have ample time to dress. Afterwards, the Emperor is accustomed to set aside some time for what he calls "recreation". Here he very often takes a walk. After that, he returns to his desk again until six o'clock, when he will dine and then spend the evening in a variety of ways.'

'Good God!' Marianne said weakly. 'How dreadful!'

'It is, indeed, rather taxing. But the Emperor may relax his rule somewhat in honour of mademoiselle. I should add that on Tuesdays and Fridays, his Majesty generally presides over his Council of State – but this is Wednesday and, by God's grace, the Trianon!'

'And it has been snowing and Paris is a long way away!' Marianne cried so impetuously that the faithful valet's eyes twinkled. 'I hope the Council of State will stay where it is until next Friday.'

'We may always hope. But at all events, mademoiselle need

have no anxiety. The Emperor will not allow her to be bored or disappointed with her stay.'

In fact, for a creature like Marianne, bubbling over with youth and vitality, it was wonderful, tyrannous, absurd, agonizing and incredibly exciting all at once. She was discovering Napoleon as he really was and also that daily life with him, even when hemmed in by protocol and etiquette, was a continual adventure. The very first meal she had alone with him was a startling revelation.

She had been slightly puzzled when, as he opened the door for her, Constant had murmured in her ear:

'Mademoiselle would be advised to waste no time at the table in contemplating his Majesty, especially if mademoiselle should be at all hungry, or she may be in some danger of rising from the table without having swallowed a morsel.'

But, once seated facing the Emperor across the large mahogany table, she forgot the warning. The table was laid with an exquisite blue Sèvres breakfast service and a great deal of cut glass, which went very well with the cutlery and the silver-gilt epergne. Napoleon attacked his food as though it were an English redoubt, but his eating habits were so eccentric that Marianne gazed at him in astonishment. He began with the cheese, swallowing a large slice of Brie, then, after selecting and disposing of a *tiubele milanaise*, proceeded rapidly to an almond cream before finishing up by gnawing at a wing of chicken Marengo. All this in the space of ten minutes, to the accompaniment of two glasses of Chambertin, and a shower of splashes and stains inseparable from such speed. Marianne, having practically fainted with horror at seeing him attack his chicken, had just decided that meals at the French court must be taken backwards, as in China, and was beginning at random on the almond cream, when Napoleon wiped his lips, threw his napkin down on the table, and exclaimed:

'What, not finished yet? You are a slow coach. Come along, hurry up, coffee will be here in a moment.'

Marianne was obliged to follow him with a sinking heart while Dumas, the butler, long accustomed to the vagaries of the imperial digestion, did his best to hide a smile. The coffee, boiling hot and strong, went down Marianne's throat like a ball of fire, but her heroism earned her a beaming smile from Napoleon.

'Bravo!' he said, slipping his arm into hers. 'I too like my coffee very hot! Now go and fetch a coat and we'll go out. We must take advantage of this weather.'

In the bedroom she found Constant waiting imperturbably with a coat lined with miniver, and a hat and muff of the same fur, also borrowed from the wardrobe of the Princess Borghese, as well as a pair of pattens for the snow. As he helped her into the warm coat, Constant murmured softly:

'I did warn mademoiselle. But don't worry, when the Emperor returns to his desk I will see that a substantial collation is served to mademoiselle in here. Otherwise, since dinner will be the same as breakfast, mademoiselle would be in some danger of death by starvation.'

'And is it always like this?' Marianne sighed, calling to mind, with a good deal of admiration, the gracious figure of Josephine who had lived this life for years on end. Then as she slipped her hands into her muff, she added in a different tone: 'Tell me, Constant, what would the Emperor's sister say if she knew I was wearing her clothes?'

'Nothing at all. Her Highness would be in no way disturbed. She has so many dresses, coats and garments of all descriptions that she scarcely knows what belongs to her. The Emperor, and with some reason, has nicknamed her Our Lady of Frippery. Mademoiselle may see for herself! But hurry now, the Emperor does not like to be kept waiting.'

Marianne ran to meet Napoleon, thinking that a faithful servant was indeed a blessing of the gods. She was duly grateful for the help, at once friendly and discreet, which she received from the imperial valet. But for him, God alone knew how many mistakes she might have made!

He was waiting outside in the pillared walk, wearing a huge, frogged greatcoat that made him look almost as broad as he was tall, striding up and down so fast that Marianne wondered for a moment whether their walk might not turn out to be more in the nature of a military exercise. But he stopped when he saw her and tucking Marianne's arm beneath his own, said quietly: 'Come, and see how lovely it is.'

Arm in arm, they strolled across the vast, snow-covered park watched over by a still, sad population of statues. They walked beside frozen lakes where a queen had once skated, and where the bronze tritons and sea gods now turned slowly green in the loneliness of forgotten things, as uncared for as the cupid with the dolphin standing by his pool in the Hôtel d'Asselnat. The farther they went from the Trianon, the more they seemed to be entering an enchanted domain where time itself stood still.

They walked for a long time in silence, happy simply to be together, but gradually the tragic stillness of this park, where everything had been created for the honour and glory of the most brilliant of all the Kings of France, seemed to have an effect upon Napoleon. He stopped by the side of a great dead pool in the midst of which Apollo's chariot seemed to be striving uselessly to break free of its icy setting. Before them a long perspective of tall trees ended in the distance in a line of large and noble buildings. Marianne's hand tightened on her companion's arm.

'What is that?' she asked in a low voice, sensing instinctively that whatever it was, it belonged to the dead.

'Versailles,' he said.

Marianne caught her breath. The sun had gone in, as though unwilling to shine on the deserted dwelling of him who had taken it for his Empire. The huge, empty palace slept in the grey light of a winter day, lightly shrouded in mist, while nature led the slow assault on its pure line with the relentless advance of moss-grown terraces and neglected gardens. The great spectre of departed royalty was so poignant that Marianne turned to the Emperor with eyes filled with tears. But the face she saw might have been carved from the same stone as the statues in the park.

'I can do nothing for it,' he said at last, gazing with brooding eyes on the huge, hollow monument. 'The people might rise against me if I so much as tried to restore it. The time is not yet. The people could not understand.'

'A pity. It would suit you so well—'

He thanked her with a smile and laid his hand over hers as it rested on his arm.

'I have sometimes dreamed. But one day, I too shall build a palace worthy of my power. On the hill of Chaillot probably. There are plans already. But there are still too many memories attached to this one, too many memories which the people still hate.'

Marianne said nothing. She dared not say that the imminent arrival of a niece of that martyred Queen might well affect the French people more than the employment of a few hundred workmen at Versailles. Besides, she too had her memories. It was in the chapel of this palace, visible from where they stood, in the days when it seemed that Versailles must live for ever, that her mother had been married. But she made no attempt to ask him to go nearer so as to see the chapel. She was too much afraid of feeling again the grief that had pierced her heart as she pushed open the door of her own ruined house. Instead, she only pressed a little closer to Napoleon and asked to go back.

In silence, as they had come, wrapped up in their own thoughts, they made their way back to the Trianon from which a troop of mounted couriers was at that moment setting out in all directions, carrying the morning's letters. It was also time for the changing of the guard and all this gave to the palace an air of bustling activity.

But instead of returning to his desk as Constant had predicted, Napoleon led Marianne straight back to their bedroom and shut the door. Without a word, but with a desperate ardour that seemed as though it would never be quenched, he made love to her as he had never done before. It was as though he sought to draw from her young body all its reserves of fresh strength and energy to help him fight the invading shadows of the past. Perhaps he was trying in some way to combat an unacknowledged dread of the unknown Viennese in whose veins ran some of the blood of the Sun King himself.

Then, with no explanation beyond a long kiss and a brief 'See you later', he vanished, leaving her alone in the untidy room, an island of quiet in the midst of the palace humming like a hive with military orders, the clatter and the coming and going of servants. But when, a few minutes later, Constant entered gravely bearing a laden tray, Marianne had done her hair, restored some order to her clothes, and even made the bed, so embarrassed was she at what the solemn valet might think. She was very far, yet, from having acquired the traditional shamelessness of a royal favourite.

However, this did not prevent her from devouring everything Constant set before her with the utmost enjoyment. The keen morning air and the love-making which followed had sharpened an already considerable appetite. When she had finished, she glanced at the valet gratefully.

'Thank you,' she said. 'That was lovely – though I doubt I shall be able to eat a mouthful at dinner.'

'I should not be so sure of that. In theory, dinner is at six, but if the Emperor takes it into his head to work later, he may well dine three or four hours after that.'

'It can't be fit to eat.'

'Not at all. The cooks have orders to keep something always ready, even if only a roast chicken. They put a fresh one on the spit every quarter of an hour, so that one is always ready when his Majesty wishes to sit down.'

'And – do they get through a great many that way?'

'On one occasion, mademoiselle, we attained the figure of twenty-three,' he told her with pride. 'So mademoiselle has plenty of time in which to recover her appetite. I might add that most of those honoured with an invitation to the imperial table are accustomed to take some precautions beforehand. If not, they are unlikely to satisfy themselves in ten minutes, especially as they are generally obliged to answer the Emperor, who talks incessantly without missing a mouthful.'

Marianne laughed. She enjoyed discovering Napoleon's little oddities, but, however surprising, she was much more inclined to find them funny than shocking. She loved him too well for that.

'Never mind, Constant,' she said. 'One does not need food when one is with the Emperor. That is enough in itself.'

The valet's broad, pale face was suddenly serious. He nodded.

'Mademoiselle says so because she truly loves the Emperor. But not everyone thinks as she does.'

'Are there really people who do not love him? Truly, I can't imagine it.'

'How could it be otherwise? He is so great, so powerful, so far above the common run of men! But he was not born to a throne and there are those who would a hundred times rather see the crown on the head of some half-witted scion of a royal house than worn by a man of genius who frightens them and makes them see themselves for what they are. Inferiority is never an agreeable sensation. There are some who avenge themselves by jealousy, hatred and ambition – he can trust no one. His marshals are envious and think for the most part that they would have made better sovereigns than he, his family plague him constantly, his friends, or those who claim to be his friends, are for the most part only thinking of what they can get out of him – only his soldiers give him a simple, honest love. And that poor, sweet Empress who loved him and cared for him like the child she was never able to give him.'

Constant was speaking now without looking at Marianne and she realized that this was probably the first time he had spoken his thoughts aloud for a very long time. And he was doing it because he had sensed that Marianne truly loved the master he revered. When she spoke, it was so softly as to be almost a whisper.

'I know all that. The Grand Marshal said something of the kind yesterday and I have met the Empress. But what do you think of the one who is to come?'

Constant seemed to come back again to the real world. He shook his head, picked up the tray and moved a few steps towards the door as though unwilling to reply. But before opening it, he turned to Marianne and smiled rather sadly.

'What do I think, mademoiselle? Saving the respect I owe him, exactly what the grumblers of his Old Guard think as they sit round their fire. "The Tondu ought not to have sent his old woman packing! She brought him luck – and us too!"'

'The Tondu?'

'That's what they call him, and sometimes the Little Corporal, or Puss in Boots, or Père la Violette. I told you they worship him! They're old devils who fought their way through a good many campaigns and they are not often wrong! I'm afraid they may be right again. It wasn't an Empress from the Danube that he needed.'

That night, just as she was dropping off to sleep, her body overwhelmed by a delicious weariness, Marianne was surprised to see Napoleon leap out of bed, stark naked, as though the building were on fire. He put on his white flannel dressing-gown and slippers, wound a white silk scarf about his head and, picking up a candlestick, was already making for his office when Marianne sat up amid the pillows and asked, like any young bride: 'Where are you going?'

'To work. Go to sleep!'

'Again? But what time is it?'

'Half past twelve. Go to sleep I tell you.'

'Not without you! Come here—'

She held out her arms, confident in the power her beauty had over his awakened senses. But he frowned and made as if to go. Then he seemed to change his mind, put down the candle and came back to the bed. Marianne closed her eyes, but instead of kissing her parted lips he merely tweaked her ear hard.

'I have already told you you are a dreadful siren, *mio dolce amore*, but don't abuse your power. I have just sent the Comte de Narbonne back to Munich as Ambassador with the King of Bavaria and I have important dispatches to send him. Besides that, some rogues have been circulating counterfeit coins among the soldiers of one of my Irish regiments stationed at Limoges and I forgot to deal with it—'

'State affairs, never anything but State affairs!' Marianne complained, tears starting to her eyes. 'I have so little of you to myself – and for so little time! You promised me a week.'

'And you have it. If you were the Empress, you would not have me for more than a few minutes a day, or not much more at least. I have cleared a space around us so as to be able to love you. Do not ask for more—'

'I wish I could help you – I mean, be useful to you in some

way. I am nothing but an instrument of pleasure, a kind of odalisque for a busy sultan!'

He was not smiling now. Taking Marianne's head in his two hands he forced it gently back on to the pillow and then bent over her until all he could see were her wide eyes, ringed now with a faint bluish shade.

'Do you really mean that?'

'With all my heart — don't you know I am all yours?'

He kissed her, a long, passionate kiss, then muttered rapidly: 'One day, I shall remind of you of those words. When I need you I will tell you as frankly as today I tell you that I love you. But just at present, what I need is your love, your being here, your wonderful voice — and your body, of which I can never tire. Sleep now — but not too deeply. I shall wake you when I come back—'

Later, Marianne would often look back on those days at the Trianon. It was broken by the meals taken helter-skelter in the pretty room looking out over the bare, winter woods, by the long excursions on foot or on horseback in the course of which Marianne had been able to note that Napoleon was nowhere near as good a rider as herself, by long fireside talks and by the sudden bursts of passion which hurled them into one another's arms at the most unexpected moments and then left them panting and exhausted, like shipwrecked mariners washed up on some strange shore.

During the hours Napoleon devoted to his exhausting work, Marianne also worked. On the second day, the Emperor had taken her into the music room and reminded her that before very long she would have to face the public in Paris. She had flung herself into her work with a new ardour, perhaps because she was conscious of him there, close by, and because sometimes he would slip quietly into the room to listen to her for a moment.

It was true, she had to do her studying alone, but she soon discovered in her lover an expert capable of appreciating the most obscure musical points. He was astonishingly versatile. He might have been as good a teacher as Gossec, just as he could have been a talented writer or a remarkable actor. As time went on, the admiration he inspired in his young mistress became stronger than ever. She longed desperately to be worthy of him, one day perhaps to reach those arid, inaccessible regions where he moved.

Yet perhaps conscious of the extent to which his bewitching Marianne had given herself to him, Napoleon gradually began to confide in her a little more. He would talk about certain problems, small ones perhaps, but which gave her an insight into the vastness and complexity of his task.

Each morning, she saw Fouché, her old tormentor now become the most gallant and attentive of her admirers, appear in person to give the Emperor his daily report on all that was going on in his vast Empire. Whether in Bordeaux, in Anvers, in Spain, Italy or the smallest villages of Poland or the Palatinate, the Duke of Otranto's fantastic organization seemed, like some gigantic Hydra, to have an eye hidden everywhere. Let a grenadier be killed in a duel, an English prisoner escape from Auxonne, a ship from America dock in Morlaix with dispatches or cargo from the Colonies, a new book appear or a vagabond commit suicide, Napoleon would know it all the next day.

In this way Marianne learned, incidentally, that the Chevalier de Bruslart was still at large and the Baron de Saint-Hubert had managed to make his way to the island of Hoedic, where he had boarded an English cutter, but she felt no great interest in the news. The only thing she wished to talk about was the one subject that no one mentioned in her presence, that of the future Empress.

There seemed to be a conspiracy of silence on the subject of the Arch-Duchess. And yet, as time passed, her shadow seemed to loom ever larger over Marianne's happiness. The days were so short and passed so swiftly. But every time she tried to bring the conversation round to the Arch-Duchess, Napoleon side-stepped the issue with depressing skill. She sensed that he did not want to talk about his future wife to her and feared to see, in his silence, a greater interest than he cared to admit. And meanwhile, the hours flew by ever more swiftly, the wonderful hours that she so longed to hold back.

However, on the fifth day of her stay at the Trianon,

something occurred which came as an unpleasant shock to Marianne and very nearly spoiled the end of her stay.

Their walk that day had been a short one. Marianne and the Emperor had intended originally to go as far as the village where Marie-Antoinette had once played at being a shepherdess, but a sudden fall of snow had forced them to turn back halfway. Soon the flakes were falling so thick and fast that in no time at all they were up to their ankles.

'Wet feet,' Napoleon said with finality, 'are the worst thing possible for the voice. You can visit the Queen's village another day. But instead—' a gleam of mischief danced in his eyes '—instead, I'll promise you a first-rate snowball fight tomorrow!'

'A snowball fight?'

'Don't tell me you never played at snowballs? Or doesn't it snow in England nowadays?'

Marianne laughed. 'Indeed it does! And snowballs might be thought a proper pastime for ordinary mortals – but for an Emperor . . .'

'I have not always been an Emperor, *carissima mia*, and my earliest battles were fought with snowballs. I got through a prodigious number of them when I was at college in Brienne. I'm a devil of a hand, you wait and see!'

Then he had slipped his arm about her waist and half-leading, half-carrying her, had set off at a gallop back to the rose-coloured palace where the lamps were already bright against the darkening sky. There, since the time set aside for 'recreation' was not yet over, the two of them had retired to the music room, where Constant brought them an English tea with buttered toast and jam which they ate in front of the fire, as Napoleon said, 'like an old married couple'. Afterwards, he asked Marianne to sit at the great gilded harp and play to him.

Napoleon was passionately fond of music. It calmed and soothed him and in his frequent periods of abstraction he liked to have it as a murmurous background to lend wings to his thoughts. Besides, the sight of Marianne seated behind the graceful instrument, her slender white arms etched against the strings, was to him an exquisite enchantment. And today, in a

gown of watered silk the same green as her eyes that rippled to
the light with every inclination of her body, her dark curls
clustered high on her head and bound with narrow ribbons of
the same subtle shade, pearl drops in her ears and more pearls,
round and milky, like a huge cabochon between her breasts
and joining the high waist, she was irresistible. She knew it,
too, for while her hands played without effort the slight air by
Cherubini, she could see dawning in her lover's eyes a look
which she had learned to know. In a little while, when the last,
vibrating notes had died away, he would rise without a word
and take her hand to lead her to their room. A little while –
and once more she would know those moments of blinding joy
which only he could give her. But meanwhile the present, filled
with sweet anticipation, had its own charm.

Unfortunately for Marianne, she was not allowed to enjoy it
to the end. Right in the middle of her sonata, there came a
timid scratching on the door which opened to make room for
the furiously blushing face of a youthful page.

'What is it now?' Napoleon spoke curtly. 'Am I not to have
an instant's peace? I thought I said we were not to be disturbed?'

'I – I know, Sire,' stammered the wretched boy. It had obvi-
ously taken more courage on his part to enter the forbidden
room than to storm an enemy redoubt. 'But – there is a courier
from Madrid! With urgent dispatches!'

'Dispatches from Madrid invariably are,' the Emperor commented dryly. 'Oh, very well, let him come in.'

Marianne had ceased playing at the first words and now she
rose hurriedly, preparing to withdraw, but Napoleon signed to
her briefly to be seated. She obeyed, divining his annoyance at
being disturbed and his reluctance to leave his comfortable
fireside for the draughty corridors leading to his office.

The page vanished, with significant haste, to return a
moment later and throw open the door to allow the entrance of
a soldier so liberally plastered with mud and dust that it was
impossible to see the colour of his uniform. The soldier ad-
vanced to the middle of the room and stood to attention, chin
up, heels together, his shako on his arm. Marianne stared

thunderstruck at a face fringed with a few days' growth of
golden beard, a face she knew from the first moment, even before he fixed his eyes in a blank, military stare on the grey and
gold silk covering the wall and spoke.

'Sergeant-Major Le Dru, with special dispatches from his
Excellency the Duke of Dalmatia to his Majesty the King Emperor. At your Majesty's service!'

He it was, the man who had made a woman of her and to
whom she owed her first, disagreeable experience of love. He
had not changed much in these past two months, despite the
ravages of fatigue upon his face, and yet Marianne had the
feeling that she was looking at a different man. How, in so
short a space of time, had Surcouf's sailor become transformed
into this stony-faced soldier, the messenger of a duke? On his
green jacket she noted with surprise the brand new mark of the
Légion d'Honneur. But Marianne had been long enough in
France to realize the kind of magic which surrounded Napoleon. What might have seemed preposterous or absurd elsewhere was the daily bread of this strange country and the giant
who ruled it. In no time at all, a ragged sailor out of an English
prison hulk could become a hero of the Army, galloping like a
centaur from one end of Europe to the other.

Napoleon, hands clasped lightly behind his back, walked
slowly round the newcomer who, stiff with pride and awe,
strove desperately to overcome his weakness under this august
scrutiny. Marianne sat wondering how long it would be before
Le Dru's glance fell on her and what would happen then. She
knew the Breton's impulsive nature too well not to fear the
worst. Who could tell how he would react on seeing her?
Better to slip away quietly now and disarm Napoleon's prob-
able wrath later.

She rose, intending to make her way unobtrusively to a side
door. As she did so, the Emperor stopped in front of Le Dru and
put out a finger to lift the cross that glittered on his breast.

'You are a brave lad, it seems. Where did you get this?'

The soldier's set face flushed with pride.

'At Ciudad Rodrigo, Sire. From Marshal Ney in person.'

'What for?'

'For – a peccadillo, Sire.'

The Emperor's face lit briefly with his rare and wonderful smile. He put up his hand and tweaked the boy's ear. The young eyes filled with tears.

'I like such peccadilloes,' Napoleon said, 'and I like your modesty. What is your message, my friend?'

Marianne had stayed where she was, held in spite of herself. After all, she thought, why should she run away? Her past was no secret from the Emperor now and even if Le Dru dared to attack her in his presence, he could not hurt her. Somewhere inside her, there was an irresistible curiosity, tinged perhaps with perversity, urging her to stay and watch this young man of whom at one time she had been so afraid, and towards whom she was no longer very sure what her feelings were. Quietly, she resumed her seat at the harp.

Le Dru was feverishly pulling a large sealed package from inside his jacket. His colour had faded and now he looked to Marianne to be growing paler with every second, as though about to collapse. The spasm of pain that crossed his face as he held out the dispatch told her all she needed to know. She found her voice at last, experiencing a sense of excitement in thus challenging the danger.

'Sire,' she said tranquilly, 'this man can hardly stand. I am sure he must be wounded.'

At the sound of her voice, Le Dru turned to look at her. Marianne saw with some amusement the erstwhile sailor's blue eyes widen with astonishment.

'True, by thunder,' Napoleon began. 'Are you—'

The sound of the man's fall cut short his words. Le Dru had only held himself upright by a supreme effort of will but the unexpected shock of finding himself gazing full at Marianne had been too much for his overstrained nerves, and the courier from Madrid had fainted clean away at the Emperor's feet.

'Well, well,' commented his Sovereign, 'if my dragoons take to swooning like green girls . . .'

But even as he spoke he was on his knees ripping open the high collar of the green dolman to give the man air. Blood spread in a widening stain across his shirt near the shoulder.

'You were right,' Napoleon said to Marianne, 'this man is wounded. Come and help me.'

She had already fetched a crystal decanter from a side table and was pouring a little water on to her handkerchief. Kneeling beside the Emperor on the carpet she began bathing Le Dru's temples, but without effect.

'He needs a cordial,' she said, 'and a doctor as well. Have we any brandy?'

'We call it cognac in this country,' Napoleon retorted. 'As for the doctor—'

He went quickly to the hearth and pulled the bell. The frightened page reappeared, his eyes growing rounder than ever with horror as he saw the man he had let in stretched unconscious on the floor.

'A doctor, at once,' the Emperor commanded. 'Also a stretcher and two footmen to see this man put to bed in the soldiers' quarters.'

'Send a wounded man out in the cold in this weather?' Marianne protested. 'Your Majesty cannot be serious?'

'You may be right, though my soldiers have tough hides, you know. Never mind. Have a room made ready for him here. Well, go on, hurry, imbecile! What are you waiting for?'

Le Dru must have been in the last stages of exhaustion. He was still deeply unconscious when the palace doctor appeared, accompanied by the servants who were to carry him to bed.

While the medical man made his brief examination, Marianne retired to an armchair and watched Napoleon break the seal on the dispatches and cast a quick eye over them. She was disturbed to see him frown and look grim. The news must be bad. When he had finished reading, the Emperor crushed the thick sheet angrily in his fist.

'Incompetents!' he muttered between his teeth. 'I am surrounded by incompetents! Could there not be one person in my whole family capable of making reasonable plans, or at least of carrying mine out with disinterested greatness!'

Marianne said nothing. The words, she knew, were not addressed to her. For the moment, Napoleon had forgotten her, preoccupied as he was with the new problems raised by the dispatch. He was talking to himself and to have risked a reply would inevitably have been to seek a rebuff. In any case the doctor was on his feet again.

'The man may as well be put to bed, Sire,' he said. 'I will be able to attend to him more readily there.'

'See to it, then. But make sure he is fit to talk soon. I have several things to ask him.'

While the servants, acting on the doctor's instructions, were getting the unconscious Le Dru on to the stretcher, Marianne approached the Emperor who, with the letter still in his hand, was clearly about to depart for his office.

'Sire,' she said, 'have I your permission to go and inquire how the man does?'

'Are you afraid he will not be well cared for?' Napoleon sounded half angry, half in jest. 'My medical men know their job, I promise you.'

'It's not that. The reason I wish to learn how he goes on is because I know him.'

'What, another? You are as bad as Talleyrand for being intimately acquainted with half Europe! Do you mind telling me how you come to know this fellow who is sent from Spain when you yourself came straight from England?'

'I met him in England, on a stormy night in Plymouth Sound, on board the vessel belonging to Nicolas Mallerousse. He was escaping from the hulks. He had sailed under Surcouf and was with me when I was taken by the wreckers.'

Napoleon frowned. Evidently the story did not altogether convince him.

'I see,' he said sardonically. 'You are old comrades-in-arms! But what intrigues me is what your friend is doing in the dragoons? There is still fighting at sea and Surcouf needs men more than ever. And, I might add, his men are generally so devoted to him they would rather lose their right arms than leave him. So what is he doing on land? Was he seasick?'

Marianne began to wish she had not spoken. Napoleon's ironic tone boded no good and she even had a vague suspicion that he did not altogether believe her. But it was too late now to draw back. She could only go on to the end.

'He was indeed devoted to Surcouf but he loved the Emperor more,' she began cautiously, wondering how she was going to explain the episode at the Compas d'Or without provoking a storm and, still more important, without finding herself obliged to go into the mortifying happenings in the barn. It had not occurred to her that he could ask so many questions and as she paused, searching for a way to go on, she was expecting every instant to hear a dry: 'That is no explanation,' or something equally forbidding.

But to her surprise, the ominous crease vanished from the imperial brow, to be replaced by an indulgent smile.

'There are some such,' Napoleon said complacently. 'Very well, my heart, go and visit your fellow fugitive whenever you wish, you have my permission. The page on duty, young St Géran, will take you. But don't forget what time we sup. Until then, farewell.'

A second later, to Marianne's intense relief, he was gone. She heard his quick tread fading down the corridor and could not repress a grateful sigh. It had been a near thing and she sank into a chair to recover. She was in no hurry to visit Le Dru. First, she needed time to think what she meant to say to him.

She was certainly under no obligation to go and see a person she had no cause to remember with kindness. If she made no move he might even think when he recovered consciousness that he had been under a delusion and had dreamed her sudden appearance. But the idea no sooner presented itself than Marianne rejected it. Le Dru might be a superstitious Breton, but he would hardly believe in hallucinations of that order. At least he would ask the doctor whether the woman in the green dress he had seen with the Emperor had been dream or reality. And how could she be sure that once he had learned the truth he would not commit some folly in order to see her again? As a result of which Marianne would undoubtedly find herself compelled to furnish explanations infinitely more detailed than those she had already provided . . . No, her request to visit the injured man had been an inspiration. In that way she had every hope of doing away with misunderstandings and putting matters to rights with him without the Emperor suspecting anything.

Her mind made up, Marianne went to her room to fetch a large cashmere shawl in a mixture of autumnal shades from dark green to palest gold, and with this draped round her shoulders over the low-cut gown, she went in search of young St Géran to ask him to take her to the bedside of the wounded man.

The page was killing time out in the gallery, staring out with a disillusioned air at the sentries marching to and fro in the snow outside with their bearskin hats pulled well down to their eyebrows. He welcomed Marianne with eagerness.

'Do you know where the injured courier was taken?' she asked him. 'The Emperor wishes me to inquire how he does and would have you lead me to him.'

'It will be an honour, madame! He has been put in one of the small rooms upstairs.'

The boy was clearly delighted at the chance and Marianne suppressed a smile as she caught the admiration in his gaze. He could not have been more than fourteen or fifteen, but even at that age boys know beauty when they see it and Henri de St Géran had instantly constituted himself her slave. With the utmost dignity he went before her up the staircase and flung open the door of one of the rooms, then stood back for her to enter, inquiring politely if she wished him to wait for her.

'No, thank you. And I should prefer not to be disturbed.'

'As you wish, madame.'

With a lordly gesture he beckoned to the woman who sat by the bed and went out with her, closing the door behind him. Marianne was left alone with the wounded man. A deep silence reigned in the room and she hesitated a trifle nervously before going forward.

The curtains, patterned with exotic flowers, had been drawn against the early dark outside and the room was un-lighted except for the glow of the fire in the hearth and the nightlight burning on a table by the bed.

The bed was placed in such a way that its occupant was unable to see the door and Marianne moved forward softly in case he should be asleep. It would scarcely be wondered at if he were after his long ride, and with his wound and the sedatives

which the doctor must have given him. But then she heard a
very human sound: someone sniffing hard, like a person who
had been crying.

Without more hesitation, Marianne stepped up to the bed
and into the pool of light thrown by the nightlight. Once there
she saw that the man who had once sailed with Surcouf and
was now a soldier of Napoleon was indeed crying like a baby.

At the sight of Marianne, however, Jean Le Dru stopped
short and stared at her, without surprise this time but with
sudden anger.

'What do you want?' he asked abruptly.

'To know how you feel – and also, perhaps, a little how we
stand, you and I. Don't you think it might be time you confessed
at last that you were wrong about me? And that we were both
serving the same cause, you knowingly, I without yet being
aware of it?'

She spoke with great gentleness, firstly because she was
dealing with an injured and exhausted man, and secondly because she genuinely wished to make an end of the tragic misunderstanding which had developed between them as a result
of the mischievous words of Morvan's vindictive mistress,
Gwen. But the boy was determined to regard her as an enemy
and no amount of sweetness in her voice could have any effect
on him. He gave a short, bitter laugh.

'The same cause? When we know where you came from?'

Marianne shrugged, hugging the big, soft shawl more closely
round her.

'When will you make up your mind to understand? Or are
you really too stupid to accept the truth? When we met, I was
escaping from the English police and you from the hulks. We
were equal then. I had nothing left but my life and I did my best
to keep that.'

'You seem to me to have succeeded admirably. When I asked
just now who was the woman in the green dress I saw with the
Emperor, no one could tell me your name but they said you
were his latest love and that you were living here in this palace
with him – and if I wept just now, it was for rage and help-
lessness because I was powerless to save him from you!'

Marianne had heard that Bretons were accounted unusually obstinate but she would never have believed they could be so to this extent. She sighed resignedly and sat down on the bottom of the bed.

'Suppose we have a little talk — if you are not too feverish.'

'I have not yet lost my reason.'

'Then try to use it. Let us take matters up from where we left off. When you denounced me and had me thrown into prison you were convinced, if I remember rightly, that I was an English spy sent here especially to bring about the downfall of the Corsair, Robert Surcouf. Is that correct?'

'Correct,' Le Dru admitted unwillingly.

'I was therefore thrown into prison, only to be released through the intervention of that very Surcouf who did not seem to appreciate your part in the affair.'

'He sent me away,' the Breton said sourly. 'Sent me packing just like a felon, me, one of his best seamen who loved him more than anything in the world, except the Emperor, of course.'

'And I realize that is something you find hard to forgive me for. But afterwards, I had every chance to do what I liked with Surcouf. With you out of the way, I could carry out my supposed purpose at leisure?'

'Yes.'

'Are you trying to tell me that anything untoward has happened to the man you admire so much? I have not seen the Baron since but I do know that he is at present at St Malo and threatened by no worse dangers than those he ordinarily runs at sea. So what do you think happened? Did I betray my masters and abandon my mission? Or will you finally admit that I was never a spy except in your own imagination?'

'The fact that you are here with the Emperor is the best answer to that. Beside him, even Surcouf is a poor prize! You'd be a fool to stick to the first when you could have the second!'

Marianne exclaimed angrily. She had a sudden, strong desire to slap the stubborn face which looked at her with such implacable sternness from the shadow of the bedcurtains, but she controlled herself with an effort and managed to ask in a tone of the utmost detachment:

'And what, according to you, am I supposed to be doing with him? Am I to persuade him to abandon his Empire and his subjects and go with me to England to live in perfect love so that, no doubt, I can hand him over duly bound and gagged to the British Government? Or do you expect me to open the palace gates one dark night and let in a band of secret conspirators? Unless, of course, I am hiding a dagger under my clothes—'

Sarcasm was, to all appearances, lost on Jean Le Dru. He was a Breton, solemn, obstinate and utterly without imagination. He answered roughly:

'I don't know. But I daresay you are quite capable of any of those.'

'Simply because I failed to return the sentiments you were pleased to feel for me,' Marianne finished for him calmly. 'It has not occurred to you that I too could love the Emperor as much or even more than you do, that I could be his in soul as much as in body?'

Jean Le Dru said nothing but his eyes closed for a second and Marianne could have sworn that a fresh tear slid furtively from beneath his lid.

'And yet, suppose it were so?' she persisted gently. 'Don't you think, you who serve him with such blind devotion, that he has charm and glory enough to make a woman mad about him? For that is what I am. Believe me or believe me not, Jean Le Dru, but I love Napoleon as no one, except perhaps the Empress Josephine, has ever loved him. And, let me tell you, you are wrong once again if you think me at the peak of happiness. There is a poison in my joy. My days here can have no future to them because the future belongs to the one who comes here to marry him, the Austrian stranger who will take from me – and from you too, perhaps – a little of his heart! And you can never know how wretched I am!'

Le Dru spoke slowly, as though speech were infinitely painful to him.

'You love him – so much?' Then he added, as if to himself: 'Of course! How could it be otherwise! Even if you were the lowest of the low, you could not help it! I know he casts his spell on women almost as readily as he dominates men. No woman has been able to betray him yet and why should you be the first? No one can help but love him . . .'

'And yet, I know those who hate him, though it is true that they are men . . .' She was silent for a moment, allowing the Breton to think his own thoughts. She knew, all her quick woman's intuition told her, that she was gaining ground and that his doubts were gradually lessening. After a few seconds, she stretched out her hand and laid it on the boy's hot, feverish one.

'Since we both love and serve the same master, can we truly not be friends, Jean Le Dru?'

'Friends? You and I?' he said slowly, as though striving to weigh the words he uttered. Then, with sudden anger: 'No! It cannot be!'

'Why not?'

'Because—' A pause, followed by an explosion. 'Because you are you. And because there has been that between us which I cannot forget! And yet, God knows I have done my best! When I entered the Army, I knew it was for Spain but I was glad to go because it was a long way off and perhaps I might not think of you when I was there. But you would not let me go, not for all the distance I travelled, not for the battles, the sun and the snow, the blood and all the horrors that I saw! You can have no idea what it is like, those frozen sierras where nothing seems to live, where one is cold and hungry and yet where death is hidden behind every rock, in every hollow – and such a death!'

Jean had forgotten Marianne. His eyes were wide open as if on a present terror. Marianne held her breath and when she spoke it was very gently, so as not to break in too suddenly on the tragic scenes she sensed were in his vision.

'Was it – so very dreadful?'

'Worse than that. The men there are savages! And worse than savages. I have seen savages in my seafaring days and none of them had faces so twisted with hatred and hideous cruelty. But these – these olive-skinned devils can make our poor fellows suffer endless tortures before they let them die. They are worse than animals! Woe betide any isolated detachments or any stragglers! They'll soon be carried off into some barn or other lonely spot by a band of leering demons, as often as not led by a priest waving a crucifix, and tortured cruelly. They even mutilate the wounded and not even dead men can be left in peace without their corpses being treated to fearful indignities. We found them all along the road, some half burned, others with their limbs lopped off, yet others nailed to trees or hung up by their feet, their eyes and nails torn out . . .'

Marianne shrank with horror and put her hands before her eyes.

'For pity's sake – no more!' she cried. 'Don't say such things!'

He started at her cry and turned to look at her in vast surprise.

'Why not? They talk of us in drawing-rooms as barbarians. They say we burn villages and shoot the Spanish *guerrilleros*, but how can any man not give way to fury after seeing such sights? All we want is to give them back a taste of what they have done themselves, make them pay – for all that.' His voice changed suddenly as he added, quite calmly, as though making a simple statement of fact: 'There have been times in that hell when I have thought I was going mad – yet even then, I never managed to forget you. I think I even accepted it all because of you.'

'Because of me?'

'Yes, as if it were a price I had to pay.' And suddenly he turned on Marianne a pair of eyes so blue and innocent that she almost gasped. 'I know that you are far from me by birth, that you are an aristocrat, but all that counts for very little in the Emperor's armies, because there are ways of lessening the distance. Men whose fathers were innkeepers or blacksmiths have been known to rise to high rank, earn pensions and titles and marry duchesses. And however much I might pretend I had gone there to forget you, the truth was that I was hoping to become someone – someone who could address you as an equal. But now, it is all up with that – all up with everything! What can I do to compete with the Emperor? I have not even the right to be jealous of him, while as for bearing him a grudge – that I could never do.'

He turned on his side abruptly, and hid his face in his folded arm. Marianne found herself gazing in perplexity at the shirt covering one thin bony shoulder and a mop of tousled fair hair.

For a second she was unable to speak. The boy's naïve and touching confession that he had done his best to hate her and only succeeded in loving her the more, and had undergone the most frightful dangers in the vague hope of one day winning her, wrung her heart. She suddenly wanted very much to be done once and for all with all misunderstandings and get back to the comradeship they had shared on board Black Fish's boat, when they were no more than escaped prisoner and fugitive. She realized that those were the only moments which had really mattered to her and that this odd, rough, unsophisticated boy was dearer to her than she knew.

As she bent over him, she heard him muttering:

'I cannot fight my Emperor – all I can do is go back there, when I am better, and hope that this time it will make an end of me.'

Tears sprang to her eyes and she put out her hand and began gently, very gently to stroke the roughened hair.

'Jean,' she said softly, 'please, don't cry! I do not wish to cause you such unhappiness. I can't bear to see you so distressed.'

'There's nothing you can do about it, is there?' he answered in a muffled voice. 'It isn't really your fault that I fell in love with you . . . and not your fault at all if you love the Emperor . . . if anyone's to blame it is myself.' He looked up suddenly and his blue, tear-drenched eyes fastened on Marianne's. 'It is true that you do love him, isn't it? That, at least, was no lie?'

'It is true – I swear it on my mother's memory and it is true that I am very nearly as wretched as you are yourself and you would do wrong to be jealous of him. I may not have the right to love him for much longer. And so – I wish we could be friends now, you and I.'

Jean sat up suddenly and, taking Marianne's two hands in his, drew her down to sit beside him on the bed. He was smiling a little wistfully but his anger had gone.

'Friends? You are sorry for me, is that it?'

'No. It is not pity. It is something else, something deeper and warmer than that. I have met many people since I saw you last, but very few have made me want their friendship. But I do want yours. I – I think I am fond of you.'

'In spite of everything that happened between us?'

Before Marianne could answer, a harsh voice spoke from behind the curtains close to her ear.

'And I should like to know precisely what it was that did happen between you.'

At the sudden appearance of Napoleon, Jean Le Dru gave a cry of alarm but strangely enough, Marianne showed no sign of shock. She stood up quickly, hugging her shawl more closely around her, and folded her arms.

'Sire,' she said boldly, 'I have learned to my cost, on more than one occasion, that listeners hear nothing to their advantage and in general miss the real sense of what they overhear.'

'By God, madame,' the Emperor said in a voice of thunder, 'are you accusing me of listening at keyholes?'

Marianne curtsied, smiling. This was in fact precisely what she meant, but he must be made to admit it without an outburst of wrath for which the injured man might suffer.

'Not at all, Sire. I merely wished your Majesty to know that if you desire any further information as to my past dealings with Jean Le Dru I shall be happy to supply it myself, later on. It would be unkind to question one so truly devoted to his Emperor, and who has suffered so much in his service. I cannot think your Majesty has come here with that in view.'

'I have not. I desire to ask this man some questions . . .'

The curt voice left no doubt of his intentions. Marianne sank into a deep, respectful curtsy and, with a smile and a pleasant word of farewell to Jean Le Dru, left the room.

Back in her own apartment, she had little time to prepare herself for the storm she guessed was coming. This time she would not escape close questioning. She would have to tell him everything, except the episode in the barn which nothing on earth would force her to confess. And this not for her own sake alone. She was herself too much in the grip of jealousy not to feel strongly tempted to tell Napoleon frankly that Jean Le Dru had been her first lover. But there would be no enjoyment for anyone but herself in arousing the imperial jealousy and poor Le Dru would very likely have to bear the consequences. Moreover, she was under no obligation to mention an amorous incident which she only wished to forget. It was enough – but Marianne's reflections were interrupted at this point by the Emperor's return.

At first Napoleon merely threw her a glance loaded with suspicion and began striding nervously up and down the room, his hands clasped behind his back. Marianne forced herself to keep calm, and going to a chaise longue near the fire reclined upon it in a graceful posture, arranging the shimmering folds of her dress becomingly about her ankles. Above all, she must not appear ill at ease, must not let him see the small, nagging fear within her or the unnerving effect his anger always had on her. Any moment now, he would come to a halt in front of her and fire his first question . . .

Almost before the thought was formulated, he was there, saying in a harsh voice:

'I imagine you are now ready to explain, madame?'

The formal address made Marianne's heart contract. No hint of softness or affection showed in the marble severity of his face – no trace of anger, either, which was infinitely more disturbing. Even so, she managed to conjure up a gentle smile.

'I thought I had already told the Emperor the circumstances of my meeting with Jean Le Dru?'

'Indeed. But your confidences did not extend to the most intriguing parts of what – er – happened between you. And it is just this which interests me.'

'And yet it is hardly worth it. It is a pathetic tale, the tale of a boy in unusual and tragic circumstances falling in love with a girl who could not return his feelings. Out of pique, perhaps, he preferred to listen to certain slanderous stories presenting her as the irreconcilable enemy of his country and of all he held most dear. The misunderstanding grew to such an extent that the time came when he denounced her as an agent of the Princes and an émigrée returned to France illegally. That is more or less the whole of what happened between Jean Le Dru and myself.'

'I do not care for "more or less"! What else?'

'Nothing, except that his love changed to hatred because Surcouf, the man he worshipped most next to yourself, dismissed him for what he had done. He entered the Army, was sent to Spain – and your Majesty knows the rest.'

Napoleon gave a short laugh and resumed his walking up and down, although more slowly now.

'From what I saw, not an easy tale to believe! I'll take my oath that had I not come in, the fellow would have taken you in his arms. I'd like to know then what faddle you'd have told me.'

Stung by the contempt in his voice, Marianne rose, white-faced. Her green eyes met the Emperor's, flashing a greater defiance than she knew.

'Your Majesty is in error,' she retorted proudly. 'Jean Le Dru would not have taken me in his arms. It was I who would have taken him in mine!'

The ivory mask had grown so deathly pale that Marianne found herself exulting wickedly in her power to hurt him. Disregarding the menacing gesture he made, she stood her ground as the Emperor bore down on her, eyeing her relentlessly. Nor did she flinch when Napoleon caught her wrists in a grip of steel.

'*Per bacco!*' he swore. 'Do you dare?—'

'Why not? You asked for the truth, Sire, and I have told it you. I was about to take him in my arms, as one would do to anyone one wished to comfort, like a mother with a child—'

'Cease this farce! Why should you comfort him?'

'For a bitter grief – the grief of a man who finds his love

again only to see her in love with another, and worse than that, with the one man it is forbidden him to hate, because he worships him! Can you dare say that does not merit some comfort?'

'He has done you nothing but harm and yet you could feel such compassion for him?'

'He harmed me, yes, but I think that I did worse to him unwittingly. I want to forget the wrongs that lay between us and remember only what we suffered together and that Jean Le Dru saved my life, and more than that, when I was washed up from the sea into the hands of the wreckers.'

Napoleon was silent. Marianne could see his taut face close to hers. His fingers bruised her wrists until the pain brought tears into her eyes. He was breathing hard and she was conscious of his hot breath on her eyeballs.

'Swear to me,' he rasped into her face, 'swear to me that he has never been your lover . . .'

The moment she dreaded had come and Marianne almost swooned with the anguish of it. She could not lie and yet she had to lie to him, to the man she loved more than all else. If she refused him the oath he demanded he would banish her without mercy. Within the space of a few minutes she would have left the Trianon, banished like a slave who had ceased to please, for she knew that he would give no quarter. Already he was growing impatient, was shaking her roughly.

'Swear, I tell you! Swear, or get out!'

No, that she could not take. He could not ask her to tear out her own heart. Mentally praying for forgiveness, she closed her eyes and with a little moan—

'I swear,' she said. 'He has never been my lover . . .'

'That is not enough. Swear by the great love you say you bear me!'

The pain of her wrists made her cry out.

'For pity's sake! You're hurting me!'

'Never mind. I want the truth—'

'I swear, swear there was never anything between us – I swear it by the love I bear you!'

'Take care! If you are lying, our love will not endure . . .'

'I am not lying!' she cried in terror. 'I love only you . . . and I have never loved that boy. I feel nothing for him but pity – and a little kindness.'

Only then did the terrible fingers relax their hold.

'Good,' the Emperor merely said. He took a deep breath. 'Remember you have sworn.'

Superstitious, like all Corsicans, he attached an almost fanatical importance to oaths and feared the vengeance of fate on perjury. But the ordeal had been too much for Marianne. Once the cruel hands no longer supported her, she fell to the ground, convulsed with sobs. She was broken by the fright she had endured and also by shame that was already overwhelming her for her perjured oath. But she had been forced to do it, as much for Napoleon himself as for the wretched Le Dru.

For an instant longer, the Emperor remained motionless, as though petrified, listening perhaps to the chaotic pounding of his own heart as it slowly returned to normal. The hand he brushed across his forehead was trembling slightly. Then, suddenly, he seemed to become aware of the desperate weeping that filled the room. He looked down and saw the girl huddled at his feet in heartbroken tears, and at the pitiful sight the demon jealousy relaxed its grip at last. Kneeling swiftly, he put his arms around her and gently raised the tear-stained face to his and began covering it with kisses.

'Forgive me – I am a brute but I cannot bear the thought of another man touching you. Don't cry now, *mio dolce amore* – it's all over now. I believe you—'

'T-truly?' she sobbed. 'Oh, you must believe me – or the grief of it would kill me. I couldn't bear it.'

He laughed suddenly, the young, lighthearted laughter that sometimes followed his worst rages.

'I will only let you die of love. Come, we must wipe out all this.'

He helped her to her feet and holding her close against him led her softly to the bed. Marianne went with him, scarcely conscious. But he was right, only love could restore them to what they had been before the arrival of the courier from

Madrid. She felt the silk counterpane beneath her shoulders and closed her eyes with a sigh.

Some while later, as Marianne emerged from her happy trance, she saw Napoleon leaning on his elbow gazing earnestly at the great purple bruise that marked one of her wrists. Thinking that she could guess his thoughts, she tried to draw her hand away but he held it fast and laid his lips to the place. She expected some word of regret but all he said was:

'Promise me you will not try to see that boy again.'

'What! Are you still afraid—'

'Not in the least! But I should prefer you not to see him. Love is too strong.'

She smiled a little sadly. What a man he was, and how hard it was to understand him. When he himself was actually on the point of taking a new bride, he could still demand that his mistress break off all connexion with another man whose only fault was that he loved her. She might perhaps have said something of this, when another idea came to her. Very well, it should be tit for tat. She would make a bargain with him.

'I promise,' she said sweetly, 'but on one condition—'

He stiffened at once and jerked away from her a fraction.

'A condition? What is it?'

'That you repair the hurt I inflicted without meaning to. Don't let him go back to that dreadful Spain where he will get killed for nothing, for a country he does not know and cannot understand. Send him back to Baron Surcouf. One word from you and he will certainly forgive him and take him back. Then he will have the sea again, and the life he loves, and a man he loves to serve under, and so he will more easily forget me.'

For a moment there was silence. Then Napoleon smiled. He gave Marianne's earlobe a gentle, loving little tug.

'There are times, *carissima mia*, when you make me feel ashamed, and I tell myself I do not deserve you. Of course I promise. He shall not go back to Spain . . .'

When Marianne took her seat at the supper table two hours later, she found beside her place a green leather case stamped with the imperial arms. Inside, were two wide bracelets of chased gold set with a pattern of seed pearls. But when, the next day, she sought discreetly for news of Jean Le Dru, she learned that he had left the palace at dawn in a closed carriage for an unknown destination.

She experienced a momentary sadness but she was bound by her promise and, when all was said, only one thing mattered to her. The single cloud that had nearly overshadowed these few days of happiness had disappeared, leaving her free to enjoy the last hours of this wonderful gift from heaven in peace. There was so little time.

On the last evening, though she desired above all to leave him with an unforgettable memory, it was all Marianne could do to smile. She felt deathly sad. For dinner, the last they would have alone together, she dressed with special care, striving to make herself more beautiful than ever. Her dress of heavy, pale-pink silk moulded every line of her body. Her neck and shoulders rose from the draped and silvered corsage as though from a huge, dew-bespangled flower, and not a single jewel broke the pure line of her throat. The high-piled curls held in place by silver ribbon showed off the graceful poise of her head. But the green eyes under their soft, sepia lashes were bright with unshed tears.

For once, the meal took longer than usual, as though Napoleon too thought to prolong these last private moments. When at last they rose from the table, he took Marianne's hand and kissed it tenderly.

'Will you sing for me tonight? Just for me?'

Her eyes said yes, and leaning on his shoulder, she went with him to the music room. Gently he seated her at the gilded harpsichord but instead of going away and sitting down, he remained standing behind her, his hands gripping her shoulders.

'Sing,' he told her softly.

Marianne could not have said what made her, in that grieving moment, choose the sad song which Marie-Antoinette had once sung, here in this very Trianon, for the handsome Swede with whom she was secretly in love.

*'C'est mon ami, rendez-le moi,
J'ai son amour, il a ma foi,
J'ai son amour, il a ma foi.'*

Sung by her warm voice, the words of love and regret became charged with such a poignant sadness that on the last note the melody broke and Marianne's head drooped. But the hands on her shoulders became hard and commanding.

'Don't cry,' Napoleon said. 'I forbid you to cry.'

'I – I can't help it. It's stronger than I am.'

'You have no right! I have told you, I must have a wife who will give me children. No matter whether she is pretty or ugly, so long as she can give me fine boys! I will give her that which is due to her rank, but you, you will always be my escape. No! Don't turn around! Don't look at me! I want you to trust me, as I trust you – she shall never have what I have given you and will give you again. You shall be my eyes, my ears – my star.'

Overwhelmed Marianne closed her eyes and sank back against Napoleon. The burning hands on her shoulders came to life, slowly caressing the smooth skin, moving down towards her breasts.

The little room was warm and very private. A deep silence fell, scarcely broken by Marianne's trembling sigh.

'Come,' Napoleon murmured hoarsely. 'We still have one night left.'

Early the next morning, a closed carriage left the Trianon at full gallop bearing Marianne back to Paris. This time she was alone, but to avoid any risk of a repetition of what had occurred on the way back from La Celle Saint Cloud, a company of dragoons was to follow at a distance as far as the barrière de Passy.

Never had Marianne's heart felt so heavy. Muffled in the big green velvet cloak she had worn on her arrival, she gazed out absently at the passing wintry landscape. The morning was very cold and grey. It was as though the world had used up all its store of joy. It made no difference that she knew nothing was at an end between Napoleon and herself. It made no difference that he had sworn to her that the ties between them were now too strong for anything to harm them, not even the marriage of convenience which he was bound to make. Still Marianne could not help thinking that never again would things be as they had been during those few days. For an instant, her love had shone out in the broad light of freedom, now it must return to shadows and secrecy. For however strong the passion which bound her to the Emperor, in future there would always be between them the figure, vague as yet, of the wife who officially would have all and who must not be offended. And Marianne, in an agony of fear and jealousy, could not help trembling at the thought of what might happen if Marie-Louise had only a fraction of the irresistible charm of the unfortunate Marie-Antoinette. Suppose she were to resemble her ravishing aunt, that proud bewitching creature for whom so many men had been prepared to die? Suppose he were to love her? He was so easily won by women's charms.

Furiously, Marianne dashed away the tears which ran unbidden down her face. She was impatient now to return to Fortunée Hamelin and her friend Jolival. For the present they alone were real to her. Never had she felt such a rush of warmth and affection as she did now. At the thought of Fortunée's little bright salon where, very soon, she would be sitting down to the fragrant morning coffee which Jonas made so well, Marianne felt her pain ease a little.

The coach descended the hill of Saint Cloud towards the bridge. But shimmering in the mist beyond the trees and beyond the quick silver band of the river, she saw the blue-tinged roofs of Paris topped by so many grey-white plumes from the smoky chimneys. For the first time, she was struck by the sheer size of the city. Paris lay stretched at her feet like a huge, tame animal and suddenly she had an irresistible desire to master this beautiful quiet monster, and make it cry out for her more loudly still than it would cry out for her rival when she drove for the first time through its streets.

To conquer Paris, to win first Paris and then all France and all the vast Empire — that, surely, was a task inspiring enough to soothe the bitterest regrets of the heart? In a few weeks'

time, Marianne would be facing her first battle with this great
and fiercely artistic city, whose seething life she could feel
almost like the blood in her own veins. There was no time to
waste now if she were to be prepared to face that fight.

Filled with a sudden impatience, she leaned forward and
tapped on the little window to attract the coachman's attention.

'Faster!' she told him. 'I am in a hurry.'

At the bridge of Saint Cloud, the rough-shod horses sprang
into a gallop and at the barrière de Passy, while the dragoons
vanished into the morning mist, the carriage with the imperial
arms plunged hell for leather across Paris, as though already
charging to the attack.

That night, a proclamation appeared on all the walls of the
capital.

'A marriage will take place between his Majesty the Emperor
Napoleon, King of Italy, Protector of the Confederation of the
Rhine, Mediator of the Swiss Confederation and her Imperial
and Royal Highness the Arch-Duchess Marie-Louise, daughter
of his Majesty the Emperor Francis, King of Bohemia and of
Hungary . . .'

There was no going back now. Fate was on the move, and,
while Marianne was endlessly rehearsing with Gossec a melody
from *Nina, or the Lovesick Maid*, Napoleon's sister Caroline
Murat, Queen of Naples and Grand Duchess of Berg, and
Marshal Berthier, Prince of Neufchâtel and Wagram, were
already making ready for their journey to Vienna to bring back
the bride.

CHAPTER EIGHT

Time Returns

Marianne kicked with one small gold satin slipper at a log which had rolled out of the grate. She picked up the tongs and rearranged the smouldering logs before returning to curl up again in the big armchair at one side of the fire and resume her musings. It was Tuesday, March 13th, 1810, the day on which she had moved into the Hôtel d'Asselnat, repaired in record time by one of those miracles which only the Emperor knew how to create. This was her first evening in her own home. For the first time for many weeks, Marianne was absolutely alone.

This was how she had wanted it. She would have no one to come between herself and the ghosts of her family for this, her first acquaintance with the old house in its new dress. Tomorrow, the doors would open wide for her few friends, for Arcadius de Jolival who had taken lodgings in a house nearby, for Fortunée Hamelin with whom Marianne meant to celebrate her entry into possession worthily, for Talleyrand who, in these last weeks, had been a discreet and attentive friend, for Dorothée de Périgord, who had promised to bring the best society to call on her, and, lastly, for her teacher Gossec, who would come tomorrow as he did every morning, to help prepare her for her first contact with the public of Paris. Tomorrow, there would be all sorts of things, known and unknown, faces that would all soon be familiar. But tonight, she wanted to be alone, to listen to the silence of her house. There must be no stranger, however friendly, to disturb her first meeting with her own memories.

The servants, carefully hand-picked by Madame Hamelin, would not arrive until tomorrow. Mademoiselle Agathe, the young ladies' maid, would not be coming to take possession of the little room which had been set aside for her near Marianne's own until after eight o'clock. Only young Gracchus-Hannibal Pioche, newly promoted to the rank of coachman, was in the house, and even he had his own quarters in an outbuilding. He had orders not to disturb Marianne on any account. She had found it by no means easy to escape from the attentions of her friends. Fortunée in particular had been decidedly unwilling to leave Marianne all alone in the great house.

'I should die of fright if it were me!' she had declared roundly.

'What is there to be afraid of?' Marianne had answered. 'There I shall really be at home.'

'Yes, but remember the portrait, and the prowler comes here—'

'I think he must have gone for good now. And besides, the locks have been changed.'

It was true that all attempts to trace the mysterious visitor had been unsuccessful. There was no sign of the missing portrait of the Marquis d'Asselnat in spite of all Arcadius' investigations. A time had come when Marianne had begun to wonder if she had not really dreamed it all. If Fortunée and Arcadius had not been there also, she would have begun to doubt her own memory.

Wrapped in a long housegown of white cashmere, its high neck and long sleeves edged with ermine, Marianne looked round her at the big, bright, cosy room which tonight had become her own.

Her eye rested in turn on the soft blue-green hangings, the exquisite lacquered corner cupboards, the small chairs upholstered in a gaily-flowered Aubusson, the great bed draped in changeable taffetas, and came to rest at last on a big caledon vase filled with lilac, irises and huge tulips. The blaze of colour and freshness made her smile. Those flowers were like a presence in themselves, his presence.

They had arrived that morning, armfuls of them, brought by the gardeners of Saint Cloud, and the whole house was full of them, but the best of all were in Marianne's own room. She

found them better company than any human being because she
was conscious of their fragrance even when she was not looking at them.

Marianne closed her eyes. Several weeks had passed since
those days at the Trianon, but she was still living under their
spell. And it would be much, much longer before she ceased to
regret their brevity. It had been an instant of paradise which
she would cherish for ever in her inmost heart, like a tiny,
delicate and fragrant plant.

Marianne got up from her chair with a sigh, stretched and
went across to one of the windows. On the way her foot
brushed against a newspaper that lay on the floor. It was the
latest number of the *Journal de l'Empire* and Marianne was all
too familiar with its contents. In it the people of France were
informed by the writer, Joseph Fievée, that on this day, March
13th, their future Empress had left Vienna with her household.
She had already been married to the Emperor by proxy in the
person of Marshal Berthier. In a few days, the Empress would
be in Paris and then Marianne would no longer have the right
to cross the threshold of the great bedchamber in the Tuileries,
where she had been so many times since her return from the
Trianon that she had finally begun to feel at home there.

When she tried to picture this unknown Marie-Louise, who
would so soon become a part of the Emperor's life, Marianne
still found herself shaking with an anger and jealousy all the
greater because she had neither the right nor the opportunity
to show them. Napoleon was marrying for purely dynastic
reasons. He would listen to no arguments that went against his
determination to have a son. He himself was endlessly jealous
and watchful, and had questioned Marianne more than once
about the real state of her relationship to Talleyrand and, even
more, with Jason Beaufort, who he seemed unable to forget.
But he would not have countenanced a similar display on her
part, or not where his future wife was concerned. And, little by
little, Marianne had come to feel an all-embracing sympathy
for his divorced wife, Josephine.

One day in the middle of February she had gone with
Fortunée Hamelin to call on the ex-Empress. She had found her

as melancholy as ever although apparently resigned, but when the Empress' name was mentioned, tears were never far away.

'He has given me a new château,' Josephine had said pathetically. 'The château of Navarre, not far from Evreux, and says he hopes that I shall like it. But I know why, it is because he wants me to be out of Paris when she arrives — that other!'

'The Austrian!' Fortunée spoke angrily. 'The French have been quick to call her that. They have not forgotten Marie-Antoinette.'

'Oh no. But they are sorry now, and they will do their best to make the niece forget the sufferings of her aunt.'

To Marianne, Josephine was especially kind. She seemed delighted to learn of the distant kinship between them and immediately embraced the younger woman with a quite motherly affection.

'I hope that you, at least, will remain my friend, although your mother gave her life for the late Queen.'

'I hope you cannot doubt it, madame. Your Majesty shall have no more faithful or loving servant than myself. Make what use of me you will.'

Josephine smiled faintly and brushed Marianne's cheek with her finger.

'Indeed — you love him too! And I have heard that he loves you. Look after him, I beg of you, as far as you may. I foresee grief and disappointment ahead. How can this girl, brought up as a Hapsburg to hate the victor of Austerlitz, how can she love him as I do when only six months ago he occupied her own father's palace?'

'And yet, it is said your Majesty approved this marriage?'

There had been many rumours to the effect that Josephine had been personally concerned in the choice of her successor.

'One must choose the lesser of two evils. The Austrian was better for the Emperor than the Russian. And I shall always place the Emperor's good before my own personal satisfaction. If you love him truly, cousin, you will do the same.'

Marianne had devoted much thought to those words of Josephine's. Had she, the newcomer, any right to raise the slightest protest; to make any complaint of her own sufferings when this woman was prepared to wipe out so many years of glorious memories? Josephine had left a throne as well as a husband. The sacrifice that Marianne must make seemed very pale in comparison, though none the less cruel in her own eyes. But at least she had hope for the future in looking forward to a great career as a singer. That in itself was no small blessing.

She had been standing leaning her burning forehead on the cold glass to cool it when she started suddenly. Penetrating the mists of melancholy into which she had fallen, she had heard the sound of footsteps, stealthy, but distinct, on the small wooden straicase that led up to the attic floor.

Wide awake now, Marianne went to the door, holding her breath. She was not afraid. The sense of being at home in her own house sustained her. It occurred to her that Gracchus-Hannibal might have come into the house for some reason, though why she could not think. Besides, had it been he she would have heard him walking about downstairs, not over her head. No, it was not Gracchus. Then she thought of the mysterious person who had been there on their first visit, of the hiding place which they had never discovered. Had the unknown prowler returned? Yet how could he have got in? He could hardly have lived in the Abbé's old hiding place all these weeks without being discovered by the workmen swarming over the house. Softly, with infinite caution, Marianne opened her bedroom door. It gave on to the broad landing at the head of the great stone staircase, and she was just in time to see a glimmer of candlelight in the doorway of the main salon. This time, it was beyond a doubt. Someone was there.

Marianne glanced about her for some weapon. If this were a prowler, then she must have something to defend herself with. But there seemed to be nothing apart from a china vase or a jade statuette standing on a chest of drawers, neither of which would be of much use if it came to a fight. The mysterious visitor might be armed. Suddenly she remembered.

Turning back into the room she went quickly over to a beautiful Venetian cabinet which Fortunée had found and presented to her, insisting that she absolutely must have something in the way of local colour. Opening it, she took out a long, flat, satinwood case inlaid with silver. When opened this revealed a pair of magnificent duelling pistols. Napoleon himself had given his mistress this unusual present, one of many.

'A woman like you should always have the means of self-defence to hand,' he had told her. 'I know that you can handle a gun and these may be useful to you one day. The times we live in are not so secure that a woman can be safe, alone and unarmed in her own house.'

Grasping one of these pistols firmly, Marianne loaded it and then, slipping it into the folds of her white gown, made her way back to the landing. She could still see the yellow light. It seemed to be moving about slowly, as though whoever was carrying it were looking for something. Unhesitatingly, Marianne began to walk downstairs.

Before leaving her room, she had kicked off her slippers at the foot of her bed. Now barefoot on the tiled floor, she neither felt the cold nor made the slightest noise. She was not in the least afraid. The weapon cradled in her hand put her on an equal footing with any burglar. What she felt was more a kind of exultation, and a sense of heightened curiosity like that of someone who, after living with a mystery for a long time, suddenly finds the key put into his hand. She no longer had the slightest doubt that the stranger moving about in the salon with a candle at this hour was the same person who had removed the portrait.

She reached the foot of the stairs, but although the double doors leading into the main salon stood wide open, she could see nothing beyond the candlelight, now stationary, and the restored fireplace with the last embers dying in the hearth, and the great, empty panel of yellow damask above it. By Marianne's wish nothing hung there because it seemed to her that nothing should be put in place of the vanished picture.

Thinking that the thief, if thief there was, must be going round the room, probably estimating the value of the works of

art it now contained, she decided not to go in through the main
door. Facing her, the smaller one leading into the music room
was part open. From there she thought she might be able to see
her nocturnal visitor without being seen. Very gently she
pushed the door wider and went into the little room to which
there already clung a faint fragrance of her chosen scent of
tuberoses. Enough light came in from the salon next door to
enable her to move about without bumping into the furniture.
She saw the music she had put out ready for her lesson
tomorrow on the pianoforte, stepped round the big, elabor-
ately gilded harp and reached the door. The velvet curtain
offered her a refuge from which to peep into the salon. It was
all she could do to hold back an exclamation of surprise. Her
visitor was a woman.

From where she stood, Marianne could see her only from the
back, but there was no escaping the dress, which seemed to be
grey, and the hair bundled up in an untidy knot. She was a
small frail-looking woman, but she carried herself as straight
as a ramrod. In her hand she carried a heavy silver candlestick
and she did seem to be making a circular tour of the room. She
paused for a moment before the fireplace and Marianne saw
her lift her arm so that the candlelight fell on the empty space.
She heard a short, dry laugh with such a note of mockery in it
that she could no longer doubt that she was looking at the
thief. But who was she, and what did she want?

A dreadful thought struck her. Suppose this woman were
something to do with Fanchon-Fleur-de-lis and the crone were
once more on her track? Who could say whether the rest of the
gang were not also in the house and any moment the hideous
creature and her two associates, the frightful Requin and the
pale Pisse-Vinaigre would not suddenly appear? Already, it
seemed to her that she could hear the tapping of a stick on the
stone floor in the hall.

Then, suddenly, Marianne stopped thinking and sprang forward, driven by an impulse stronger than any reason. The
woman had moved on beyond the fireplace and was making for
a damask curtain with an air of unmistakable purpose. Marianne realized with horror that she was going to set fire to it. In

a flash, she had left her hiding place and taken several strides into the room, the muzzle of her pistol levelled at the unknown. Her voice rang coldly in the silence.

'Can I help you?'

The woman swung round with a cry. Marianne saw a face of no particular age or beauty, or rather one that might perhaps have been beautiful, but for the great arrogant beak of a nose which dominated it. The skin on the fleshless face was dry and sallow and the thick, grizzled hair seemed too heavy for the little head that carried it, but the eyes, an innocent baby blue, were so round with terror as to relieve Marianne instantly of any fears she might have felt. The mysterious wanderer looked exactly like a frightened hen. Calmly, although still without lowering her weapon, Marianne walked towards her, but to her surprise the other woman backed away fearfully holding out trembling hands as though to ward off some nightmarish vision.

'Pierre!' she muttered in a shaky voice. 'Pierre, oh my God!'

'Are you unwell?' Marianne inquired pleasantly. 'And do please put down that candle before you set the house on fire.'

The woman seemed completely overcome. Still staring at Marianne with eyes almost starting out of her head, she reached out a trembling hand and let the candlestick down on the table with a clatter. Her teeth seemed to be actually chattering, and it occurred to Marianne that her behaviour was extremely odd coming from one who had appeared to harbour such violent intentions. She regarded the stranger in some perplexity, convinced that she must be dealing with a mad woman.

'Will you be good enough to tell me who you are and why you are trying to set this house on fire?'

Instead of answering, the woman asked a question of her own, but in a voice that trembled so much as to be scarcely audible.

'For – for the love of heaven! Who are you?'

'The owner of this house—'

The stranger shrugged, her eyes still fixed on Marianne's face.

'You cannot be. Your name?'

'Don't you think it is rather for me to ask the questions? But I will tell you. I am called Maria Stella. I am a singer and in a few days' time I shall appear at the Opéra. Does that satisfy you? No. Don't move—'

But ignoring the pistol still trained on her, the strange woman closed her eyes and passed a trembling hand across her brow.

'I must be mad!' she murmured. 'I must have been dreaming! I thought – but it is only some opera singer.'

The inexpressible contempt in her voice aroused Marianne's anger afresh.

'You are insufferable! For the last time, I ask you to tell me who you are and what you are doing here. There are no more portraits to steal.'

The stranger's thin lips, so pale and narrow as to be almost non-existent, curved in a disdainful smile.

'How did you know it was I?'

'It could be no one else! Where have you put it?'

'It is no concern of yours. That portrait belongs to me. It is a family heirloom.'

'Family?' Now it was Marianne's turn to be surprised. 'What family?'

'My own, of course! I fail to see how it can interest an Italian singer, but this house belongs to my family. I say "belongs" because you may not keep it long. It is said that Napoleon means to honour his forthcoming marriage to the niece of Marie-Antoinette by making the purchasers of émigré property disgorge it again.'

'No doubt that is why you wished to set fire to this house?'

'I could not see the house in which the d'Asselnats had lived and suffered become the setting for an actress' wanton revels! As for my name—'

'I will tell it you,' Marianne interrupted her, realizing at last who stood before her. 'Your name is Adelaide d'Asselnat. And I will tell you something else as well. When I came in just now, you looked at me with a kind of terror because you were struck by a resemblance—'

'Perhaps, but that was an illusion—'

'Was it then? Look at me more closely!' Now it was Marianne's turn to seize the silver candlestick and hold it near her face. 'Look at my face, my mouth, my colouring! Go and find the picture you took away and put it beside me. You will see that I am indeed his daughter!'

'His daughter? But how—'

'His daughter, I tell you. The daughter of Pierre d'Asselnat, Marquis de Villeneuve and of Anne Selton! Maria Stella is not my real name, only a pseudonym. My name is Marianne Elizabeth d'As—'

She had no time to say more. Mademoiselle d'Asselnat must have had more than her share of excitement for one day. With a little sigh she subsided on to the salon carpet in a dead faint.

Marianne succeeded, with something of an effort, in getting the little old spinster on to one of the sofas standing near the fireplace. Next, she stirred up the fire as best she could, lit some more candles to give a better light, and then made her way down to the kitchen in the basement in search of something to revive her cousin. The evening's melancholy had flown away as though by a miracle, and, all things considered, the discovery of this remarkable Adelaide she had believed confined to the depths of Auvergne under the watchful eye of the imperial police, an eye which now seemed somewhat lacking in watchfulness, might well qualify as a miracle. She had earlier promised to plead her cousin's cause with the Emperor but, with the selfishness of all those in love, she had let it go out of her mind during the enchanted days at the Trianon. Yet now that this d'Asselnat had dropped from heaven like a dusty, grey spider, she was suddenly as happy as though she had been given a present.

As she moved about filling a tray at random with a bottle of wine, glasses, plates, a pâté which she happened to come across in the larder and a big chunk of bread, she caught herself humming the tune from *The Vestal* which she was studying at that moment. At the same time she was racking her brains to remember what the Duc d'Avaray and then later on Fouché had said about her turbulent relative. 'An old mad creature', the first had called her, 'the friend of Mirabeau and La Fayette', 'a somewhat undesirable relative for one in your situation', the second had said. From all this and from her own observations, Marianne concluded that Adelaide was certainly no ordinary person and this pleased her.

Whatever the case, mad or not, dangerous or not, Marianne had firmly made up her mind to try and make friends with this one remaining member of her family. When she returned to the salon with her tray, she saw that the few hearty slaps she had administered to her before leaving had produced the desired effect. Adelaide's eyes were open and she was sitting upright on the sofa where Marianne had left her lying down, gazing about her with the bemused expression of one who had seen a ghost. She looked up suspiciously at the pale smiling figure coming towards her.

'Are you feeling better now, cousin?' Marianne asked, putting her tray down on a small table.

Mechanically, the little spinster pushed back a lock of hair that had fallen over her eyes and stretched out her hand for the proffered glass of wine. She swallowed a full glass with an ease denoting a certain familiarity and then sighed deeply.

'Yes, I feel better now. And so you are his daughter? You are so like him. I should not even have to ask. Except for the eyes. Pierre's eyes were black, and yours—'

'I have my mother's eyes.'

Adelaide's thin face hardened with a look of anger.

'The Englishwoman's eyes! I know!'

'Did you – did you dislike my mother?'

'I hate the English. I never wished to know her. What need had he to seek a wife from among our hereditary enemies?'

'He loved her,' Marianne said gently. 'Does that not seem to you a sufficient reason?'

Adelaide did not answer, but her expression told Marianne much more than any words. She guessed the tragedy of the plain girl, secretly in love with her handsome cousin only to see him one day fall in love with a girl so exquisitely lovely that there was no longer any question of fighting. She understood why Adelaide d'Asselnat had begun to live somewhat apart from her family, why she had sought her friends among the intellectuals whose heads were full of great, revolutionary ideas. The brilliance of Versailles which had suited the young married couple so well must have been painful to this night bird who had sucked in the new ideas as greedily as a thirsty traveller coming upon an unexpected spring of fresh water. But then—

'What did you do during the Terror?' Marianne asked suddenly, seized by a terrible suspicion. Surely this old maid's frustrated love would not have driven her to associate with those who had turned the idea of a revolution into a blood bath? But there was no shadow in the candid blue eyes that looked into hers. Adelaide shrugged.

'What could I do? I went to ground in Auvergne. Those great minds which had worked for the people's good had become the enemies of the Convention. To Robespierre's men, I was simply an aristocrat, and hence meat for the guillotine. I had to go. My house in the Marais was given to a ropemaker from the Faubourg St-Antoine who turned it into a livery stable. And I knew that I had nothing to fear from our peasants at Villeneuve who were all devoted to the family. I had thought to end my days there, but when Bonaparte became Napoleon I, I had a mind to see just what kind of a man he was who could make victory follow at his heels like a well-trained dog. I came back to Paris—'

'To this house?'

'No. That was not possible. But I came here very often to think about – about those who were no more. That was how I came across the portrait in one of the attics. Probably your father had it put away because its warlike subject could not help but remind your mother how often France and England had been at war. I liked coming here. For all its dilapidated condition, it made me feel at home.'

'Where did you live?'

'With a friend. She died, three months ago, and I was forced to look for somewhere else. But while there, I had met someone who had a house nearby and was willing to rent me a pair of rooms—'

She broke off and, for the first time, she smiled, a smile so amazingly young and mischievous that Marianne was astounded. Suddenly, her frosty cousin was twenty years old.

'—and now I am going to surprise you,' she went on, 'my landlady is English, she is that famous Mrs Atkins, who also tried to save the royal family and especially the unfortunate little King Louis XVII. But she was drawn to me by my name and her extraordinary kindness made me forget her nationality.'

'But you have been in this house? I heard you just now come down from the attic. I suppose you must know the secret hiding place?'

'Of course I know it. It was made such a long time ago. And I used to play there as a child. The d'Asselnats have not always been the most obedient subjects and there have been troubles from time to time with the King – or with the Regent as the case might be. The hiding place was useful. I hid there when you came with those others who were with you. But I did not see your face. You wore a veil. What I suffered to think that this old house, so full of memories for me, was to belong to an actress!'

She stopped abruptly and a deep blush spread over her plain features. Marianne understood her feelings and knew a moment's anxiety. She was discovering that this woman who, a moment ago, had been no more than a vague name to her, had suddenly become someone almost dear. Perhaps it was the fact that the same blood ran in both their veins, but more probably because of the strange life which Adelaide herself had led, an unconventional life which had even taken her to prison. The two of them ought to understand one another. And so Marianne decided to have done with half-truths once and for all.

'I am not an actress,' she said gently. 'Indeed I have never sung in public yet, except in a few private houses. The reason I have chosen to be a singer, is because I want to be free to live my life. I make my first appearance in a few days' time. Does that shock you dreadfully?'

Adelaide thought for a moment, though the cloud which had come over her face did not lift.

'No,' she said at last. 'I think I can understand that. But it is also said that the new owner of this house is a special favourite of the Emperor's and—'

'I love him,' Marianne interrupted her firmly. 'And I am his mistress. That too, you must understand. Unless it is too difficult—'

'Well, one can at least say that you do not mince your words,' Adelaide said when she had recovered from the shock of Marianne's announcement. 'That you should love him does not surprise me. I did myself until this senseless divorce! I cannot forgive him his Arch-Duchess.'

'I have been forced to forgive him. He must have an heir.'

'There were other ways he could get one. The Hapsburg blood is worthless. They should know that in France. But this fool has let it go to his head! What can he hope to gain in the way of offspring by mingling his own good Corsican blood, that is pure and rich and noble, with an old strain thinned by inter-marriage and hereditary weakness? What Marie-Louise brings him is the inheritance of Mad Jeanne and of Philip II. Much cause for rejoicing there is there! And, by the way, tell me how it is that you, a Frenchwoman, with English blood in you, are passed off as an Italian?'

Marianne sighed and poured another glass of wine for herself. She felt she needed it, if only to recover from hearing Adelaide abusing Napoleon so freely.

'It's a long story.'

'Bah!' the old maid retorted, settling herself more comfortably. 'I've plenty of time. And if I may have a little of this pâté – I'm always hungry!' she finished up triumphantly. 'And I'm passionately fond of stories.'

As though they had known one another all their lives, the two of them sat one either side of the little table and attacked the food and Marianne's story with equal relish. Marianne herself had never felt so comfortable. She could not wait, now, to tell the whole story to this quaint old spinster whose twinkling blue eyes regarded her with such a spontaneous sympathy. The words seemed to come of their own accord and in telling Adelaide of all that she had been through, she felt as though she were telling it to the spirits of her house as well. She was making her confession to all the past members of her family and she discovered at the same time that all the hatred and resentment she had built up suddenly left her, as though she were recovering from an illness. She had only one fear, that Adelaide would think that she was mad. But the old lady was not without experience. When Marianne had finished she merely patted her young cousin's hand as it lay on the table and sighed.

'And to think I thought that I had led an exciting life! If you go on at this rate, my dear child, I don't know where you might not end up! But it will be interesting to watch.'

Marianne looked up almost timidly and asked:

'You are not shocked? You do not blame me? I am afraid I may have surrendered my honour too cheap!'

'You had no choice! Besides, in all justice, it was Lady Cranmere's honour which suffered. Marianne d'Asselnat has merely followed her heart. You would not have me weep for an English honour? Especially one of such melancholy origin—'

She rose suddenly, shaking crumbs off her grey dress. Then, with a thoughtful look at Marianne, she asked suddenly:

'This American — you are quite sure you are not in love with him?'

What could Adelaide be thinking of to ask such an apparently preposterous question? Had she not understood anything Marianne had told her, or had she some special picture of Jason? For a second, the sailor's tall figure seemed to invade the quiet room bringing with it a rush of sea air, but Marianne thrust it back.

'In love with him? How could I be? I feel friendship for him now, and a certain gratitude, but I told you I loved—'

'So you did. But too much gazing on the sun can make one blind, even to one's own heart. I don't know whether you realized it, but you have just described to me an extraordinarily attractive man, and if I were in your shoes—'

'Well?'

'Well – I think I might have paid my stupid husband's gambling debt! Just to see! He seems to know what he is about, that one – and there's no doubt but he's madly fond of you!'

At the sight of Marianne's stunned face as she sat wondering whether she could have heard right, Adelaide suddenly burst out laughing.

'Don't look at me like that,' she exclaimed. 'One would swear you had set eyes on the Devil! Let me tell you, my girl, I'm not such an old maid as you may think. Believe me, there is some good even in the most troubled times! But for the Revolution, I should still be a canoness in some aristocratic convent and no doubt bored to death! But thanks to it, I have been able to discover that virtue does not have all the charm it is cracked up to have and I have stored up one or two fragrant memories that I may tell you about later, when we know one another better. But just remember this. There has always been hot blood in the family, and you won't be the first! And with that I'll bid you goodnight—'

Marianne could not have been more astonished if a thunderbolt had fallen on her. She was discovering that nothing she had ever thought about Adelaide came halfway near the truth, and she would have to begin all over again. The mere fact that she had mentioned Beaufort had been enough to bring him back, tenacious and encroaching, into Marianne's mind though she still persisted in trying to drive him out again. Why? Marianne began to have strange doubts. Could she perhaps have loved the American? Oh dear, it was clear that she was still very young and there was still a great deal she had to learn!

She became aware that Adelaide was walking purposefully in the direction of the kitchen staircase and called out to stop her.

'But – where are you going?'

'Down to the cellar, child. I forgot to tell you it communicates with that of Mrs Atkins. A circumstance I discovered not long ago but one which I have found very useful ever since you changed the locks. Goodnight.'

She walked on but Marianne called after her.

'Cousin!'

It was only one word but there was a world of feeling in it. It suddenly seemed to Marianne that in Adelaide she had rediscovered something of her Aunt Ellis and that cry was the product of her need for some of the warmth of kinship. Adelaide paused in the doorway as though something tangible had struck her. She turned slowly, a look of strain on her face.

'Yes?'

'Why – why must you go on living with a friend when there is this house, our house? It is too big for me. I – I need someone – you! I will ask the Emperor to pardon you and then we can—'

She could not go on. There was silence. Blue eyes and green eyes met and held one another with an intensity that was far beyond words. Was it an illusion, or was that a tear that gleamed for a moment under the older woman's lashes? She pulled out a handkerchief and blew her nose vigorously.

'I dare say I'd better move,' she muttered. 'It's dreadfully gloomy here with nothing over the fireplace.'

Patting her tottering pile of hair into place with an air of stern determination, Adelaide turned and marched firmly in the direction of the cellar.

Left alone, Marianne gazed at her surroundings in triumph. It seemed to her that now, suddenly, the old house was really itself again, that only now had the old walls begun to live and to accept their new dress. The wheel had come full circle. The house had got its soul again and Marianne a home.

Six days later, on March 19th, the streets around the Théâtre Feydeau were crammed with carriages all turning in to deposit their elegantly dressed contents beneath the round arches of the former Théâtre de Monsieur. Women muffled in expensive furs from beneath which came the occasional gleam of jewels, heads crowned with flowers, feathers and diamonds; men in huge overcoats that concealed splendid uniforms or dark coats studded with decorations. In spite of the persistent rain which had been drenching Paris for some days, all that was most distinguished by rank or fortune in the French capital was thronging to the doors of the famous Théâtre.

The choice of the Théâtre Feydeau was a late one and due particularly to the size of the auditorium which was much larger than that of the Opéra in the rue de la Loi. It had also been thought that an Italian singer would find herself more at home on a stage traditionally the preserve of the Italian Comedy and then of the Opéra Comique, rather than at the Opéra where ballet was generally the chief spectacle. The dancers were notoriously averse to sharing the limelight, while the Théâtre Feydeau was truly the temple of *bel canto*. If the Director of the Opéra, Picard, had felt some twinges of regret at the fabulous takings which would not come his way, he consoled himself by thinking of the trouble it would have called down on his head from the temperamental Auguste Vestris, that 'god' whom age did not mellow and who ruled as a despot over a theatre which he regarded as his own personal property.

The members of the Feydeau company, the celebrated Dugazon, the lovely Phyllis and Madame de Saint-Aubin and their male counterparts, the irresistible Elleviou and his colleagues Gavaudan, Martin, Solie and Chenard, had all displayed great deference to the imperial command and declared their willingness to welcome the singer Maria Stella whose great fame, most of it due to the efficient publicity which sprang full-grown from Fouché's fertile brain, had gone before her.

The four Parisian daily newspapers, *Le Moniteur*, the *Journal de l'Empire* the *Gazette de France* and the *Quotidienne*, duly instructed, had all published laudatory articles about the new star of *bel canto* whom none of them had yet seen. Meanwhile, the streets of Paris became covered with bills announcing the forthcoming event at the Théâtre Feydeau presenting 'for the first time in France, the celebrated Venetian diva Signorina Maria Stella, the golden voice of the peninsula'. As a result, Paris was talking quite as much about the mysterious new singer as about the new Empress still making her slow way towards France. Fashionable gossip had done the rest. The Emperor was rumoured to be wildly in love with the beautiful Maria, to have installed her secretly in an apartment in the

Tuileries and to spend a fortune covering her with jewels. The magnificent preparations for the marriage went almost unnoticed: the alterations to the *salon carré* in the Tuileries for the ceremony, the overworked dressmakers and seamstresses, the endless drilling of troops, and even the transformations taking place on the site of the triumphal arch at the Etoile, where a false arch was being erected out of scaffolding and canvas until the real one could be built. This, too, was not without set-backs caused by the carpenters going on strike for more pay every five minutes.

Marianne was both amused and terrified by all the fuss. She was well aware that on the great night, all the eyes in Paris would be on her, that her figure and her clothes would be subjected to the closest scrutiny and that the slightest weakness in her voice would be fatal. And so she had worked to the very utmost of her strength until her friends became actually worried about her.

'If you wear yourself out,' said Dorothée de Périgord, who now came to the rue de Lille every day in order to encourage her friend, 'you will be too tired on Monday night to bear the fatigue and excitement of the evening.'

'Who would travel far must spare his horse,' cousin Adelaide, who now watched over her like a mother, would remark sententiously, while every morning, Napoleon sent his personal physician Corvisart to check on her health. It was the Emperor's command that Mademoiselle Maria Stella should take care of herself.

But Marianne, scared to death, would listen to none of them. It took Gossec himself to declare that he refused to practise with her more than one hour a day and Arcadius de Jolival to take it upon himself to lock up the piano for the rest of the time before she would finally agree to take a little rest, and even then the harp had to be shut up in the attic and the guitar in a cupboard before she could be brought to resist temptation altogether.

'I'll be a success,' she cried, 'if it kills me!'

'If you go on like this, you'll not get the chance,' retorted Fortunée Hamelin, who was constantly obliging her to swallow mysterious concoctions from her native islands, intended to sustain her, and waging a daily battle against Adelaide who prescribed eggnogs. 'You'll be dead first!'

The Hôtel d'Asselnat, so peaceful a few weeks before, had become a forum for the expression of everybody's opinion and was filled all day long with seamstresses, bootmakers, furriers, milliners and purveyors of endless frills and fancies. Rising above the general uproar was the greedy voice of the couturier Leroy, who ordered everyone about. The great man had not slept for three nights while he was designing the clothes that Marianne was to wear on stage, and in between times had wandered about his salons with such a distracted and distant expression that three princesses, five duchesses and the wives of half a dozen marshals had practically died of rage. A fortnight from the imperial wedding day and Leroy could think of nothing but one lovely figure!

'The evening will either be my triumph, or it will not!' was all he would say, wading through miles of satin, tulle, brocade and gold thread, to the even greater confusion of the scribblers for the various journals, who one and all concluded in their articles that Maria Stella would be dressed with such splendour that even the glories of the most fabulous sultans of Golconda would pale in comparison. They claimed that she would stagger under rivers of diamonds, that she was actually to wear the crown jewels, that the Emperor had had his largest diamond, the 'Regent', mounted in a necklace for her to wear, that he had given her permission to wear a diadem like a princess and a great deal more nonsense of the same kind. Paris retailed it with all the more assurance when it was known that the Austrian Ambassador had gone anxiously to visit Fouché in private to find out how much truth there was in it all.

Meanwhile, Picard, the Director of the Opéra, locked himself firmly in his office while his artists gathered round his door weeping with fury, and the performers of the Théâtre Feydeau exulted as though in a personal victory. Everyone, right down to the most insignificant member of the chorus, felt immensely proud and considerably flattered to be taking part in an event of this importance.

Several times in the last few days, Marianne went to rehearse on stage, accompanied by Gossec and Arcadius, the latter taking his role of impresario very seriously indeed. There she met Jean Elleviou, the fashionable tenor who was to sing with her in the first part of the evening. Since there had been too little time for her to learn and rehearse a whole opera, it had been decided that she would begin with a scene from Spontini's opera *The Vestal,* an elaborate Roman piece, which was one of Napoleon's favourite works. As a curtain raiser, therefore, they would sing the duet for Julia and Licinius, after which Marianne would sing Zétulve's aria from the *Calif of Baghdad* followed by a longish extract from *Pygmalion* by Cherubini. The second half of the concert was confined to Marianne alone when she would sing a number of arias from Mozart, Austrian being decidedly the coming fashion.

Everything had gone very well for Marianne. She had met with great kindness from her new colleagues and a good deal of gallantry from Elleviou, whose numerous feminine conquests left him by no means insensitive to the charms of the new star. He did his best to make her feel at home on the great stage whose dimensions had terrified her when she set foot on it for the first time.

'When the footlights are alight,' he told her, pointing to the impressive array before them, each with its own small reflector, 'you can scarcely see the audience. Besides you will not be alone on the stage for your entrance, since we are to sing together.'

To help familiarize her with her surroundings, he took her on a tour of the theatre from top to bottom, showing her sets, dressing-rooms, the auditorium decorated in the style of the last century in pink velvet and gilt bronze, with clusters of candles on the front of the balconies and the huge, glittering crystal chandelier. The whole of the centre of the first circle was taken up by one vast box, the Emperor's, and Marianne swore to herself that she would look nowhere else throughout the performance.

She was determined to be quite calm for this most important evening of her life. She spent most of the day in her room, resting in semi-darkness, watched over by Adelaide, who had already taken charge of the household and herself prepared the light meals which were all that Marianne would take on the all-important day. Apart from Fortunée Hamelin, who was almost as nervous as Marianne herself, no one was allowed near her, although three or four notes of tender encouragement had been delivered from the Tuileries.

But in spite of everything, in spite of all the affectionate care of her friends, Marianne's hands were icy cold and her throat dry when she reached the theatre that night. She was trembling like a leaf in the great pelisse of white satin lined with sable which Napoleon had given her, in spite of all the foot warmers which her maid Agathe had stuffed into the carriage. She had never been so nervous in her life.

'I can't do it,' she said again and again to Arcadius, who looked almost as pale as she in his black coat. 'I can't do it – I'm too frightened!'

'Stage fright,' he told her with a coolness he was far from feeling. 'All great artists have it. Especially for their first appearance. It will pass.'

Elleviou was waiting for Marianne at the door of her dressing-room with a huge bouquet of red roses in his hands. He presented them with a bow and an encouraging smile.

'Already you are the most beautiful,' he told her in his deep voice. 'Tonight, you will also be the greatest – and we two, if you will, may perhaps be friends for life.'

'We are friends already,' she told him, and gave him her hand. 'Thank you for giving me such a comforting welcome. I needed it.'

He was a fair, good-looking man, whose figure did not betray his forty years, and although his eyes showed a somewhat disagreeable inclination to linger on her bosom, he was pleasant and kind in offering to help her past a difficult moment. His support was not something to be scorned. Moreover, Marianne had to get used to her new and rather strange surroundings, very different from anything she had known before, but in which she meant not simply to make a place for herself, but a reigning one.

The dressing-room which they had given her had been transformed into a flower garden. It seemed as though there could not be a single rose, carnation or tulip left in all Paris, her friends had so conspired to outdo one another. There were huge sprays sent by Talleyrand, by Fortunée and her friend the banker Ouvrard, even, in a wild burst of unusual extravagance, from Fouché, as well as from the Grand Marshal of the Palace, and a host of others. One small bouquet bore the timid signature of M. Fercoc. Inside the great cushion of violets sent by Napoleon was another bouquet, this one made of diamonds, and with it three words which tripled it in value: 'I love you, N.'

'You see,' Arcadius told her softly. 'How can you fail to be brave with so much affection all around you? And think, he will be there. Come and see!'

While Agathe took possession of the dressing-room and endeavoured to make some room among the flowers, Arcadius took Marianne by the hand and led her behind the stage curtain. Stage hands and members of the chorus were moving about in all directions, busy with last-minute preparations. In the orchestra pit, the musicians were tuning their instruments and men were beginning to light the footlights. From beyond the great velvet wall, they could hear the hum of the audience.

Arcadius made a tiny crack. 'Look.'

The theatre was literally sparkling with the countless points of light from the great chandelier. All the foreign ambassadors were there and all the dignitaries of the Empire, dressed in the slightly fantastic uniforms ordained by Napoleon. Marianne's heart beat faster as she caught sight of Madame de Talleyrand in one box with a group of friends, Talleyrand himself in another surrounded by lovely ladies and Dorothée's sharp little face in a third. Prince Eugène was there, with his sister, Queen Hortense. In a low voice, Arcadius pointed out the chief of those present: Old Prince Kurakin, the Arch-Chancellor Cambacérès, the beautiful Madame Récamier, dressed in silver gauze with long pink gloves, Fortunée Hamelin, brilliant and dazzling as the bird of paradise beside the crafty-looking Ouvrard. In a box facing her sat Adelaide d'Asselnat, resplendent in the dress of plum-coloured velvet and white satin turban which Marianne had given her, her lorgnettes held insolently to her eyes fixing everything and everyone with a proud, imperious stare. This was her moment of glory, and her re-entry into society. A wooden-faced lackey guarded the door of her box where she sat enthroned in splendid isolation while every box around her was filled to overflowing.

'The whole Empire is here – or very nearly,' Arcadius whispered. 'And on time, too! One can see the Emperor is coming. In a little while, all these people will be in love with you!'

But Marianne's eyes had fastened on the great box, empty as yet, where Napoleon would sit with his sister Pauline and one or two of his court.

'Tomorrow,' she murmured half under her breath, overcome by a sudden sadness, 'he leaves for Compiègne to meet the new Empress. What do I care if others are in love with me. Only he matters and he is going away!'

'But he will be yours tonight!' Jolival said quickly, realizing that if Marianne gave way to melancholy she was lost. 'Run and get ready now. The orchestra is beginning the overture – quickly!'

He was right. Marianne had neither the time, nor the right, to think only of herself. In this final moment, she belonged to the theatre. She had become truly an artist and, as such, must do her best not to disappoint those who had trusted her. Marianne d'Asselnat was gone and Maria Stella took her place. Marianne meant it to be a dazzling change.

Returning the friendly greetings which met her on all sides, she made her way back to her dressing-room where Agathe stood waiting for her in the doorway holding a big bouquet of pure white camellias, lace-edged and tied with a bunch of green ribbon. She handed it to Marianne with a little bob.

'A messenger brought them.' Marianne could not help a sudden feeling of excitement as she read the little card that came with them. On it were only two words, a name, 'Jason Beaufort'. Nothing else.

So he too had been thinking of her? But how, and where?

Had he come back to Paris after all? Suddenly, she wanted to go back on stage and peep through the curtains again to see if she could catch a glimpse of the American's tanned face and tall, loose-limbed figure anywhere in the audience. But it was too late now. The violins were already striking up. The chorus must be already on stage. In a moment, the curtain would go up. Marianne had just time to slip into her dress. Yet even then, as she laid the white bouquet down on her dressing-table, something stirred in her, despite herself, that almost made her forget her fear. Merely with his name pinned to a few flowers, Jason had brought into that crowded, hot-house dressing-room, something of his own fierce personality, a breath of the open sea and his keen love of struggle and adventure. And Marianne discovered that no other evidence of affection had done as much for her as those few syllables.

While Agathe was putting the finishing touches to her hair and setting a few diamond stars among the thickly piled locks, Marianne remembered Adelaide's astonishing question: *'Are you sure you're not in love with him?'*

It was ridiculous, of course she was sure! How could she hesitate for a single moment between the American and Napoleon? She was honest enough to admit the American's charm, but the Emperor was something different. Besides, he loved her with all his heart and all his power while there was absolutely nothing to show that Adelaide's supposition was right. She had decreed, without ever seeing him, that Jason loved her but Marianne herself thought differently. The American felt guilty towards her and whatever she might have thought before, he was a man of honour. He was sincerely anxious to wipe out the wrong he had done her, that was all. None the less, Marianne admitted that she would be very glad to see him again. It would be so wonderful if he too were there tonight to share her triumph.

She was ready and the image reflected in her mirror was indeed very lovely. Leroy's much-talked-of dress was, in fact, a masterpiece of simplicity. The heavy, pearly satin with its long train lined with cloth of gold was moulded to her body like a wet sheet, only widening a little at the hem, with an effrontery which only a woman with her figure and her legs could have carried off. With its dizzily plunging neckline that showed off to the full the emeralds and diamonds Napoleon had given her, the dress undressed more than it covered her, but what might have been indecent on another became, on her, merely the height of beauty and elegance. Leroy had predicted that by the next day his salons would be besieged by a host of women all wanting a dress like it.

'But I shall not let them have it,' he had declared firmly. 'I have my reputation to think of and there is not one in a thousand could wear such a dress so regally.'

Slowly, and without taking her eyes from herself, Marianne pulled on the long, green lace gloves. Tonight, she was fascinated by her own reflection. Her beauty seemed to her like a promise of triumph. The diamond stars in her black hair flashed fire.

For a fraction of a second, she hesitated between the two bouquets that lay before her. The violets or the camellias? She was tempted to choose the latter, which would have gone better with her dress, but could she slight the flowers of the man she loved for such a reason? Quickly, with one last look at the delicate white flowers, she picked up the violets and made her way to the door while outside in the passage the stage manager was calling:

'Mademoiselle Maria Stella, on stage, please!'

The duet from *Vestal* had just finished in a storm of applause led by Napoleon himself with uncharacteristic enthusiasm. Her trembling hand clasped firmly in that of Elleviou, who was flushed with pride, Marianne made her bow with a feeling of triumph so fierce that her head seemed to spin with it. But her eyes were less on the packed house now giving them a standing ovation, than on the man in the uniform of a colonel of chasseurs sitting up there in the big, flower-filled box and smiling back at her with such love in his eyes. Next to him, was a very pretty, dark woman with a chiselled profile, his youngest and favourite sister, the Princess Pauline, and from time to time he leaned towards her as though asking her opinion.

'You've got them!' Elleviou muttered under his breath. 'Everything will be all right now. Courage! They are all yours.'

She scarcely heard him. The applause was like triumphal music filling her ears with its wonderful tempestuous sound. Was there any more intoxicating noise in the whole world? Her eyes never left the man in the box, and she looked up at him, seeing nothing else but him and dedicating all this dazzling success to him alone. He dominated the vast black hole which had almost made her faint with terror when she came on stage so little time ago. But the panic had passed. She was herself again and not afraid any more, Elleviou was right. Nothing could touch her now.

Silence fell once more, an expectant silence that was yet more living than all the bravos that had gone before. It was as though the whole audience were holding its breath. Marianne's fingers tightened on the bouquet of violets as she began to sing the aria from the *Calif of Baghdad*. Never had her voice, trained now to cope with the most difficult tests, been so wholly at her command. It soared out across the audience, warm and flexible, containing in its pure notes all the pearls and jewels of the East, the burning scent of the desert and the joyous happiness of children playing in a fountain's spray. Marianne herself, bent like a bow string towards the Emperor's box, sang for one man alone, forgetting all the others whom she carried with her along the magic pathway of her music.

Once again, it was a triumph, noisy, uproarious, indescribable. The theatre seemed to explode into frenzied applause and a sweet-smelling storm of flowers began to rain down on the stage. Across the orchestra pit, a radiant Marianne could look out on a standing audience, wild with applause.

On all sides there were cries of 'Encore! Encore!'

She took a few steps forward to the front of the stage. Her eyes left the imperial box at last and, meeting the conductor's look, she nodded to him to begin the aria again. Then she lowered her eyes while gradually the audience quietened down and the musicians resumed their instruments. Once again, the music began to spin its enticing thread.

But suddenly a movement in one of the stage boxes caught Marianne's attention. A man had just come in and instantly her eye was drawn to him. She thought for a second that it was Jason Beaufort, whom she had sought in vain among the rapt faces before her. It was not he but someone else at the sight of whom Marianne's blood seemed to freeze in her veins. He was very tall with broad shoulders encased in dark blue velvet and thick fair hair brushed in the latest style and the face above the high, white muslin cravat bore a cynical expression. He was a handsome man in spite of the thin scar that ran across one cheek from the corner of his mouth to his ear, but Marianne gazed at him with the incredulous horror of someone who has seen a ghost.

She wanted to cry out, to try and overcome the terror which was taking possession of her, but no sound came. She felt as though she were in a bad dream, or else going mad. It could not be true. This frightful thing could not be happening to her. At one blow she saw the wonderful, delicate world she had built up for herself at the cost of so much suffering, crumble to pieces at her feet. Her mouth opened, gasping for air, but the impression of nightmare became more terrifying while the audience, the imperial box with its dark red roses, the great velvet and gold curtains, the footlights and the conductor's startled face all merged into one infernal kaleidoscope. Marianne put up her hands with a small pitiful movement, trying with all her strength to push the spectre back into the darkness from which it had risen. But the spectre would not go. He was looking at her now, and he was smiling ...

Marianne gave one small desperate cry and then collapsed on to the flower-studded stage while, towering above the uproar which arose all about him, her husband, Francis Cranmere, the man she had believed that she had killed, bent forward to look down on the stage and on the slender white form that lay there, twinkling with tiny stars in the stage lights. He was still smiling.

*   *   *

When she opened her eyes, some minutes later, Marianne saw a ring of anxious faces bending over her, against a background of flowers, and realized that she was in her dressing-room. Arcadius and Adelaide were there, Agathe was bathing her temples with something cool and Corvisart was holding her hand. Elleviou was there too and Fortunée Hamelin, while towering over them all was the resplendent figure of the Grand Marshal Duroc, dispatched no doubt by the Emperor.

Seeing her open her eyes, Fortunée immediately seized her friend's free hand.

'What happened?' she asked affectionately.

'Francis!' Marianne murmured. 'He was there — I saw him!'

'You mean — your husband? But that is impossible! He's dead.'

Feebly Marianne shook her head.

'I saw him — tall and fair, dressed in blue — in Prince Cambacérès' box.' She struggled to raise herself and her eyes met Duroc's imploringly. The Grand Marshal understood and disappeared at once. Marianne allowed Corvisart to push her gently back on to the cushions.

'You must calm yourself, mademoiselle. His Majesty is in the gravest anxiety on your account. I must be able to reassure him.'

'The Emperor is very good,' she said faintly. 'I am ashamed to be so weak—'

'There is no need to be ashamed. How do you feel? Do you feel able to continue the concert or should we ask the public to excuse you?'

The cordial which the imperial physician had given her was gradually having its effect on Marianne. She felt a little warmth and life return to her body. Now she felt nothing beyond a general lassitude and a slight headache.

'Perhaps I can go on,' she began, a little hesitantly. It was true, she felt strong enough to return to the stage but at the same time she was afraid of the audience, of seeing again the face which had filled her with such terror. In a flash, in the moment of seeing it, she had understood why Jason Beaufort

had done all he could to make her go with him and what the
mysterious danger was, the precise nature of which he had
always refused to divulge. He must have known that Lord
Cranmere was alive. But he had wanted to spare her the knowledge. In a moment, perhaps, when Duroc had found him,
Francis was going to cross the threshold of this very room and
come to her. He was coming now. There were footsteps in the
passage. The footsteps of more than one man.

Marianne clung desperately to Fortunée's hand.

'Don't leave me – at all costs, don't leave me!'

There was a knock. The door opened. Duroc was there but
the man he brought with him was not Francis, it was Fouché.
The Minister of Police looked grave and anxious. With a wave
of his hand he dismissed all those gathered about Marianne
with the exception of Fortunée, who stayed holding tightly to
her friend's hand, 'I fear, mademoiselle,' he said speaking very
deliberately, 'that you have been the victim of an hallucination.
At the Grand Marshal's request, I myself went into the Prince's
box. There was no one there corresponding to the description
you gave.'

'But I saw him! I am not mad, I swear to you! He was
dressed in blue velvet – the moment I close my eyes, I can see
him still. The people in the box must have seen him!'

Fouché raised one eyebrow and made a helpless gesture.

'The Duchess of Bassano, who is in Prince Cambacérès' box,
thinks that the only blue habit she saw just after the interval
belonged to the Vicomte d'Aubecourt, a young Flemish noble-
man just recently arrived in Paris.'

'Then you must find this Vicomte. Francis Cranmere is an
Englishman. He would not dare to come to Paris under his own
name. I want to see this man.'

'Unfortunately, he cannot be found. My men are turning the
theatre upside down in search of him but so far—'

He was interrupted by three quick raps on the door. Fouché
went himself to open it. Outside was a man in evening dress
who bowed briefly.

'There is no one in the theatre, Minister,' he said, 'who seems
able to tell us where the Vicomte d'Aubecourt can be found.

He appears to have vanished into thin air during the uproar which followed mademoiselle's illness.'

There was a silence so profound it seemed that everyone had stopped breathing. Marianne was once more white as a sheet.

'Nowhere to be found! Vanished!' she said at last. 'But he can't have done! He was not a ghost—'

'That is all that I can tell you,' Fouché said shortly. 'Apart from the Duchess, who believed she saw him, no one, do you hear me, no one has seen this person. Now will you tell me what I am to tell the Emperor? His Majesty is waiting!'

'The Emperor has waited long enough. Tell him, if you please, that I am at his service.'

A little unsteadily, but with determination, Marianne rose to her feet and, putting aside the woollen shawl they had wrapped round her, went to her dressing-table for Agathe to restore some kind of order to her hair. She forced herself not to think of the spectre which had risen from the past to appear so suddenly against the red velvet background of a stage box. Napoleon was waiting. Nothing and no one should ever keep her from going to him whenever he was waiting. His love was the one really good thing in the world.

One after another, her friends left. Duroc and Fouché first, followed by the singers and then by Arcadius, though with evident reluctance. Only Adelaide d'Asselnat and Fortunée Hamelin remained until Marianne was ready.

A few minutes later, a storm of applause shook the old theatre to its foundations. Marianne was back on stage.

JEAN PLAIDY

'One of England's foremost historical novelists'–
BIRMINGHAM MAIL

The story of Henry of Navarre
EVERGREEN GALLANT   30p

The story of Jane Shore
THE GOLDSMITH'S WIFE   30p

The persecution of witches and puritans in the 16th and 17th centuries
DAUGHTER OF SATAN   30p

The Tudor Novels
THE SPANISH BRIDEGROOM   30p
GAY LORD ROBERT   30p
THE THISTLE AND THE ROSE   30p

The reign of Henry VIII
MURDER MOST ROYAL   35p
ST THOMAS'S EVE   30p
THE SIXTH WIFE   30p

The story of Mary Stuart
ROYAL ROAD TO FOTHERINGAY   30p
THE CAPTIVE QUEEN OF SCOTS   35p

The infamous Borgia family
MADONNA OF THE SEVEN HILLS   30p
LIGHT ON LUCREZIA   30p

Life and loves of Charles II
THE WANDERING PRINCE   30p
A HEALTH UNTO HIS MAJESTY   30p
HERE LIES OUR SOVEREIGN LORD   30p

Catherine de Medici
MADAME SERPENT   30p

Robert Carr and the Countess of Essex
THE MURDER IN THE TOWER   30p

A SELECTION OF POPULAR READING IN PAN

FICTION

THE GODFATHER Mario Puzo	45p
THE FORTRESS Hugh Walpole	30p
VANESSA Hugh Walpole	30p
MADAME SERPENT Jean Plaidy	30p
THE ROSE AND THE SWORD Sandra Paretti	40p
IMMORTAL QUEEN Elizabeth Byrd	40p
SYLVESTER Georgette Heyer	30p
FREDERICA Georgette Heyer	30p
COUSIN KATE Georgette Heyer	30p
HEIR TO FALCONHURST Lance Horner	40p
THE COUNTESS ANGELIQUE Book One: In the Land of the Redskins Sergeanne Golon	30p
THE COUNTESS ANGELIQUE Book Two: Prisoner of the Mountains Sergeanne Golon	30p
AIRPORT Arthur Hailey	40p
HOTEL Arthur Hailey	35p

NON-FICTION

OLD YORKSHIRE DALES (illus.) Arthur Raistrick	40p
THE COUNTRYMAN WILD LIFE BOOK (illus.) Edited by Bruce Campbell	30p
THE SEAL SUMMER (illus.) Nina Warner Hooke	25p
MY BEAVER COLONY (illus.) Lars Wilsson	25p

These and other PAN books are obtainable from all booksellers and newsagents. If you have any difficulty please send purchase price plus 5p postage to PO Box 11, Falmouth, Cornwall. While every effort is made to keep prices low, it is sometimes necessary to increase prices at short notice. PAN Books reserve the right to show new retail prices on covers which may differ from those previously advertised in the text or elsewhere.